MUDDLED THROUGH

Barbara Ross

Kensington Publishing Corp.
www.kensingtonbooks.com

"Julia? Come right away! I'm at the shop." The vibration in my sister's voice said it wasn't time to ask questions.

"Be right there." I jumped into my Bean boots and pulled on my jacket. The sky was steel gray and the air was so damp I could feel the moisture on my face as I ran. It was going to rain, hard and soon.

My mind raced as I sped down Main Street. Lupine Design had been vandalized again. That had to be the reason for the shakiness in Livvie's voice.

Once again, there were three police cars in front of the store, lights ablaze. But this time there was also an ambulance with its back doors opened wide.

Out of breath and sweating in my waterproof jacket, I skidded to a stop in front of Lupine Design. I registered that there was no one in the ambulance, and the two EMTs lounged behind it. When I glanced through the display window, my instant impression was that everything was as it should have been—the shelves were upright, the was floor clean—but I didn't take time to process what that meant.

Then I saw the uniformed Busman's Harbor officer, standing, arms crossed, in front of the door . . .

Books by Barbara Ross

Maine Clambake Mysteries
CLAMMED UP
BOILED OVER
MUSSELED OUT
FOGGED INN
ICED UNDER
STOWED AWAY
STEAMED OPEN
SEALED OFF
SHUCKED APART
MUDDLED THROUGH

Collections
EGG NOG MURDER
(with Leslie Meier and Lee Hollis)
YULE LOG MURDER
(with Leslie Meier and Lee Hollis)
HAUNTED HOUSE MURDER
(with Leslie Meier and Lee Hollis)
HALLOWEEN PARTY MURDER
(with Leslie Meier and Lee Hollis)

Jane Darrowfield Mysteries
JANE DARROWFIELD, PROFESSIONAL
BUSYBODY
JANE DARROWFIELD AND THE MADWOMAN
NEXT DOOR

Published by Kensington Publishing Corp.

This book is dedicated to our Maine Friday night Zoom group, especially the regulars: Dick and Anne Cass, Brenda Buchanan and Diane Kenty, Gayle Lynds and John Sheldon, and Barbara Kelly. Bill and I couldn't have made it through the pandemic without you all!

CHAPTER ONE

I spotted the whirl of blue lights the moment I left my mother's house. I squinted into the morning sun, trying to make out what was happening. There were three police cars stopped in front of Lupine Design, the pottery shop and studio at the end of the last commercial block on Main Street. I started down the sidewalk, picking up my pace from walk to jog to run as I went. For the past two years, my sister Livvie worked at Lupine Design during the off-season.

The closer I got, the faster I ran. The door of one of the police cars hung open, as if the driver had leapt out in a rush. The double doors of the pottery shop were open, too. I couldn't imagine what was going on inside. My heart hammered, not only from the run.

I stopped outside the big display window and looked into the store. Livvie stood talking to Jamie Dawes, one of Busman's Harbor's police officers and a childhood friend. I exhaled with relief. My sister was okay.

But all around her the shop was in chaos. Broken pottery littered the floor. Display shelves were tipped over. Cabinet doors hung open.

Livvie leaned in to say something to Jamie. A thick lock of her auburn hair fell across her profile, obscuring her face. She was almost his height, and Jamie was tall. He said something and Livvie nodded.

I hurried inside. "What happened?"

They turned, surprised to see me. "I found the place like this when I opened the store this morning." Livvie was unnaturally pale, and her voice shook. Her trembling hand swept around the shop, where the glass display shelves were empty, knocked over, some leaning against others. The dark wood floor was littered with ceramic shards in Lupine Design's signature ocean colors—blues, greens, grays, and white. I recognized the rounded body of a teapot, the lip of a serving platter, the handle of a pitcher. The original shape of most of the pieces had been obliterated.

On a side wall of the shop, a door I had never noticed before stood open. Beyond it, a blue-gray staircase led up to a landing, then turned and disappeared out of sight. "Zoey?" I gasped. Livvie's boss, Zoey Butterfield, the owner and entrepreneur behind Lupine Design, lived in the apartment over the store.

"Not here," Jamie reassured me. "We've checked." As he said it, I heard the clomp of footsteps overhead, then the clearing of a throat from the basement below us. The other Busman's Harbor cops were moving around the building.

"Where is she?" I asked.

"We were just getting to that." Jamie took back control of the conversation. It was his interview. He was in charge.

"Yesterday she told me she was going early to collect local clay," Livvie said. "She warned me I'd be opening the studio this morning because she probably wouldn't be back in time."

Jamie pulled his cell phone out, thumb at the ready.

"You won't be able to reach her with that unless she's already on the way home," Livvie told him. "I know where she goes and there's no service there."

Jamie dialed the number Livvie gave him and left a message carefully worded not to cause panic. "Following up on some inquiries," he said after introducing himself. "Please get back to me right away."

"Can you think of anyone who might have done this?" Jamie's voice was calm, businesslike but not abrupt. I imagined he used it with all the upset citizens he dealt with. But then he put his hand on Livvie's shaking arm and squeezed, a gesture reserved for a good friend.

Livvie swallowed hard. "No. No one."

Jamie slipped his phone back into his pocket. "The officers will be here for a while, taking photos and fingerprints. It would be helpful if you could figure out if anything is missing, beyond what's broken."

Livvie gave a curt nod to indicate she accepted the assignment. My body had relaxed the moment I'd seen her standing in the shop unharmed. She, in contrast, was still tensed like a jungle cat about to pounce. I moved next to her, fit myself beneath her shoulder and hugged her rib cage. I was the older sister, but she had been the bigger one since adolescence.

"I can't imagine we'll find any usable prints." Jamie

looked around at the mess. "This stuff probably gets touched by all of the staff when you're shelving, and by lots of customers, too."

"Over here." Livvie led us to the other side of the shop where high counters ran along the wall, left over from the nineteenth-century apothecary that had originally occupied the building. Zoey had painted the once dark wood the same blue gray as the stairs to her apartment. The paint had been applied in wide strokes that allowed a bricky-pink undercoat to show through in places. Normally, the effect was warm and gorgeous against the white walls of the large, light-filled store. Today, the cabinet doors hung open, broken pieces of glass still in some of their panes.

Livvie pointed at the mess on the wide planks of the floor. Pieces of glass were mixed with the ceramic shards. "If you're looking for fingerprints, the broken pottery around here will be your best bet. Our most expensive pieces were kept locked in these cabinets. I washed them myself and placed them in there at the end of the fall season. I doubt anyone has touched them since."

"Thanks," Jamie said. "I'm going to let the other officers know what you've told me and then I'm going out to look for Ms. Butterfield. The sooner she gets here, the better. I'd like to spare her being unprepared for the sight of patrol cars in front of her place when she returns. You said you know where she is?"

Livvie rattled off a set of directions that I immediately recognized led to the Old Culver property. Back when he was alive, with the Culver family's permission, our dad had used the easy access to a protected inlet that their private road provided, to load firewood into the small boat we used to take it out to Morrow Island.

During Maine's all too brief summer season, twice a day, the Snowden Family Clambake brought two hundred guests over to the island and provided them with an authentic Maine "dining experience." I managed the business. Livvie's husband, Sonny, ran the crew that cooked lobsters, clams, potatoes, onions, ears of corn, and eggs under saltwater-soaked tarps and over the fire the wood provided. Livvie was in charge of the kitchen where she and two other cooks put out the clam chowder we served for the first course and the blueberry grunt we offered for dessert. My mother did all the buying for and managed the gift shop.

Livvie's directions to the Old Culver property included a lot of "turn at the green house" and "take the veer left, not the slight left or the turn left," and "look for the break in the hedge," type directions. I could tell by the furrow in Jamie's brow he was having trouble keeping up. He was a native and a first responder, but there was no dwelling on the Culver property, no town or county road. He would never have been there, and he wouldn't be able to get GPS directions where he was going.

"I know where it is," I volunteered. "I'll go with you." We hadn't used the Old Culver property for years. Now we trucked the wood directly to our boat at the town pier, but I was confident I could still find it.

Jamie hesitated, wanting to argue, but then gave in to relief. "Great. Give me a minute and we'll go."

CHAPTER TWO

We drove in the easy silence that comes from long friendship. Jamie steered us out of Busman's Harbor, across the swing bridge onto Thistle Island, then over the second bridge to Westclaw Point. He didn't need me to give him directions for this early part of the ride.

The sky was bright blue with high puffy clouds riding on a stiff breeze. In mid-April there were mere suggestions of buds on the trees. When I'd lived in New York City for eight years for business school and then work, I'd fallen in love with spring. The warm days, full of promise and renewal. The flowering trees and shrubs in Battery Park, where I went for my evening runs.

But when I'd moved back to Maine five years earlier, I'd had to move my favorite season allegiance back to the fall. Spring, such as it was, arrived in Maine almost a full month later than in New York. When it came it brought gray, cold, rainy days, broken occasionally by sunny ones like today. Reacquaintance had taught me that these rare nice days were a tease. Maine spring was like Lucy Van Pelt jerking the football from Charlie Brown. As soon as we began to believe warmer weather would come, Mother Nature would pull it away. You could almost hear the wind call, "Blockhead."

April was mud season. The snow had melted, bathing the landscape in water. The trees and shrubs weren't yet absorbing the moisture from the soil. April's torrential rains, added to all that, created a boggy, miserable mess. In Maine, April was to be endured, not celebrated.

"I'm not looking forward to this conversation." Jamie adjusted the visor to keep the sun out of his eyes. "How much do you think all that stuff was worth?"

"At retail, a lot." Lupine Design, pronounced LU-pin, like the wildflowers that filled Maine meadows and lined the roads in June, specialized in gorgeous, sophisticated, expensive, handmade pieces. "At cost, I have no idea. I also have no idea how long it will take to remake the inventory they need to fill orders." The retail shop was, for Lupine Design, a showcase but something of a sideline. Zoey made most of her money selling her wares through high-end gift shops and online orders. She was a prime example of the new kind of entrepreneur Maine had attracted in recent years. She lived and worked in Busman's Harbor because she wanted to, not because her business depended on the location.

We fell silent again. I glanced at Jamie's profile as he drove, focused on the road. He was one of those blonds with tannable skin, dark brows and dark lashes, a state of affairs Livvie pronounced, "desperately unfair." His parents' property backed up to my parents' yard and we'd grown up together. He'd gotten tall, his face had lengthened, and his features sharpened, but a slight fullness in his cheeks still gave me glimpses of the boy I'd known.

Over the winter, Jamie and I had gone out to eat or to the movies a few times. I suspected these outings had been engineered by my mother and sister to distract me from my tragic, single state. Nothing had come of it. Probably we'd been friends too long to change our status. At least that was my assessment.

My family refused to give up hope. They, and by *they* in this case I meant Mom and Livvie, fervently hoped I would stay in Busman's Harbor. They believed that without a romantic partner and meaningful winter work it would be hard to hold me. They weren't wrong. Only the inertia born of a bad set of circumstances kept me from exploring my options more actively. Besides, there were worse things than being loved and wanted by your family.

I pointed out the turn at the green house to Jamie and set us on the right road at the intersection with the slight left, veer left, and hard left turns. Together he and I hunted for the break in the thick vegetation that could only charitably be described as a hedge. The opening would be almost impossible to spot once the buds on the branches turned into leaves. When we were through the hedge, the dirt road was familiar to me. The heavy patrol car, built for speed but not for traction, spun its wheels. They don't call it mud season for nothing. Jamie cursed under his breath, but kept the big car moving.

The road came around a long, wide curve and ended at a sweep of marsh that opened to the West Bay, a protected spot surrounded by summer houses up on the rocky hillside. The faded browns of the winter marsh grass spread out toward the deep blue of the bay. Jamie parked behind a big, bright red SUV. We got out and walked to the edge of the marsh.

I spotted Zoey before he did. Or I assumed it was Zoey, a figure in a puffy navy-blue vest and tall army-green rubber boots. She was bent over, digging in the mud with a shovel. I waved and called out, but a stiff wind coming off the water blew my words away. I poked Jamie in the arm and pointed. We trudged in the figure's direction.

Eventually she straightened up and watched us come toward her, a puzzled but not panicked expression on her face. I'd been introduced to her before, a few times, when I'd buzzed in and out of Lupine Design to pick up Livvie or deliver a message. Zoey was a pretty woman with a cascade of curly brown hair that she had tamed with a blue bandana. She was broad-shouldered, broad-hipped, and pleasantly curvy. With her large brown eyes and generous smile, I guessed she attracted her share of attention. I judged her to be in her midthirties, same as me.

"Can I help you, Officer?" she shouted when we got closer.

Jamie waited to speak until we reached her. "Ms. Butterfield?"

She swallowed and nodded that she was.

"I'm Officer Dawes with the Busman's Harbor P.D. This is Julia Snowden. Her sister Livvie Ramsey works for you."

"Hi. We've met," I said.

Zoey nodded again, brows pinched together, clearly troubled by the interruption in her morning.

"I'm sorry to tell you there has been an incident of vandalism at your shop." Jamie spoke quickly but clearly, ripping off the Band-Aid.

Zoey looked from one face to the other. "You mean like graffiti?" Her voice was high-pitched and quavery. Cops didn't come out to the back of beyond to tell shop-owners about graffiti.

"I'm afraid it's more serious." Jamie's tone matched the gravity of the situation. "Most of the contents of the shop have been destroyed."

Zoey's mouth dropped open and she stutter-stepped backward. Whatever awful thing she'd been expecting Jamie to say, this wasn't it. "Is everyone okay?"

"Livvie discovered the damage when she came to open this morning," I said. "She's shaken up, as you must be, but she's fine. No one else was there."

Zoey stood for a moment, absorbing. The wind blew her brown hair around the bandana into her face. She brushed it away with her hand.

"I'd like you to come back to town," Jamie said, "to inspect the premises, file a report, let us know if anything is missing."

Zoey nodded. "My car . . ."

Jamie understood her question. "You can come in your own vehicle. You've had quite a shock. If you prefer not to drive, Julia can drive you back in your car."

Zoey hesitated, and then gave me a hint of a smile. "I'd like that. Thank you."

"If that's settled, I'll go," Jamie said. "I'd like to get back to the scene as quickly as possible."

"The scene." Zoey's brow puckered, then comprehension dawned. "The crime scene."

"One thing before I go," Jamie said. "When I told you what happened, did any person jump to mind that you suspect might have done this?"

Zoey looked truly baffled. "No."

"Have you had a recent beef with anyone, anyone at all?"

She smiled, a tentative smile, but a smile nonetheless. "It depends on what you mean by beef. It's a small town. I've become accustomed to people having their differences."

That was putting it politely.

"Let me say it this way," Jamie pressed. "Has anyone threatened you recently, even in the most abstract way? Unhappy customer? Ex-boyfriend? Angry neighbor?"

Zoey started to shake her head, no, but then stopped abruptly. "I do have an angry neighbor," she said. "Phinney Hardison. His shop shares the building with mine."

That got Jamie's attention. "Why is Mr. Hardison angry with you?"

Zoey opened her mouth to answer, then closed it, then opened it again, in a series of false starts. "Let's just say, he's a local and I'm From Away," she finally answered.

An old story, and a generic answer. Barely an answer at all. I wondered what she was holding back.

Jamie looked like he wanted to follow up, but then thought better of it. "Thank you for the information. I'll see you back at your store." He turned and walked away.

"I'm not accusing Phinney," Zoey shouted at Jamie's back. "It's just, you asked if I had an angry neighbor."

Jamie looked over his shoulder. "I understand. We'll have a longer conversation in town."

The dirt road was too narrow to turn around. Zoey and I waited until Jamie's patrol car backed around the big curve and was out of sight. Then we stowed Zoey's shovel in the back of her SUV and hurried to the spot where she'd been digging when Jamie and I arrived.

Four big, clear plastic bags stood at the site, filled with—well, it looked like mud, only maybe a bit bluer. Zoey picked up one, squatting and putting her legs into it, just like they teach you.

I copied her, grabbed another and almost fell over. "Oof."

Zoey moved quickly toward her car. "Careful. They're twenty-five pounds, give or take."

I tried to remember what Livvie's son Jack had felt like when he was twenty-five pounds. Not nearly so heavy, I was sure. My work boots sank into the mud in the dirt road as I walked.

We rushed back for the other bags and loaded up the car. The back of the SUV was protected by a blue tarp. Zoey exchanged her boots for sneakers.

"Do you still want me to drive?" That was why Jamie had left me, but maybe she'd changed her mind.

"If that's okay, I'd feel better."

"Of course." I went around to the driver's side and climbed in.

The outside of Zoey's big vehicle wasn't clean, no car in Maine was during mud season. But under the spray of brown on its sides, red paint gleamed. Inside, the seats were comfy and the car was spotless. I could tell it was new, and luxurious. Livvie had told me Lupine Design was hugely successful, but financial success was a relative thing in a small town. I hadn't expected this. I felt bad about my muddy boots.

Zoey climbed into the passenger seat, reached into the glove compartment, and put on a pair of sunglasses with brown lenses. I stared at the vehicle's unfamiliar dash-board. "How do you—" I finally asked.

"Put your foot on the brake. The keys are in my vest pocket."

"Did it start?" I couldn't hear or feel a thing.

"It's electric. Put it in reverse and ease back slowly."

"I need to move the seat forward." I was at least four inches shorter than she was.

"Lever's on the side."

I found the lever and, after one false start when I found myself lying flat on my back staring at the glass moon roof, got it adjusted. Then I did the front and side mirrors.

"And how do I . . . There's no prindle."

"Prindle?" Zoey was clearly as baffled by the question as I was by the car.

"Prindle," I repeated. "Park-Reverse-Neutral-Drive-Low. How do I put this thing in gear?"

"On the steering wheel."

I pushed the little lever into reverse. A screen the size of my tablet sprang to life so quickly I jumped in my seat. I had to admit the clear picture on the screen did help as I backed the big car up the long dirt road. I held my breath until we reached the pavement at the end of the track where I could turn around. The last thing I wanted was scratches on Zoey's new car.

Once we were on the road, Zoey turned in her seat to face me fully, which only made me more nervous about driving the unfamiliar car. "How bad is it?" she asked. "The shop I mean."

I took a deep breath. "I'm sorry. I think it's a total loss. It looked like every piece of pottery in the store was bro-ken."

"What about the studio? The inventory in the basement? My apartment?" Her voice rose higher and louder with each word. She'd been eerily calm as we'd loaded the car. Now Jamie's words were sinking in.

"I only saw the store. I'm sorry." I said it again because I was.

"*Why* did this happen?"

I didn't have an answer, so I said nothing. We lapsed into an uneasy silence.

"Livvie's told me a lot about you," Zoey finally said as I eased the SUV onto Westclaw Point Road.

"Same here." That wasn't quite true. Livvie had told me *some* about her.

"Thank you for driving me, but how come you were with the officer?"

I explained how I'd seen the police-car lights flashing in front of the store and knew Livvie was there. "I know where the Old Culver property is, so I volunteered to come along."

"Thank you," she said again.

The silence returned for a bit. "Do you dig all the clay for your pottery?" I asked.

Zoey laughed, but not unkindly. "Good heavens, no. It gets delivered on pallets, twenty-five hundred pounds, two at a time, four times a year."

"Then why do you . . ."

Zoey leaned back against the headrest. A bit of the tension seemed to seep from her body. "Digging in the earth reminds me why I got into pottery, before my life was taken over by phone calls, emails, and spreadsheets. I love being outdoors. Early spring is my favorite time to dig. The ground has thawed, and the black flies aren't out yet. Spring and the fall. I love to dig in the fall."

Black flies were the other bane of a Maine spring,

emerging just as the mud was disappearing. They swarmed and bit and drove you crazy whenever you ventured outside. From Mother's Day to Father's Day they would eat you alive.

"The clay I dug today will require hours of processing to make it usable," Zoey said. "You have to get rid of the twigs, stones, and dirt. I use the clay I dig to make special things like gifts for friends or experimental pieces I keep for myself."

"How do you know where to find the clay?" How had she, after three years in the area, found the Old Culver property when Jamie, who'd lived here all his life, didn't know where it was?

"Clay is everywhere in Maine, especially within forty miles or so of the coast. And it's often close enough to the surface to dig. The glaciers only left here twelve thousand years ago. There hasn't been much time, earthwise, to develop a deep layer of topsoil. That's what causes the mud. Not enough soil to absorb the rain and snow melt. That and the water can't drain through the clay that's underneath."

She looked out her window. From the high seat in the SUV, it was easy to see the side of the road as we sped by. Even on this sunny day, there was standing water in the muddy ruts on the shoulder.

"When I'm hiking, I look for depressions in fields, places where gardens won't grow," Zoey continued. "Flat land near water is almost always good. Of course, then you have to get permission from the owners. Three years ago, when I first moved here, I was having my building renovated. I lived in this awful rental, an old farmhouse that never got warm. My studio was in the barn. I was so depressed I started studying geologic maps in my spare time, looking for likely places to dig clay. That's how I found the Old Culver place. The Culvers have been so generous letting me dig there."

"They are generous." I told her how my dad used to load firewood there. "That's why I knew where you were."

"I think Livvie mentioned she'd been there."

"How did you go sideways with Phinney Hardison anyway?" I asked. I figured after three years in town she'd be used to the Maine habit of directness.

A flush rose in her cheeks. "I didn't accuse him of trashing the store. Officer Dawes asked if I had a beef with anyone. Do you know Phinney?"

"Kind of." Phinney was a friend of my friend Gus and his compatriot Bud Barbour. They often gathered in Gus's restaurant in the quiet times between meals, three old guys jawboning while Gus cleaned. I'd heard enough to know what they hated: a) change, b) people who wanted change, and c) most especially of all, people From Away who wanted change. I jokingly referred to the place where they sat at the counter as "Curmudgeon's Corner." Sometimes they would do me the favor of looking mildly amused.

Phinney's store, filled with shelves of dusty "antiques" and "collectibles," occupied about a quarter of the main floor at the front of the Lupine Design building. It had its own entrance and big display window.

"I was so excited when I signed the lease on the building," Zoey said. "I did a lot of improvements and customizations. In the studio I added the kilns, a sink, worktables, and shelving. I renovated my apartment up-stairs. You know how we're the farthest shops down Main Street?" She looked over at me until I nodded. "Lots of times, tourists don't make it down the street that far. So I had this brilliant idea, or so I thought, that we would put bright yellow and white striped awnings over each of our display windows, to attract people's attention." She took a breath. "I suggested it to Phinney."

"Let me guess. He didn't go for it."

"He acted as if I had asked him to pay to have graffiti dripping in blood and curse words painted on the front of our stores. He said he had plenty of customers and maybe I'd get some someday, too, although since I'd destroyed the inside of my space, he doubted I'd last long. 'Nobody can pay ninety-two dollars for a dinner plate,' he said. Well, ha-ha, Phinney, they can, and they do. By the thousands."

Zoey's issues with Phinney didn't surprise me. Not only had she entered the nuclear code for c) change suggested by someone From Away, but she'd also asked Phinney to spend money, which was the biggest sin of all. "How long ago was this?" I asked.

"Two-and-a-half years ago, before I opened the store." She paused. "Anyway, after the blowup about the awnings, things settled down and we got along pretty well. We had arguments about little stuff, but nothing major. Until this thing with the pedestrian mall."

Ah, the pedestrian mall. Busman's Harbor's current swirling controversy. There was a proposal to block traffic on the four commercial blocks of Main Street on Friday and Saturday evenings during July and August. The idea was that shops would put their wares out and restaurants would expand their outdoor dining, and it would turn into something of a street festival. I hadn't paid much attention to the controversy. It wouldn't have an effect on the Snowden Family Clambake. We'd be serving our second seating out on Morrow Island during that time. Main Street was a game of dodge 'em on weekend nights in the summer, anyway, with tourists crossing without looking, people walking in the street, and zero parking anywhere. I did know that Gus, Bud Barbour, and Phinney Hardison were vehemently opposed to the proposal, for no rational reason that I could see. Gus's restaurant closed at three in the afternoon and Bud pretended to run a small boat repair business outside of the pedestrian zone, but was mostly retired. Phinney might actually have benefited from the extra foot traffic the pedestrian mall would bring, but he insisted on closing his store at 6:00 p.m. every day, in every season, regardless of the opportunity.

"You're for the mall I take it?" I said.

"Absolutely," Zoey answered. "I think it will be wonderful. More customers, less car exhaust, and a fun party atmosphere. What's not to love?"

What indeed?

CHAPTER THREE

When we turned the corner onto Main Street, a group of twenty people or so had gathered in front of Lupine Design. Phinney Hardison and Jamie were visible in the center of the crowd. Phinney was red in the face, his mouth opening and closing in rapid speech. Jamie was three feet away from him, gesturing for calm, getting nowhere.

"My parking spot is in the back," Zoey said. I pulled into the driveway. When we got out of the SUV, I could hear Phinney yelling. We hurried around to the front.

Zoey pushed her way through the crowd. I followed in her wake.

"What 'er ya tryin' to say?" Though well into his seventies, Phinney had the size to intimidate. He was over six feet with a broad chest and thick neck. The rest of his weight seemed to have left his extremities and gathered in his midsection, but he was still a bull of a man. His white hair was so short that his scalp, currently bright red, was visible through it. He held a paper coffee cup with a plastic lid in his right hand.

"Perhaps, Mr. Hardison, you'd prefer to discuss this inside your shop," Jamie suggested.

"I got nothin' to hide. Ask me right here, in front of these people." Phinney gestured around the crowd with his coffee cup. Jamie's partner, Pete Howland, stood in the front row, frowning, his arms crossed over his pudgy belly. Phinney caught sight of Zoey. "You!" he thundered. "What's the drama queen cooked up this time?"

"Take a look for yourself." Officer Howland cleared the way so Phinney could approach Lupine Design's display window. Phinney put his face against the glass and peered inside. "Well, well. That's a mess." He turned back to face Jamie. "Ask me anything." Phinney was calmer, his attention captured.

"What time did you leave this building last night?" Jamie asked.

"Six o'clock on the dot, same as always," Phinney answered.

"And what time did you return this morning?"

Phinney gave the crowd an exaggerated look of disbelief. "Just now. Didn't you stop me on my way in?"

"When I approached you ten minutes ago, that was the first time you'd come to your store today."

"I was carrying my coffee, was I not?" Phinney challenged.

"That's why I thought you might be returning from a coffee break," Jamie responded, still calm.

"Well, I'm not."

They had lowered their voices by this point, but Jamie

was obviously uncomfortable with conducting an interview in front of the crowd. "Let's go inside," he suggested again.

"Am I under arrest?" Phinney demanded.

"Are you unwilling to help with a police investigation?" Jamie shot back.

"No." Phinney shrugged his broad shoulders. "I'm willing to help with it right here." He pointed at the sidewalk with his left hand.

Jamie's jaw clenched. He was angry, trying to remain calm. "In the last few days or weeks, did you hear or see anything unusual on the Lupine Design premises or around the property?"

"Aside from females chattering, machines banging and scraping, supplies getting dropped off by noisy delivery trucks, and other trucks getting loaded with that ugly stuff and hauling it away, aside from that?" Phinney looked hard at Jamie. "Nah. None of that's unusual. I didn't see or hear anything unusual."

"Did you hear anyone make threats against Ms. Butterfield or her property?"

Phinney put his skinny arms out, palms up. "Why would anyone bother?"

"When was the last time you were inside Lupine Design's side of the building?" Jamie asked.

"Now you're accusing me." Phinney dug the worn-down heels of his unlaced leather boots into the sidewalk.

"No. Eliminating you from our inquiries."

"Our stores share a basement," Phinney conceded. "I may have accidentally stepped into her side down there once in a blue moon. As to being in the store itself, I've never been in there. Why would I?"

"To sum up," Jamie said, "you heard nothing, you saw

nothing, you've never heard any threats against Ms. Butterfield, and you've never been in the shop."

"You got it," Phinney said. "I got a store to open if it's all right with you."

The crowd began to drift away and Jamie, Zoey, Howland, and I went through the double doors into Lupine Design. Livvie was in an office chair behind the checkout counter, looking miserable. There were no cops visible in the store, but I could hear heavy footsteps in the apartment above and from the studio behind the shop. Livvie joined us and we huddled in a circle.

Zoey's head turned as she took in the shambles in her store, her eyes slightly glazed. Her lip quivered and she bit it hard. I could scarcely imagine the fear, rage, and worry she must be feeling, though she was fighting hard not to show us.

"Did you come into the store before you left this morning?" Jamie asked Zoey.

"I have to go through the shop to enter or leave my apartment." Zoey pointed to the staircase on the side wall of the display room.

"And everything was fine, I assume," Jamie said. "Or you would have called us." Zoey nodded and Jamie continued. "What time did you leave?"

"A couple of minutes before six o'clock." Zoey sounded confident, certain. "I noticed the time on my car dashboard and was pleased with myself for getting out before the deadline I'd set in my head."

"Livvie found the mess when she arrived at nine." Jamie reviewed the available information. "This happened between six and nine."

It seemed like an odd time for vandalism. The sun would be fully out, and carpenters, plumbers, and electricians would be picking up supplies at Gleason's Hardware, a few blocks away. People would be driving to Gus's, the only restaurant open for breakfast in the off-season. On the other hand, the few shops operating at this time of year wouldn't open until ten, and there were no tourists to walk by the store in search of a place to eat. So someone could have trashed Lupine Design in broad daylight in full view of the shop's display window. They could and they had.

As if he'd been tracking with my thoughts, Jamie said, "We'll put a call out on the police social media channels to ask witnesses to come forward." He looked over at the front door to the shop. "We saw no signs of a break-in. How many people have keys?"

Zoey counted on her fingers. "Three of my employees, including Livvie. They take turns opening up." She looked up at him and shrugged. "That's it, I think, besides me."

Jamie took the employees' names. "No cleaners, repair people," he confirmed.

"We clean ourselves. The goods are too delicate to let anyone else do it. And I live here. I can always let repair people in. So no one else."

"Did you change the locks when you did your renovation?" Jamie asked. "We didn't see a security system."

"I wanted to change the locks, but Phinney wouldn't hear of it. It seemed ridiculous to change only mine, since we share the basement, so I left them. As for a security system, who would want to steal my pottery? It's not like you can fence the stuff."

She had a point. Or she would have had, if we weren't

standing in a store littered with destroyed ceramics. "Does your landlord have keys?" I asked.

"I don't know. All my dealings were with the agency that rented me the place."

Jamie nodded. "Ms. Butterfield, I'd like you to walk Officer Howland and me around your entire space and tell us if you see anything missing. You'll need to do a complete inventory later for your insurance company. I want your first impressions."

Zoey nodded and the three of them walked toward the open door in the middle of the back wall of the shop. Livvie and I looked at one another and followed.

The doorway opened up to a large, light-filled studio. Lupine Design and Phinney's shop divided the front half of the building, but the entire back half belonged to Zoey. The space looked more like a place for light industry than a craft studio. There were big presses for making the molded pieces and a large shipping area lined with stacks of cardboard boxes and rolls of bubble wrap and newsprint. Six big kilns, which looked like bank vaults from an old western movie, lined an outside wall. There was an area for the pottery wheels and a huge table speckled with paint and glaze. There was even a forklift in one corner. But then there would have to be to move twenty-five-hundred pounds of clay.

There was clay everywhere, long rolls wrapped in plastic. Hundreds of pottery items, white and dull, sat on the wooden shelves that lined the inside wall.

Livvie saw me looking at them. "Those are the pieces that have been in the kiln once to dry out the clay, but haven't yet been glazed or had their second firing. Pieces at that stage are called bisque."

Silent and still, the room felt abandoned, like the workers hadn't gone home for the day, but had disappeared forever.

Zoey flitted around the space, her face puckered with concern, though even I could tell the studio hadn't been vandalized.

"Anything missing or out of place?" Jamie asked.

"No, thank goodness." Zoey was visibly relieved.

Jamie walked purposefully to the big barn door that took up almost half the back wall. "We don't see any sign of forced entry." He twisted the handle to unlock the door and pushed it open. It led to a concrete loading dock.

Zoey stepped forward and examined the door. "I don't see anything either."

"Let's go to the basement." Jamie led the way to the stairs. Zoey followed immediately behind him. Then came Livvie, then me, with a silent Pete Howland bringing up the rear.

"Thank goodness!" Zoey halted the minute she reached the doorway at the bottom of the enclosed staircase and the rest of us piled up behind her. She turned excitedly to Livvie, smiling broadly. "Everything is fine."

The rest of us continued down the stairs as the damp basement smell wafted up to us. The space was lined with shelves and shelves of ceramics—stacks of finished plates, bowls, platters, vases, pitchers, and lamp bases all in Lupine Design's distinctive ocean colors. Zoey took her forms from nature. The plates were shaped like tide pools. The platters mimicked the curve of a cresting wave. One shelf held bud vases shaped like sea urchins. I had always admired the work and had been proud that Livvie was a part of creating such beautiful things.

"We have enough inventory to fill our orders. We're saved." Zoey and Livvie hugged each other tight. Zoey turned to Jamie. "Most of this needs to be shipped out in the next couple of weeks."

She pointed to three tall shelves in the corner laden with plates, mugs, and other tableware. "Those are all custom orders for wedding gifts. I was so worried." She sounded like she might finally break down and cry.

From Livvie I knew that Lupine Design's busiest time was in the spring when they shipped off the bulk of their goods to retail stores. That's why Livvie could work at Lupine Design fall to spring and at the Snowden Family Clambake in the summer. She was available when Zoey needed her.

Jamie went to a basement door made of beadboard painted gray and rolled it aside. Concrete steps led up to angled metal doors to the outside, a common setup called a bulkhead in New England. Jamie climbed the concrete stairs and checked. The doors were bolted from the inside.

He came back down and walked over to a second staircase leading up on the other side of the space. "Where does this go?"

"Phinney's shop," Zoey answered. "He uses it to get to his storage area down here. It's also the legally required second egress from his store." A quarter of the basement was partitioned off by chicken wire tacked to wooden scaffolding. Peering into the dark space, I spotted an old mahogany dining table, and several massive bureaus, the kind of stuff nobody wanted anymore. Every surface was covered with ceramic figurines, mismatched teacups, heavy glass ashtrays, and all manner of flotsam and jetsam.

Jamie flipped on a light in the stairwell. "No lock on this side."

"Wouldn't be," Howland said, "if it's his legal egress. Couldn't take the chance in case of fire."

Jamie climbed the stairs and tried the door. "It's locked from the other side." He came back down and looked at Zoey. "Phinney has pretty much unfettered access to your space. Does that make you uneasy?"

"Never," Zoey answered. "What would he want with my stuff? Or I with his, for that matter? I have a lock inside the door at the bottom of the stairs to my apartment, which I use at night. Phinney's long gone by then anyway. I've never felt unsafe." She paused. "For any reason."

Jamie turned to Howland. "Can you check Phinney's store for signs of a break-in?"

Howland gave a sharp, quick nod, unusual for him; in general he moved slowly, and went up the main stairs back into the studio. We heard him tramp across the floor, calling out to another officer. The rest of us followed.

Back in the store, Jamie turned to Zoey. "Ms. Butterfield, I'd like to accompany you upstairs to your apartment so you can check it out. Julia, Livvie, thanks for your help. Why don't you stay down here?"

CHAPTER FOUR

After the police left, Zoey took hundreds of photographs of the mess for her insurance company. Livvie grabbed a snow shovel and big, rolling rubber barrel from the studio and began dumping the pottery shards. I found a bottle of dish soap, a bucket, and cloth by the studio sink. I diluted the dish soap in warm water and started in on the black fingerprint powder that covered the countertops and cabinet door frames by the specialty display. It wasn't the biggest mess in the place, but I knew from sad experience how hard it was to clean off. They would thank me later.

Zoey finished with the photos and all of us worked. When we ran out of rubber barrels, I went to Gleason's Hardware to buy heavy plastic contractor bags "These must be for Zoey's store," Al Gleason, the owner, said as he scanned the items. "I should have known you'd be in that up to your neck. Give Zoey my condolences."

Ah, small town life. Everybody knows everything.

Back at Lupine Design I grabbed a broom and kept working. Clearing away the broken pottery was a sad business. On the back or the bottom of each piece was a delicate, painted lupine, in one of an array of colors, along with the words LUPINE DESIGN in a stylized font. The flowers were a little off the seaside theme Zoey focused on in the shapes and colors of her pottery, but somehow the lupines made a beautiful signature for each of the pieces. Every time I dumped one of those painted pieces in the heavy plastic contractor bag, it pricked my heart. I couldn't imagine how Livvie and Zoey must feel.

By two o'clock we had the pottery cleaned away. The floor still needed the attention of a shop vac, and then a regular vac, and every surface needed to be dusted, but we'd made enormous progress.

Zoey straightened up, her hands on her hips. "I have some good cheese, bread, and hard salami upstairs. Let's eat. I'm famished."

I was starving, too, and thirsty. Livvie and I washed the dust off as best we could in the studio sink and went up the stairs. "Have you ever been in the apartment?" I whispered.

"Never."

The tight stairwell opened up into an enormous light-filled room that spanned the entire building. I should have been prepared for the apartment, given how beautiful the shop was, but I wasn't. It was breathtaking.

"Wow," Livvie said aloud, speaking for both of us.

Zoey was at the other side of the space, retrieving items from the restaurant-grade refrigerator and placing them on a wooden tray on the big island. The kitchen cabinets were the same blue-gray as in the shop, but here they were topped with gleaming white countertops.

By the time Livvie and I reached the island, Zoey had pulled three gorgeous wineglasses out of a cabinet and a bottle from a wine fridge in the island. "I think we deserve a drink."

"Water first," I said. The work downstairs had given me a powerful thirst and I'd found day-drinking made me more sleepy than relaxed.

"Suit yourself." Zoey gave me a tall glass and pointed to the fancy cold water dispenser near the deep stainless sink.

"I'll have wine." Livvie didn't share my reservations.

"We'll be more comfortable over here." Zoey carried the tray with the cheese, salami, bread, and green grapes over to the coffee table in the seating area. She sat in one of the two fifties-era chairs that faced the leather couch. The chairs were spare, with clean lines in teak, and orange cushions on the back and seat. Livvie and I headed for the sofa.

"That's wonderful." I pointed to the large abstract painting over the couch. It was a sunset over the ocean, or it least it looked that way to me. Someone else might have seen something entirely different in the slashes of blues and oranges.

"Thanks. Almost everything on the walls is stuff I got in trade from friends in art school. They got dishes, mugs, and pitchers. I got paintings, photographs, and wall-hangings." Around the big room I spotted examples of each, displayed and lit perfectly.

"Is that where you learned pottery, art school?" I asked.

"For sure. My high school education didn't offer anything of the sort and my mother never could have afforded outside lessons. It was mostly just her and me when I was growing up."

"Growing up in—" If Livvie had ever mentioned where, I'd forgotten.

"California."

"How did you end up in Busman's Harbor?"

She laughed. "You'll think I'm crazy. A photo in a magazine."

"You're kidding."

"Not at all. After school I bounced around a lot—Colorado, Michigan, Texas, New York City. When it came time to get my own studio, I bought a travel magazine and there was an article about mid-coast Maine and a photo of Busman's Harbor's Main Street shops. Instantly I thought *there*.

"It turned out the rents were reasonable, at least compared to what I was looking at in New York. There was space available, and lots of pottery businesses in the area, so I could hire experienced staff." She smiled at my sister. "Like the brilliant Livvie."

My sister smiled back, acknowledging the compliment. She'd worked as a potter in the off-season for years. Zoey had upped her wage and vowed to be flexible about Livvie's family obligations in order to recruit her.

"You signed a lease and moved your company and yourself to a place you'd never been?" I was astonished.

"I came up to see the building, of course. It needed a lot of renovation and updating to work for the business. I put so much time and money into it. But I got exactly what I wanted."

She'd made a big bet. What if she'd hated it?

"Because I did so many improvements, I demanded a

long lease," Zoey continued. "Ten years. I've never in my life lived anywhere that long."

"Is your mom still in California?" Funny she'd never considered moving back.

"She's dead."

"I'm so sorry." I glanced at Livvie. This wasn't news to her.

"It's okay. It was a long time ago."

I switched from water to wine. Zoey moved my glass and the bottle over to the coffee table so I could help myself. When I brought the delicate but perfectly balanced glass to my lips and swallowed, the white wine was delicious, crisp and dry, exactly as I'd expected. "Tell me about this pedestrian mall," I said. "Is it really so divisive it might have gotten someone wound up enough to trash your store? What's the big deal?"

"It isn't a big deal in my opinion." Zoey poured a second glass of wine for herself and for Livvie. "It's portable concrete barriers the town would have to move into place for eight weekend evenings. Apparently the public works department already owns the barriers, so the expense is the labor and some minor wear and tear on the equipment. The individual stores and restaurants would be responsible for moving displays or dining tables onto the sidewalk. Honestly, I was surprised when it turned into such a big thing."

"Some people don't like change." Livvie left it at that. I wondered where her husband stood. Sonny fought me whenever I tried to update anything at the Snowden Family Clambake. He didn't like change in the least.

"There's a public hearing at town hall tonight." Zoey looked at me. "You should come and judge for yourself."

Small towns all over Maine and New England were preparing for their annual town meeting, when every registered voter was invited to look their neighbors in the eye, say what they had to say, and vote, publicly, on everything their town would do or spend for the next year. Some called it an exercise in the purest form of democracy on earth. Others called it a crap storm. It was usually both.

If the agenda for the town meeting looked to be long, or contentious, or especially when it looked to be long *and* contentious, the elected members of the select board and the budget committee would often schedule a series of public hearings to take place in the weeks leading up to the big day. The aim was to allow everyone to feel heard and work out an acceptable compromise, which the select board would recommend to the full town meeting. Ideally, the extra meetings would cut down on the rancor and hours of debate at the main event. It was one of those hearings Zoey was urging me to attend tonight.

I made a noise that I hoped sounded neutral and then stood. The single glass of wine had hit me hard. A look at my phone told me it was almost three o'clock. "Are you sure you don't want me to stay and help?"

Zoey had to be exhausted. She'd been out doing hard physical work since early that morning, followed by the emotions of seeing her work in pieces on the shop-room floor, and then the labor of cleaning up.

"Livvie and I can finish with the vacuuming and dusting," Zoey answered. "We won't reload the shelves until tomorrow. You must have things to do. Before you go, do you guys want a tour of the rest of the apartment?"

"Yes, please!" She didn't have to ask me twice.

"You two go ahead," Livvie said. "I'll get a start on clearing up."

Livvie collected the glasses and food while Zoey led me up the stairs to the third floor. There was another big, open space painted white with trim in Zoey's signature blue gray. Windows and skylights in the slanted ceiling flooded the room with light. The only piece of furniture was a metal canopy bed, draped in swathes of sheer fabric. The effect was stunning.

Next to the bed were two framed watercolors. Both were of gardens, havens surrounded by flowers and flowering shrubs. You could almost smell the lilacs hanging from the branches. The paintings were nothing like the abstracts downstairs, but they were just as powerful. Maybe more so.

Zoey saw me examining them. "My mother's," she said. "Two of the few things I have left of her."

"They're beautiful."

"She was very talented."

Zoey led me into the large bathroom, which had one of her handmade sinks. Next to it was a closet the size of a small bedroom.

"Wow. Just wow. Everything is perfect." I meant it.

We climbed two stories down the stairs back to the store, where Livvie was waiting.

"Come to the public hearing tonight, please," Zoey said. "I know Livvie's got her family to take care of and I could use the moral support."

"I'll try." I hugged Livvie, said my good-byes, and took off.

CHAPTER FIVE

I strolled back up Main Street toward Mom's house. Zoey might not be tired, but the drama of the morning, along with the hard, physical work of cleaning up, and the big glass of wine, had caught up to me. I needed a nap.

When I crossed the street at the corner where Main Street came around the harbor hill and looped back over itself at the only traffic light in town, creating the intersection of Main and Main, I spotted John Fenwick walking toward me with his little dog.

He was somewhere in his early seventies and had a sinewy body and a jaunty gait. My impression was he was that sort of person who viewed keeping fit at any age as a virtue and failing to do so as a terrible lapse. He wore a baseball cap from his apparently limitless collection, a gray one today, and khaki shorts. His only concession to mud season was thick socks and sturdy hiking boots.

At 7:00 a.m., 3:00 p.m., and 8:00 p.m. exactly, Fenwick and his little terrier mix exited his house at the head of the inner harbor, walked down Eastclaw Point to the footbridge, crossed over into town, walked down Main Street and back home again. You could set your watch by him, if you still had a watch that needed to be set. By my quick calculation, he would have passed Lupine Design at 7:40 or so that morning. I raised my hand and hailed him.

"Mr. Fenwick," I said when I met him on the sidewalk.

"John, please. You're Jacqueline's daughter." I had many identities in my small town: Jacqueline's daughter, Livvie's sister, Page and Jack's aunt, and formerly, Chris Durand's girlfriend. "Julia." I put my hand out and we shook. "Did you hear about what happened at Lupine Design?"

"Talk of the town," he responded. "What a shame."

"You walk by there every morning, don't you?" I knew he did, but I wanted to ease my way into the conversation.

"Indeed I do." He grinned broadly, showing a good set of teeth for a man his age.

"When you were passing on your walk this morning, did you notice anything strange?"

"Not a thing." He answered without hesitation. "In my mind's eye the shelves were loaded with her beautiful designs when I passed, same as always."

"In your mind's eye?"

"Jock and I are moving pretty fast by the time we get to that end of Main. I go by there every day, and I'm usually thinking about something else. I honestly couldn't tell you if I'm remembering the shelves the way they were this morning or on some other day."

At the sound of his name, Jock, who had immediately sat when his owner stopped, stood and wagged his tail. He looked at Fenwick and walked away. Not enough to tighten the leash, but enough to say, "Let's get going."

"I'm pretty sure if I'd noticed anything, I would've walked over and looked through the window," Fenwick said. "And if the store looked like I've heard, I would've called the police."

"It looked like you've heard." Too bad he couldn't be more definitive. If he was sure the store was fine when he walked by, it would shorten considerably the time period when the destruction could have occurred. "You should probably tell the police what you think you saw," I said.

He shrugged, "Maybe. I wish I could be more certain."

When I came through the always unlocked back door at Mom's, Le Roi, our Maine coon cat, ran to greet me. Main coons have many dog-like qualities, and greeting you at the door was one of his. He rubbed up against my jeans and demanded I give his old, muscle-gone-to-fat body a rub. He was named for Elvis Presley, "the King," and was now indisputably in the Elvis-in-Vegas phase of his life.

Mom was at her job as a manager at Linens and Pantries, the big-box store in Topsham, so I went straight up the back stairs to my room. My old room. My new room.

A month earlier, my landlord, Gus, had let me know that his son, who lived in Arizona, had retired and he and his wife would be staying in Busman's Harbor for the summer. Gus planned to renovate my apartment over his restaurant so they'd have a place to stay. He felt terrible about kicking me out, but it was for family.

I had been devastated. I didn't know exactly why. Except for the beauty of its view of the back harbor, and waking up to the smells of pancakes, home fries, and coffee wafting up the stairs from the restaurant every morning, the little studio hadn't been anything to brag about.

But Gus's was the place where I'd first seen Chris again, years after he'd been my unattainable middle school crush. It was where we'd run our winter restaurant for three years. In that upstairs apartment, I'd dreamed of marriage and family. Even though Chris had moved out months earlier, leaving the apartment broke my heart all over again.

At the time, Livvie and Mom tried to tell me change was good, staying in the place where I'd lived with Chris wasn't helping me get past him. I couldn't make myself believe them.

As I'd packed up on a dismal March day, I realized how little from the apartment I wanted to keep. Gus and his wife had left most of the furniture when they'd moved out decades before. The few pieces handed down to me by friends and relatives weren't worth moving. I'd trundled my stuff—clothes and books, a lamp I'd grown fond of—up the harbor hill to Mom's in a single carload. It wasn't leaving the apartment that killed me. It was the dreams I was leaving behind. Nothing I'd believed a year ago about my life was still true.

I had instigated the breakup with Chris, as I constantly reminded myself, and therefore had no reason to be heartbroken. It had happened over Memorial Day weekend. After that, I'd worked fourteen hours a day, seven days a week at the Snowden Family Clambake for four months.

At night I fell into bed and instantly into a dreamless sleep.

Then came the awful discussion when Chris and I had concluded that attempting to run our winter restaurant as business partners and friends would be too hard. He was hurting, too.

I tried to keep busy through the fall and winter, closing out the clambake books, distributing the profits among the family and to our silent investor. I filed our taxes. I consulted to a few businesses around town, mostly solving small problems. It wasn't enough, though I tried hard to convince myself it was.

Coming on top of all that, Gus's announcement that I had to leave my apartment had thrown me for another loop, bringing back all the feelings from the first days of the breakup with Chris. An emotional loop-de-loop, as it were.

So I was back in my childhood bedroom, literally back to square one. And it wasn't my first trip around the old Monopoly board. I'd been here five years before when I'd first moved back to Busman's Harbor to run the Snowden Family Clambake.

In my teenage room, with its single bed and fading blue paint, my mind drifted to Zoey Butterfield's beautiful apartment. Everything was exactly how she wanted it. My friends and colleagues who'd stayed in finance in New York had nice homes now, too. Super nice ones.

Zoey had built what she had from nothing. She exercised ownership over her domain with a confidence and control I envied. I didn't envy the pottery business. I wouldn't want to do that. Or the apartment, specifically. But I marveled at her ability to take risks, traveling from place to place, settling in a town she knew nothing about.

I admired the way Zoey moved through the world, as if she had every right to be wherever she was, do whatever she was doing, express whatever opinion she had.

I'd been the good girl. I'd done what was expected, but at some point, my sister Livvie, the rebel, had become the one with two kids, a husband, and two marketable skills: cooking for the Snowden Family Clambake during tourist season, and creating beautiful objects at Lupine Design the rest of the year. What did I have to show for the past decade?

I sighed and lay down on top of my twin bed, chiding myself to end the pity party. Le Roi jumped up beside me and turned on his purr machine. I drifted off into a wine-induced sleep.

The sound of the back door opening and closing traveled up the back stairs.

"Mom?"

"Hi, Julia," Mom called back.

"What time is it?" I reached for my phone. Almost five-thirty and it was still fully light out. A welcome sign of spring.

"Were you sleeping?" My mother was at the bottom of the stairs.

I wasn't known for napping or day-drinking. I wanted to keep it that way. My family was already far more concerned for me than my behavior warranted, in my opinion.

"Are you here for dinner? Shall I heat the soup?" Mom asked.

Mom and I were still getting used to each other again as roommates, figuring out what we were doing communally and what we were doing individually. It had been more than four years since I'd lived in her house. Despite a long marriage, followed by a period of deep grief, my mom was generally self-sufficient and content to be on her own. I took after her in that way. We needed to learn to give each other space without neglecting one another.

"Sure. I'll be right down." Le Roi followed me to the bathroom and watched while I brushed my teeth and splashed cold water on my face. We proceeded downstairs together. Mom stood at the stove heating our dinner. I grabbed soup bowls and spoons and set our old enamel-topped kitchen table.

My arrival back at Mom's house had left the two noncooks in the family marooned together. Mom had lost her mother when she was young and was raised by a series of housekeepers, who, I gathered, ranged from nurturing to indifferent. They had left a smattering of cooking knowledge behind, but the hodgepodge of techniques and cuisines had done more harm than good. My mother was a terrible cook.

When Livvie was in middle school she had declared our family kitchen her domain, mostly out of self-defense. Since I'd moved back to Mom's house, my sister had taken pity on us and cooked a big meal for the family every Sunday. Later during the week, Mom and I had taken to combining the leftovers, along with whatever other ingredients we happened to have on hand, into something she called "refrigerator soup." Our efforts were hitor-miss, but whatever the level of culinary achievement, the soups were warm and hearty and had seen us nicely through the chill and disappointment of a Maine spring.

Mom ladled out the soup. I leaned over my bowl and breathed in the oniony, tomatoey smell. This week's effort had been particularly successful. The soup was filled with veggies and beans, chicken chunks, and pasta shells. The rich taste snapped me out of my post-nap haze.

Over dinner, I filled Mom in on the events of the morning.

She was properly horrified. "They have no idea who did it?"

"None. Zoey thinks maybe, just maybe, it's somehow connected with her advocacy for the pedestrian mall on Main Street."

"Seems like an overreaction, to put it mildly," Mom said.

"It does," I agreed. The destruction had been so complete. It seemed angry. Personal.

Mom finished her soup and put her bowl in the sink. "What's on for you tonight?"

"I'm thinking of going to the public hearing at town hall."

"A public hearing?" Mom smiled. "It's not, by any chance, about the pedestrian mall?"

"As a matter of fact, it is."

CHAPTER SIX

Busman's Harbor's combined fire-station-town-hall-police-headquarters was in an ugly, new brick building on Main Street a couple of blocks from Mom's house. By the time I walked over, the parking lot was overflowing with cars and pickups, some parked haphazardly in illegal spaces.

The multipurpose room where town meetings were held was standing room only. The state police used the big space as an incident room whenever they came to town to investigate a major crime. I was used to seeing it set up with plastic folding tables and whiteboards, with cables snaking across the faded blue carpet. Seeing it staged for its intended purpose, with rows of metal folding chairs facing front, was weirdly disorienting, like it couldn't be the same place.

I scouted for a single seat—sometimes people left them in the middle of a row—but no luck. Zoey had ob-

viously arrived early and had a seat upfront. She saw me
and waved, but there was no space open anywhere near
her. The room was hot and many people fanned themselves with pieces of white printer paper.

I found a spot along the back wall, leaned against it
and folded my arms. I was going to be standing for a
while. Over in the opposite corner, also against the wall, I
spotted my brother-in-law Sonny, with Pete Howland and
a couple of their friends. John Fenwick was in the room,
too, in a coveted aisle seat and without his little dog. It
was the first time I'd ever seen him without Jock. My ex-
landlord Gus, Bud Barbour, and Phinney Hardison sat together in the last row, also coveted seating because it was
easy to sneak out unobtrusively if the hearing got dull.

Public hearings could range from so boring that you
felt like your eyes might roll back in your head perma-
nently, to so raucous and mean that for weeks you couldn't
look your neighbors in the eye when you ran into them at
Hannaford supermarket. "There ain't no fight like a small-
town fight," the saying goes, because no matter what it's
about, it's personal.

Up at the front of the room, on one side of the podium,
the five members of the select board sat at a table facing
the crowd. The three members of the budget committee
sat at a table on the other side. The moderator stood at the
podium. He was a skinny, unprepossessing man in a flannel shirt and a terrible toupee. The town hired him to run
all these meetings and he was a master. He knew most
everyone's names and more than likely what they were
going to say on any issue. He banged his gavel and we
were off.

There was routine business to get through at the start.
The crowd chattered restlessly and had to be gaveled to

order numerous times. Everyone was there for the discussion about the pedestrian mall.

Finally, the moderator opened the floor to citizen comment about the proposal. Phinney Hardison made a bee-line for the microphone that had been placed halfway up the center aisle. John Fenwick jumped in line behind him. My brother-in-law Sonny trooped up the aisle and parked himself behind Fenwick. A man I didn't recognize got behind him. Zoey brought up the rear.

The crowd noise was so loud the moderator banged his gavel again and again. "Mr. Hardison, you have three minutes. State your name and address for the record."

"Ya know my name for blast's sake. Ya just said it."

"For the record," the moderator repeated with patience, a quality he'd need plenty of.

Phinney puckered his mouth and blew out through his lips, the portrait of aggravation. "Phinney Hardison. I've lived at 122A Eastclaw Point Road for fifteen years. I was born here at the hospital and I'm a proud graduate of Busman's Harbor High. Go Seals!"

This was part of the ritual. Any registered voter could speak at these public hearings, but everyone, and especially the old-timers, liked to emphasize their bona fides.

"Three minutes, Phinney," the moderator reminded.

Phinney shoved his big face, dotted with white stubble, forward. "This town's a beautiful town." His voice boomed, amplified by the sound system. "Those of us who go way back here know it. It's ironic, ain't it, that people move here because they say they love the place, and immediately spend all their time trying to change it." He turned around and glared at Zoey. "This pedestrian mall, or whatever you're calling it, is going to make it impossible for the merchants. Let's not do anything to make the hardworking storeowners in this town work harder than they already do. How are the stores supposed to get their deliveries?" He scanned the room, daring anyone to argue with that point. "And who is going to pay for this?" Phinney demanded. "The Busman's Harbor taxpayer, that's who, once again. We do enough for the tourists in this town. It's tourists, tourists, tourists. Let's consider the workingman for a change." His eyes swept the room as if daring anyone to disagree. "Thank you for listening. Not that it will do any good."

A murmur of conversation swept through the crowd as Phinney stepped back from the microphone. Someone near me muttered, "Same old Phinney, making the same old argument." But there were also expressions of support.

The moderator indicated it was John Fenwick's turn and he stepped up to the microphone. "My name is John Fenwick. I live at number 7 East End Road. I first saw Busman's Harbor as a young lad, visiting the summer home my grandparents built here in the 1920s."

More bona fides. A groan rippled through the audience. Clearly they had heard this opening before.

"Back then, this town was a quiet, out of the way fishing village. Yes, there were rental cottages out on the points, and motor inns, which were then groups of separate cabins. Those were accommodations for people who wanted to be here, drawn by the beauty and our quiet, peaceful way of life, not people who wanted fancy spas with massages and pedicures.

"Now, there's people everywhere all summer long. There's cruise ships, bus tours, and McMansions all along the waterfront. On a weekday you can't walk from one end of town to the other without twenty people bumping into you. And do they say, 'Excuse me?' I don't have to tell the people in this room that they do not. Try to get a parking space anywhere downtown during what we laughably call 'the season.' Season-in-hell, I call it. All the license plates are from Massachusetts and New York. Why are we going to inconvenience ourselves to do one more darn thing to accommodate these people? They can all go home and stay there as far as I'm concerned. Thank you for your time."

As after Phinney's speech, there were rumblings of agreement and disagreement when Fenwick was done. I felt bad for Zoey. The first two speeches had gone against her mall. Not encouraging. The moderator banged his gavel three times and my sister's husband, Sonny, stepped up to the mic. "My name is Sonny Ramsey. I've lived, full-time, in town all my life, as does my father, as did his father."

Sonny seemed determined to one-up the previous speakers in the legacy department. I honestly had no idea what he was going to say. Sonny and Livvie had dated all through high school. He'd been a part of my life for more than half of it. We worked together every day all summer long. But we accomplished this by carefully avoiding landmine topics, including the biggies—religion and politics—and the small: for example, what was the best route out of the harbor in the small boat we used to move lobsters and ourselves out to Morrow Island for the clambake. His fiery red hair, or what was left of it, matched his fiery opinions.

"Fishing village!" Sonny aimed his booming voice for the back row, mic or no mic. "Have you noticed, by chance, that there's not a fishing boat left in this town?"

What he said was true. When Englishmen first found

the coast of Maine, the cod were so plentiful, the fish jumped into their boats. Some said a man could walk across the sea on the backs of the magnificent fish, there were so many. But the stocks had collapsed, the grounds were closed, and what remained of the industry had become giant factory ships that left from bigger ports. Busman's Harbor hadn't had a single fishing boat in decades. Lobstering, and sometimes a small amount of scalloping, were all that remained.

"Like it or not, our main business now is tourists," Sonny continued. "The day-trippers, the weekenders, the cottage renters, the cruise ships and bus tours, they're our bread and butter. That's what we're left with, and we should give them the best time ever, to get them to come back and tell their friends. And if that means keepin' them from killing themselves by walking out between parked cars on Main Street on a summer evening, we should do it. Thank you."

There was a smattering of applause when Sonny finished. I looked at him with new eyes. He'd spoken eloquently and kept his temper. I was sorry Livvie was home with Page and Jack. She would have been proud.

The man I didn't know approached the microphone. He looked to be in his early fifties, though it was hard to tell. His face was long and he'd shaved whatever hair might have still ringed his head. Improbably, he wore a suit, which told me he'd misread his audience. "I'm Karl Kimbel," he said. "I live at 14 Ring Road on Thistle Island. I thank you"—he nodded to the elected town officers at the front—"for allowing me to speak."

So that's who he was. Karl Kimbel had been on a buying spree around town. First it was one of the big old hotels on the east side of the inner harbor. Then it was two, then three. No one paid much attention until he applied for a permit to knock the old buildings down and build big, sleek new hotel-condo-restaurant complexes.

Some people loathed him, especially John Fenwick's return-to-a-sleepy-fishing-village crowd. Others were impressed with his willingness to invest and thought he offered a vision for the town that the citizenry, locals and summer people alike, weren't supplying themselves.

"You may know me as the, shall we say, somewhat controversial owner of the Bellevue Inn and other luxury properties. I support the pedestrian mall. This is exactly the experience my guests are looking for, strolling out on a lovely summer evening to shop along Main Street, with easy access to goods to spur the impulse buy. You may think of my guests as strangers, but they are here to enjoy themselves and spend money. I emphasize *spend their money in this town*. Not just to buy T-shirts." He paused and scanned the room. "No offense to any T-shirt vendors here this evening. But high-end goods. You know what I'm talking about, Mr. Gordon."

My friend Mr. Gordon nodded his white head. He owned a beautiful little jewelry shop at the corner of Main and Main.

"Tourists can choose their destinations," Kimbel said. "We want Busman's Harbor to be their choice. We want them to come back again and again and tell all their friends. We want the town to be cleaned up, fixed up, full of charm, and filled with the goods and services tourists demand."

"It's the Disneyfication of Busman's Harbor!" Bud Barbour yelled from his place in the last row. "Any one of you who goes along with this, I hope you *personally* are cleaned up, fixed up and full of charm, or you won't be allowed downtown during the summer. These people won't stop until all the townsfolk are animatronic."

That brought a response. Loud arguments took place everywhere in the room. Kimbel stepped back from the mic. If he'd planned to say more, he thought better of it.

The moderator banged the gavel and called for order. "Thank you, everyone," he said when the room quieted. "Zoey Butterfield, one of the authors of this proposal, will now answer questions."

"If I may?" Zoey looked at the moderator, who nodded for her to go ahead. "My name is Zoey Butterfield. I own Lupine Design on Main Street. I live above my store." From my vantage point behind her I watched Zoey's head turn from side to side, tossing her brown curls. "I moved here from Brooklyn, New York, three years ago."

There was a single, loud boo from the audience. I hoped it was a boo for Brooklyn, or for New York, or for the hated New York Yankees, not for Zoey. I didn't want to think we were that rude.

Zoey squared her shoulders and continued. "There were fact sheets on everyone's chairs." She held up a white piece of paper. So that's what people had been fanning themselves with. I hadn't received one because I didn't get a seat.

Most of the questions from the audience were practical—and civil. How would B&B guests with luggage reach their destinations? How would stores and restaurants get deliveries? What if there was a fire? What kind of barriers would be used to close the road? Where would they be stored when not in use?

Zoey answered capably. Porters with carts and pedicab drivers would be hired to move B&B guests free of charge. Fire lanes would be open. She had checked with the merchants. Deliveries were unheard of after 6:00 p.m. on summer weekends. The cost for everything—the extra police detail, the public works department overtime, was detailed on the fact sheets.

Karl Kimbel watched her, beaming at how well she was doing.

The moderator scanned the audience for more questions. "Miss Rumsford." The crowd quieted, completely and immediately. Everyone craned to look as a tiny woman with snow-white hair stood to speak. A man around my age got up to help her, then retook his seat. I moved down the side wall of the big room until I was across from her, looking down an aisle full of people at her profile. The moderator didn't insist she identify herself. Sonny grabbed the microphone off its stand and rushed it to her. But he was too late.

She spoke in a thin voice we all strained to hear. "These barriers, you say they're the concrete types we see on the highway?"

"Yes," Zoey answered. "I had originally hoped for simple police sawhorses, but state regulations require something a motorist can't drive through, either accidentally or with malicious intent."

A murmur rippled through the room. The idea of someone deliberately driving into a crowd of people wasn't something we really thought about in Busman's Harbor.

"Hmm." Alice Rumsford pursed her lips. People sat forward in their seats. Miss Rumsford's opinion would be important. She was the primary funder of the new wing on our public library and the pool and changing rooms at our Y. She'd raised so much money and given so generously to the Busman's Harbor Hospital, the entire emergency suite was named in honor of her beloved mother.

Miss Rumsford cared about the minds and the bodies of the town's citizens, as these gifts indicated. But more than anything, Miss Rumsford wanted Busman's Harbor to be beautiful. Her latest project was a large sign at the end of the highway welcoming visitors to our town. As soon it was warm enough, the ground around it would be planted with flowers, no expense spared.

Miss Rumsford's proposals for changes to the town were respected and appreciated, even by Phinney, et al. She was a descendent of one of the original summer families, which didn't hurt. And she funneled her contributions to existing institutions. Most important, she paid for everything she advocated for.

The crowd waited quietly for Miss Rumsford's pronouncement on the pedestrian mall. By the time she spoke again she was holding the microphone. "I don't think those concrete barriers will be very pretty," she finally said.

The room erupted.

Zoey tried to answer her. "We thought, perhaps, we could top the barriers with flower boxes."

But Phinney seized the issue. "More expense!" he roared. "You can't put lipstick on this particular pig. Those barriers will be eyesores!"

It was chaos after that. People stood in the rows, yelling and pointing at one another. The moderator banged his gavel for order.

Phinney stood inches in front of Zoey, towering over her, his spittle hitting her face. "Go back where you came from, you stuck-up little miss, and take your fancy ideas with you!"

Karl Kimbel rushed forward to defend Zoey, but she didn't need rescuing. "I have every right to my say." Her voice was controlled, level, deadly. "I live here, too. I'm a taxpayer and an employer."

At the front of the room the moderator conferred with the people at the tables. "The board members are not pre-pared to make a recommendation tonight," he shouted above the din. "This issue is tabled. Meeting adjourned."

I zoomed toward the door before anyone could engage me on this or any other topic.

CHAPTER SEVEN

"Julia? Come right away! I'm at the shop." The vibration in my sister's voice told me it wasn't time to ask questions.

"Be right there." The morning after the public hearing, I was in Mom's kitchen, my second mug of coffee in my hand, ready to ascend the back stairs to the Snowden Family Clambake office on the second floor. Instead, I jumped into my Bean boots and pulled on my jacket. The sky was steel gray and the air so damp I could feel the moisture on my face as I ran. It was going to rain, hard and soon.

My mind raced as I sped down Main Street. Lupine Design had been vandalized again. That had to be the reason for the shakiness in Livvie's voice. What had been hit this time? The studio? The inventory in the basement? Poor Zoey, after all the work of cleaning up yesterday. The ruined pottery. The expense. How long would it be before she gave up and moved out of town?

Once again, there were three police cars in front of the store, lights ablaze. But this time there was also an ambulance with its back doors opened wide. What if Livvie had been there when the vandal came in? What if she was hurt? I ran faster.

Out of breath and sweating in my waterproof jacket, I skidded to a stop in front of Lupine Design. I registered with relief that there was no one in the ambulance and the two EMTs stood casually talking behind it. When I glanced through the window of the shop, my instant impression was that everything was as it should have been—the shelves were upright, the floor clean—but I didn't take time to process what that meant. Then I saw the uniformed Busman's Harbor officer, standing, arms crossed in front of the door.

Finally, I spotted Livvie on the sidewalk. Jamie and Pete Howland stood around her, heads bent toward her, listening intently. Livvie spoke in a low voice, eyes trained on the concrete walk. She looked fine, physically, but deeply shaken.

I ran to my sister and threw my arms around her, interruption be damned. "What's going on? Are you all right?"

The double doors of the shop opened and our local part-time medical examiner, Dr. Joellen Simpson, came outside, followed by Will Marden, the new "new guy" on the Busman's Harbor police force.

"I've pronounced him." Dr. Simpson turned to the EMTs. "That's your cue to go. There's nothing you can do here." She looked back toward Jamie and Howland. "I've called the state medical examiner's office. This is a job for them, not for me. I assume you've called Major Crimes."

I hugged Livvie more tightly. Dr. Simpson meant someone was dead. If she, a family practitioner and our part-time ME, couldn't handle the situation, it meant the cause of death wasn't either natural or obvious. The call to the state police Major Crimes Unit could only mean one thing—murder.

"Right away when we got here," Jamie assured Dr. Simpson. "They're about forty minutes out."

My heart was pounding so hard I thought I might pass out. I looked at Livvie. "Zoey?"

"Phinney," she answered, her tone flat. "Phinney is dead. In the basement."

"What! What happened?"

"That's what we were just about to find out." Jamie turned back toward Livvie.

"It was a quiet morning," Livvie said. "Strangely normal, after yesterday. Zoey and I were the only ones working in the studio. We have an alarm we can set on the door, so it rings whenever someone enters the shop and then one of us goes help the customer."

She looked at us to make sure we understood. Jamie gestured for her to continue. "Over the course of the morning, three different people stopped in to say, 'Did you know Phinney's shop isn't open?' Zoey and I talked about it. We wondered if he was mad about the public hearing, or freaked out by what happened yesterday, or maybe he even felt guilty because he did it. The vandalism, I mean. By the time the third person came in, it was around eleven o'clock and Zoey started to worry. Phinney had given her his cell number in case anything went wrong at the building during off-hours. She pulled her phone out and called him."

Livvie paused, a little breathless. "A phone started

ringing *from the basement*. Zoey called down the stairs, 'Phinney! Phinney!' but no answer. We were both freaked out. I hoped it was Phinney in the cellar, because if it was someone else down there with his phone, that would be much worse. We went down the stairs. I had my cell out with 911 entered, ready to press the button.

"Phinney was dead on the floor. In our part of the basement, between the storage shelves." Livvie began to sob. "His throat had been cut. There was blood *everywhere*."

I hugged Livvie again and looked at Jamie to see what he would add. A sharp flick of his head told me he wasn't going to tell me more. He waited for Livvie to calm down and then continued. "Did you touch anything?"

"N-no. I don't think so. I may have grabbed on to one of the storage shelves to steady myself. I pressed the call button on my phone and 911 came on the line." She gulped. "The dispatcher asked if we were safe. It hadn't occurred to me until that moment that the killer might still be in the building. She told us to go outside and wait for the police. She sent the ambulance. I didn't ask her to. I knew Phinney was dead."

"Standard procedure," Howland assured her.

"You know everything else," Livvie continued. "You two were the first ones here. Zoey and I waited outside until you came and then you separated us."

"Ms. Butterfield is being interviewed in the parking lot around the back," Jamie told me. "You didn't notice anything at all unusual when you came in this morning?" he pressed Livvie.

"No. I swear. Regular day, except for, you know, things like the display shelves are empty and the cabinet glass is broken from yesterday."

"Did you see a weapon, an instrument capable of cutting a man's throat?" he asked.

"No! Nothing. Did you see anything? You were down there a lot longer than me." Livvie was losing her stamina and her patience. I could see the adrenaline draining out of her.

"How much longer does she have to stay here?" I asked Jamie.

He relented. "You can go. Obviously the state police will want to talk to you as soon as they get here. They'll be in touch."

"My bag is in the studio," Livvie said. "My car keys. Jack's car seat—"

"Officer Howland will get it." Jamie looked at her apologetically. "He'll need to search your bag before you take it."

"I understand. For the weapon," Livvie said.

Howland talked to the officer at the door and entered the building.

"Any sign of a break-in this time?" I asked Jamie.

"Not that I could spot. The state police will do their own inspection."

"Who's coming from Major Crimes, do you know?" Like every town in Maine except Portland and Bangor, Busman's Harbor had no homicide detectives and relied on the state police to provide the service. Our unit was headquartered in Augusta, about an hour away.

"Lieutenant Binder and Sergeant Flynn. And a whole bunch of crime scene techs and the medical examiner."

"Good." I knew the detectives and they were good at their job. "And the weapon?"

"Don't know that, either. Something vicious. His throat was cut clear to his spine."

CHAPTER EIGHT

I drove Livvie up to the peninsula in her ancient, wheezing minivan. She didn't say one word and I left her to her thoughts. She and her family lived in a split-level house on a cul-de-sac, the kind of place a lot of local families lived in. No view, no charm, but big enough and warm enough, which was all that mattered.

We went up the stone steps to the front door. Livvie dug in her bag for her keys and let us inside. I left her sitting on the faux-leather couch and went to make tea, our mother's cure for all that ailed.

"They won't let Zoey stay in her apartment," Livvie called from the living room. "The whole building is a crime scene."

"I wouldn't want her to stay there anyway." I returned with two cups, one light with milk for me, the other dark and strong, the way Livvie liked it. "Someone has proven they can get in and out of that building. It's not safe for Zoey to be there."

Livvie shivered so violently it looked like an invisible being had taken her by the forearms and shaken her. Her tea sloshed in her mug. I took it from her and put it on the coffee table. "Do you think Zoey could stay at the Snuggles?" Livvie asked.

The Snuggles Inn was a bed-and-breakfast across the street from our mother's house. The proprietors, Fiona and Viola Snugg, known as Fee and Vee, had been neighbors and friends of my parents for decades and honorary great-aunts to Livvie and me. The Snuggles wasn't technically open for the season, but the beds would be made up with crisp, clean sheets and Vee would cook a hearty breakfast every morning. Though the sisters were opposites in almost every way, they both had big hearts. They wouldn't say no.

"I'd offer for her to stay here, but . . ." Livvie didn't need to go on. Three-and-a-half years earlier, their spare bedroom had been turned into a nursery for Jack, the much-wanted baby who'd arrived ten years after his sister Page. There was no room for Zoey at Livvie's house.

"You don't think there's any chance Zoey murdered Phinney, do you?" I didn't believe it was possible, but I wasn't going to send a murderer to Fee and Vee.

"No!" Livvie's response was instinctive and immediate. Then she sat for a long moment, her skin pinched above her nose. I could see her going back over every conversation she'd ever had with Zoey, thinking about how she ran her business and interacted with the world. "No," Livvie said, finally and forcefully. "I don't believe she killed Phinney. I don't believe she's capable of killing anyone."

The second no hadn't been an instinctive no; it was a considered no. But a definite no, nonetheless.

I called the Snuggles while Livvie sipped her tea. As I expected, Vee readily agreed to help. "The poor dear. It must have been so unpleasant at her shop this morning." Vee let her statement hang there, hoping, I knew, that I would fill in some details, but I didn't take the bait. "Thank you so much. We'll let Zoey know." We said our good-byes and I hung up.

Livvie's call to Zoey to tell her about Vee's offer went straight to voicemail. Livvie left a message and sent a text.

"What do you know about Zoey?" I asked when she was done. Livvie drew her knees up to her chest, resting her stocking feet on the couch. The house was quiet. Sonny was out lobstering with his dad. Jack was at daycare, Page at school. It had been a long time since Livvie and I had been alone in her house.

"Not much," Livvie said slowly. "Yesterday, when she said she'd lived in Colorado, Michigan, and Texas, it was the first time I'd heard her speak about those places. I knew she grew up in California and came here from Brooklyn, but that was it."

I was surprised. "What do you talk about in the studio all day long?"

"It's not a sewing circle, Julia. The work requires concentration. The machine that makes the molded pieces is really noisy. It's hard to have conversations." Livvie huddled farther into the corner of the couch. "When we do talk, it isn't about the past. It's about the present. Zoey talks about Lupine Design. I talk about Sonny, the kids, the Snowden Family Clambake Company. And we talk about the future. New pieces she's dreamed up. New directions to take the business. My dreams for the future."

Her dreams for the future? Livvie had never had any dream except to stay in Busman's Harbor, marry Sonny Ramsey, and raise a family. It was a dream she'd pursued relentlessly since she was fifteen, never wavering. Did she now have some vision of the future that wasn't sending the kids off into the world and growing old with Sonny? I shook my head to clear it. This wasn't the time. "If you don't know anything about her, how do you know Zoey isn't a murderer?"

Livvie took her time to answer. "I didn't say I didn't know anything about her. I see the way she runs her business—with integrity, dedicated to quality and beauty. She's kind, she's patient. She treats others with respect. She's an excellent boss. She's clear about what she wants, demands the highest standards, but she never bullies you into it. She coaches you there. I've never had a better boss." Livvie smiled at me.

Technically, at the Snowden Family Clambake, I was her boss. But it was also a family business, and she was family. It was a ringing endorsement of Zoey Butterfield's character. I would have loved to have one of my employees talk that way about me.

"Zoey's not greedy or mean," Livvie continued. "She loves being successful, but she doesn't need others to fail to make her feel like a success." She paused again, pressing her lips together. "Zoey is not a killer." Livvie sat up straight in her corner of the couch. "You should help her."

"Help her what?"

"You know. What you do. Help Lieutenant Binder and Sergeant Flynn figure out who did it."

"Livvie, it's not at all clear Zoey needs my help or anyone else's."

"The police will think she's the most obvious suspect," Livvie insisted. "You know they will. She was in the building when it happened and she and Phinney had a very public fight last night."

"Lots of people were fighting last night."

"But no one else woke up with a body in her basement." Livvie's jaw was set. It was an expression I'd seen hundreds of times since we were kids. She was not going to give up. "Zoey is not a killer."

I wanted to agree, but who knew what another person was capable of with the right provocation? But what provocation could Phinney have provided? I couldn't see Zoey killing him over a proposal for a pedestrian mall. What would that even accomplish? Someone else from his faction in the town fight would step right up behind him. "If Zoey didn't murder Phinney, someone else did."

Livvie nodded.

"Someone who had access to the building," I added. "Are you sure there's no one? Former employees? Did Zoey ever have a roommate or a live-in boyfriend?"

Livvie shook her head. "I've worked there since she moved into the building. No roommate. No boyfriend. No ex-employees who went away mad. And I don't think any of them had keys anyway."

The state police would collect that information and more. "What about former tenants? Who was in that space before?" I tried to remember.

"It was that dress shop," Livvie said. "You know, the one with the fancy resort wear. Claire Reagan owns it."

"Stowaway Resortwear." The image of the Lupine Design storefront in its previous incarnation popped into my head. "Mrs. Reagan moved the shop into one of those renovated buildings on the waterfront, across from our ticket kiosk." The Snowden Family Clambake kiosk stood on the town pier. Our customers bought or picked up tickets there and waited for our tour boat, the *Jacquie II*, to take them out to Morrow Island. Stowaway Resort-wear was newly moved to the row of stores across the road.

"Yes." Livvie looked doubtful. "Why would Mrs. Reagan want to kill Phinney Hardison?"

"I'm not saying she did. She's another potential source of keys. Along with the building's owner and the rental agency." I looked at Livvie. Her body had sagged back into the corner of the couch. "What do you want to do now?" I asked her.

"I'd love to nap until I have to pick up Jack." Then, more slowly, she said, "I owe you an apology. I never realized what it took out of you when you saw a murdered body. I am wrecked."

"I never saw one—" I almost said "one that was nearly decapitated," but I caught myself. "Like that," I finished. "But you're right. It stinks. I'm going to call a cab."

Livvie put her feet on the floor. "I'll drive you home."

"No. Grab a nap while you can. I'm fine." The couch made a crinkly sound when I stood. "Are you okay? Do you need anything?"

Livvie stretched her legs to take up the space where I'd been sitting. "Mmm, no," she said. "Thanks for everything today."

My sister scooted down and closed her eyes. Her breathing was slow and regular before I left the house.

CHAPTER NINE

I waited for the cab on the front stoop. I had carefully called the other cab company in town, not the dispatcher Chris used for the cab he owned. The taxi was one of his side gigs, supplementing the money he made from the landscaping company he owned and his other side job as a bouncer. He mostly drove on summer evenings when there were tourists to pick up from the bars. But I didn't want to take the chance. I'd seen Chris around town since we'd broken up, plenty of times. Busman's Harbor was a small town. Whenever we met, we were polite. Too polite. But I couldn't face twenty minutes alone with him in a car, especially not after the events of the morning.

While I waited, I thought about what to do next. The sensible thing would be to wait for Lieutenant Binder and Sergeant Flynn to call me. They would have learned from the Busman's Harbor P.D. that I was at Lupine Design, yesterday and today, and they'd want to interview me. But I hadn't discovered the vandalism or the body. I'd be pretty far down their list. Way lower than Zoey and Livvie. What could I do while I waited? Despite my protests, I wanted to honor Livvie's request to help her boss.

The way I figured it, the vandalism in the shop and the murder had to be connected. No place is sufficiently cursed to suffer two unrelated, violent, and tragic events in a twenty-four-hour span. The lack of a break-in both-ered me. How many people had access to the store?

I hadn't asked Livvie or anyone at the scene if Phin-ney's body was the only thing amiss in the basement. Had he fought his killer? Were ceramic pieces knocked off the shelves, other things awry? I regretted not asking, but it was probably right not to drag Livvie back over it. She would have mentioned if she and Zoey had found the place a mess. They might have noticed that before they'd noticed Phinney.

Claire Reagan might have an old set of keys. Or might have lost one. But the new location of Stowaway Resort-wear would be shuttered for the season. Mrs. Reagan ran a second boutique in Venice, Florida. She wouldn't be back until mid-May.

I recognized the cab driver, but didn't know him. We spent the whole trip in happy silence, the Maine way. The heavens opened and rain poured down seconds after I let myself into Mom's house.

Inside, I fixed myself a grilled cheese sandwich, knowing, even as I fried it, mine would never be as good as one Gus would have made for me. When it was done I carried it up to my desk and fired up my laptop. I hoped to discover who Zoey's landlord was, but no luck. I found plenty of photos of the shop and Zoey's ceramic pieces, reviews, and postings to various social media sites by happy customers. I even found the rental listing from three years earlier before Lupine Design had moved in. Looking at those photos, I was even more impressed by what Zoey had done with the place, especially the apartment, which had been pretty much attic storage when she'd rented it.

The old listing was by Oceanside Realty. They were the only game in town for residential sales, season-long or year-round rentals, and commercial property.

I listened to the rain pummel the windows while I finished my sandwich. Then I went downstairs, put on my jacket, and climbed back into my boots.

Oceanside Realty was about halfway up the highway that led to Route 1, which connected Busman's Harbor to the rest of coastal Maine. I parked in one of the half dozen empty spots in front of the low-slung wooden building and dashed to the front door.

A redheaded woman with a name tag that said JUDY came to the counter as soon as I walked in. She wore a short ponytail on top of her head like Pebbles Flintstone, and once that image had popped into my head it was all I could see. "How can I help you?" She narrowed her eyes as if trying to remember who I was.

I wasn't going to enlighten her. I'd come there looking for information before. "I understand you're the rental agents for the property at 587 Main Street."

"The Lupine Design building, yes."

"I wonder if you could tell me who the owner of the building is."

She seemed surprised by the question. I had to admit it

was kind of out of the blue. "I'm sorry," she said. "I'm not going to disclose that. At Oceanside Realty we value the privacy of our owners and renters. Besides, the property is a part of a real estate trust. Knowing the name wouldn't help you."

"Do you have keys for the property?"

"We don't have a management agreement for 587 Main, so we don't hold keys. We turned our set over to the tenant." Her red brows were furrowed, her pink-lipsticked mouth pursed. "I don't like what you're doing."

I took a small step back from the counter. "What do you think I'm doing?"

"You're trying to figure out how to go around us directly to the owner to cut us out of the deal and rent the space. Mr. Hardison died only this morning. It's disgusting."

She'd already heard. I should have guessed. I hadn't come about renting the space, but it was probably better to let her continue to believe that. Any attempt to clarify would lead to a lot of unnecessary conversation. I took another step backward, a bigger one this time. "Thanks for your time."

Before I could turn around, she had second thoughts. "Wait! Let me take your name. If the space does go on the market, I'll give you a call."

I drove back down the peninsula toward Busman's Harbor. There was more than one way to skin this particular cat. The Town Enforcement Office was the place where homeowners and business owners applied for building permits and zoning variances. More central to my current mission, the office had records on every lot and building in Busman's Harbor going back for generations.

I parked in my spot in Mom's triple-bay garage, put my jacket hood up against the rain, and walked down the hill to the town-offices-fire-station-police-headquarters building. As I passed through the parking lot, I noticed Lieutenant Binder and Sergeant Flynn's familiar unmarked state police car. I entered the building through the central door, which took me to the town offices.

"What's doing, Julia? Is there a problem?" Mark Hayman knew me well by this point. For three summers my family had been renovating Windsholme, the abandoned and partially burned mansion on Morrow Island where we ran our clambakes. The island was technically a part of the town, though it didn't feel that way when you left the protective arms of the harbor and sailed into the Gulf of Maine. Building anything on the waterfront, especially on an island, required layers and layers and layers of permits from the town, the state, and the federal government. Todd Cochran, our general contractor, had taken care of most of our interactions with Town Enforcement, but I'd been a regular visitor as well.

"No problem," I assured him. I couldn't read his expression—skepticism or surprise. It was an unusual answer from me. "I'm not here about Windsholme. I'm interested in the property at 587 Main Street. Specifically, who owns it?"

"Lupine Design? The scene of the crime." Mark was gray-haired and gray-bearded. He had to be nearing retirement, though he was spry and more than capable of climbing around building sites. "Why are you interested that space? Thinking of starting another business in town? I mean, now that you and Chris have closed the restaurant." Not only did he know everything about my building project, but he also knew the ins and outs of my not-so-private life, too.

"Just curious about the ownership," I said.

"Ah." He went to his desk and started to type. "Helping the police with their inquiries again. I get it." He squinted at the screen, moving his head slightly as he scanned the lines. "The owner is the Beautify Maine Trust."

"That's not really helpful is it? Where does the tax bill go?"

He tapped and then squinted again. "Kitty, Miles, and Meyer, a law firm, located in Cincinnati. Do you want the address?"

"Sure." It couldn't hurt, though I didn't see exactly how it would help. Lieutenant Binder and Sergeant Flynn would find their way down this path eventually and they'd have a better chance of getting a law firm to give them information.

Mark grabbed a yellow sticky pad off his desk and wrote on it with a red pen. "Anything else?"

"No," I said. "Thanks so much for your time."

"Anytime you come to me with something easy, I'm grateful."

CHAPTER TEN

I left the town offices, dashed through the rain, and re-entered the building through the public entrance for the police department. My resolution to wait until the detectives contacted me had dissolved. I decided I'd try to get Binder and Flynn to give me their early take on the case and their first impressions of Zoey. I told myself it was because I'd promised Livvie. Myself didn't believe me.

Trying to look like I'd been invited, I marched past the civilian receptionist and peered around the frame of the open door that connected the police station to the multipurpose room where I'd attended the public hearing the night before.

Lieutenant Binder and Sergeant Flynn from the Maine State Police Major Crimes Unit were inside working while their incident room was being set up. Jamie was under a plastic table wrestling with wires and plugs and Pete Howland was arranging chairs in a semicircle in front of two whiteboards. The state police detectives sat at a folding table on the opposite side of the room, each staring intently at his laptop. The crime scene techs must still be at Lupine Design.

Jerry Binder glanced up and smiled. "Julia Snowden, I can't say I'm surprised to see you."

"Or surprised you were at the scene before we were." Tom Flynn sounded a lot less enthusiastic.

Binder was in his late forties, with a ski-slope nose and a head that had gone from balding to inarguably bald in the time I'd known him. It vexed him, as did the glasses he had adopted to be able to read his laptop screen. He was a devoted husband to a woman who was also a Maine state police officer and the doting father of two boys.

Flynn was a year older than me. I would have known he was ex-military even if he hadn't told me. He was decidedly single. There hadn't been a woman in his life that I knew about since my friend Genevieve had decided roaming the world cooking on superyachts was preferable to settling down with him. He put all the energy others might have put into a relationship into his job and his workouts at the gym.

In interviews, they were naturals for good cop, bad cop, or at least good cop, scary cop. They were both dedicated, intelligent officers.

"I wasn't at the scene, exactly," I pointed out. "I didn't go into the basement."

"That was your sister," Flynn said. "She's coming in later, after her husband gets home to care for the kids."

I pulled up a metal folding chair and sat across from their makeshift desk. "The vandalism the day before and the murder have to be connected, right?"

Binder shrugged. "Probably. But you know what happens when you ass-ume, et cetera, et cetera. We'll follow the evidence."

"There was no sign of a break-in either time," I pointed out. "That has to be important."

"No sign of a break-in that we know about," Flynn corrected. "Techs aren't finished at the scene."

"Was anything taken from either shop?"

"Still determining," Flynn grunted.

"Did you find the murder weapon?"

"Not yet." Binder shook his head.

"What was it?"

"Something really, really sharp." Binder paused. "Can I ask, what's your interest in this? I mean aside from the usual."

The usual being that not knowing drove me crazy. "My sister works at Lupine Design. And I was there, like you said."

"And?" Binder prompted.

"Livvie doesn't think Zoey Butterfield killed Phinney Hardison."

This assertion was met with silence. Finally, Tom Flynn said, "We'll let your sister give us her opinion, why don't we? Then we'll come to our own conclusions."

"What motive could Zoey have?" I asked.

"We understand from Officer Dawes that Ms. Butterfield and Mr. Hardison were on opposite sides of a town issue that got heated at the public hearing last night," Flynn answered.

"Do you really think Zoey Butterfield would kill Phinney Hardison in an argument over a pedestrian mall?" I used my most incredulous tone of voice.

"Stranger things have happened," Binder answered. "Town meetings can be murder. It wouldn't be the first time."

"Could a woman have done that to Phinney? I heard his head was almost . . ."

Flynn cut me off. "With a sharp enough weapon, yes."

"Which we'll know when we find it," Binder added.

"What time did it happen?" I asked.

"Too early to know," Binder answered. "The medical examiner's best guess based on the state of the body and blood at the scene was the middle of the night sometime, two or three in the morning. We'll know more when we get the preliminary report."

"What does Zoey say?" This might be pushing it.

To my surprise, Binder answered. "Ms. Butterfield says she was in her apartment, alone, asleep."

"Is that possible?" I asked. "That she didn't hear anything?"

"Yes," Flynn admitted. "I went to the basement and yelled at the top of my lungs. The lieutenant was in Zoey's bedroom. Didn't hear a thing. That's assuming Mr. Hardison had time to yell. There's no sign of a struggle at the scene. And that's also assuming Ms. Butterfield was in her bedroom and not in the basement."

"What could Phinney have been doing there at that time?" I wondered, more to myself than to the detectives.

"Early days, early days." Binder looked at me over the top of his reading glasses. "As long as you're here, Sergeant Flynn will take your witness statement."

Mom was in the kitchen when I got home fifteen minutes later. The statement process had been quick. I'd arrived after the body was found and hadn't gone into the building, much less down to the basement.

"Hello, dear." Mom's back was turned to me as she pulled the soup pot out of the refrigerator.

"Hi." I took off my wet jacket and hung it in the back hall. Le Roi ran down the backstairs to greet me. I gave him a quick scratch behind the ears. "Mom, something happened this morning at Lupine Design."

"I heard. Or I heard some. I called Livvie, but she didn't answer. If you know more, I think you'd better tell me the rest."

Mom spooned the soup into a bowl and popped it into the microwave. As it heated the tangy, spicy smell seeped into the room. My stomach gurgled. I realized I hadn't eaten lunch. I fixed myself a bowl to heat when Mom's was done.

When we were both seated, I told Mom as much as I knew about the murder and subsequent events. "Livvie was napping when I left her. That's probably why she didn't pick up."

"I thought she might be at the police station."

"Later, after Sonny gets home," I told her.

"I'll call to see if I can help out."

We sat quietly for a moment, scraping our spoons across the bottoms of our bowls to finish the soup.

"Who would want to kill Phinney Hardison?" Mom asked.

"That's what I've been wondering, too."

Mom laughed. She had a much heartier laugh than you'd ever expect from such a petite person. "I'm sure you have."

I made a face. I don't like being so predictable. "What do you know about Phinney?" I asked.

"Not a lot. He was born here and grew up here. That I know. He went away for quite a while, and then he came back, like a lot of folks."

For decades, Maine hadn't offered much opportunity. People went away to earn a living. Then some of them returned.

"He came back to care for his mother," Mom was saying. "She was old and quite frail and needed looking after. He was a devoted son. Took her everywhere when she was still able. Stayed with her until the end."

"And stayed in town after she died," I said.

"Where else would he go?"

Anywhere? It was a sad story, a common story. Not one that would get you killed. "Has he made enemies around town?" I asked.

Mom pursed her lips, considering. "People don't go around killing other people because they disagree."

"True," I said. "Unless they passionately disagree."

"You were at the meeting last night. Did anyone seem like they wanted to kill somebody?"

"Everybody seemed like they wanted to kill everybody, but you know how those things go. They never actually do." I did a quick mental run-through of the meeting. "If anyone was going to get killed, I would have thought it would be Zoey. She was on the receiving end of a lot of the anger. More than Phinney."

"There must be some other explanation, another motive," Mom said.

"Yes," I agreed. "And then there's the vandalism at the store yesterday. No sign of a break-in either time, that the police have been able to find. I've been wondering who Zoey's landlord is. If I said the owner's lawyers were in Cincinnati, would that bring anyone to mind? I'm looking for people who own property in Busman's Harbor and who live in Cincinnati or somewhere around there."

It was a long shot, but not a ridiculous one. Most Maine summer families came from the East Coast: Boston, New York, Washington, D.C. Others did come from farther away. Still, Cincinnati might be unusual enough to yield a useful answer.

Mom's brow furrowed. "The only people I can think of are the Rumsford family. That's where Alice Rumsford's people come from."

CHAPTER ELEVEN

I pictured Alice Rumsford at the public hearing the previous evening, commenting on the aesthetics of the concrete street barriers. Why couldn't she be Zoey's landlord? Alice's family had been summer residents forever, they had money, and she was deeply invested in the town. The more I thought about it, the more sense it made.

The Rumsford cottage was a ways up the peninsula, beyond Busman's Harbor Hospital, on the water. I didn't call ahead. I thought if I talked to her face-to-face Miss Rumsford might be more likely to answer my questions.

The rain was falling in sheets as I turned off the highway. The Subaru's defroster, turned to the highest setting, fought with the noise of the downpour to see which could be louder. I sat forward, my face as close to the windshield as I could get it, as if it would help me see.

I finally found the entrance to the private road that led

up to Alice Rumsford's house, marked by a small sign, LUPINE COTTAGE. Local people's houses had numbers, summer people's houses had names. Though when I looked hard, I did spot a simple stake with reflective numbers stuck on it, a concession to the county's enhanced 911 system.

The road up to Lupine Cottage was steep and unpaved. My tires spun and the car shimmied. Subarus were the most popular cars in Maine, specifically because they ran so well on snow and mud, but even these cars had their limits. "C'mon, girl," I urged, as if she were an uncooperative steed.

I wondered why the winding road had never been paved, or at least lined with gravel. I scanned the hillside as I drove, looking for the house. It had to be around the curve behind the stand of pines near the top.

At last, I passed through the trees and pulled into a car park just beyond them. There was another vehicle parked there as well, a big black SUV with tinted windows and an out-of-state license plate, its tire tracks still fresh. I tried to find a spot to park in that wasn't inches deep in mud but didn't succeed. I stepped out of the car and the wet, gooey stuff came up to the ankles of my boots.

It was a fair walk, uphill, in mud and rain, along a winding path that led through another gate to the cottage. On a clear day there would have been a spectacular view of the Gulf of Maine. Today, there was a wall of fog that made the cottage look like a stage set with a white scrim behind it, waiting for someone to paint the scenery.

Lupine Cottage wasn't large, a couple of rooms wide at most. A single window winked out under the gable end of the second story. An old chimney poked up through the green roof shingles. There were porches on both sides, a glassed-in one on the left and a screened-in one on right that would expand the cottage living space considerably in warmer weather.

It wasn't unusual for the homes of longtime summer people to be rustic. Not every wealthy visitor built an enormous mansion like the ones in Bar Harbor, or like Windsholme, my mother's family's summer home on Morrow Island. The earliest summer visitors were called "rusticators" and they came to Maine for a simple life and communion with nature. But when families held on to their houses, as Alice's had, and held on to their money, as evidenced by Alice's many enormous gifts to the town, they usually fixed up the old places, expanding and modernizing them until the original character was gone. Alice's house looked exactly as it must have a hundred years earlier.

Nothing ventured, nothing gained. I squared my shoulders and walked up onto the small porch that sheltered the front door. There was no bell that I could see, so I knocked on the wood-and-glass storm door.

The front door opened and the man who had sat next to Alice Rumsford at the public meeting stood there. When he saw me, he flashed a warm smile. "We don't get many visitors out here." He looked at the sky. "Especially in this weather."

"I'm sorry. I didn't mean to disturb you. I wonder if I could talk to Miss Rumsford, or to both of you."

At the public hearing, I'd registered that he was a good-looking guy, but up close the man was even better looking, handsome actually. He had large brown eyes, full lips, and a strong chin. His chestnut-brown hair was short on the sides and longer on the top, and flopped appealingly over his right eyebrow. He wore a heavy sweater in a gorgeous sea blue, jeans, and leather bedroom slippers.

"Of course," he said. "You've traveled all the way out here." He stuck out a hand. "Ben Barlow. Welcome to my Aunt Alice's house. Come in."

I used the toes of one boot to pull off the heel of the other and stepped out of it and then bent to remove the other one. I left them on the porch in the rain, because there was no possible way I was bringing them into the house. Inside, Ben took my soaked rain jacket and hung it on a peg in the narrow front hallway.

"Julia Snowden," I said, trailing behind him through the dark corridor next to the stairs.

"You were at the public hearing last night."

"Yes," I admitted, surprised. I hadn't said a word. There was no reason he would have noticed, much less remembered me.

We came out of the hallway into a large two-story room. A fire burned in a wood stove. Alice Rumsford sat in a big green velvet chair, swaddled in blankets. "You'll pardon me, dear, if I don't get up."

"Of course. Thanks so much for seeing me. And without any notice. I apologize for bursting in like this."

"It's lovely to have company," she said. "And so rare at this time of year. Ben, perhaps you could get us all tea and some of those delicious cookies you baked yesterday."

Ben smiled and left the room.

"Welcome." Alice's reedy voice rose out of the pile of blankets. She wore at least two sweaters, a bright red one under a mustard-yellow one. Her hair was snow white, with a wave that rolled across the top of her head like a cresting sea.

"Miss Rumsford, I'm Julia Snowden." I wasn't sure if she would have heard me introduce myself in the hallway.

"I know who you are." She seemed delighted to see me. "You're Jacqueline and Jack's daughter. Your mother and I worked as volunteers at the Busman's Harbor Opera House for years. I've always admired her. She's a brave woman. And your father, Jack, was a dear, dear man."

"He was," I agreed. I thought in the moment "brave" was perhaps a strange word to describe my mother, who was kind, supportive, smart, and on occasion, slyly funny, but I supposed it was true. After a long period of mourning after my father died, she'd pulled her life together and moved forward. It had taken conscious effort. And bravery.

"You must call me Alice. Everyone does."

The inside of the house was as rustic as the outside. The walls were varnished beadboard nailed to scaffolding. The wooden dividing wall between this room and the kitchen stopped a foot short of the ceiling. Ben moved around behind it, getting the tea things together. An open wooden staircase climbed to a landing then reversed itself and continued to the second story over the kitchen. I'd been in enough of these kinds of cottages to be sure it led to a single large room, also clad in unfinished wood, filled with enough old cast-iron beds for an entire family. Which brought up an interesting question about Alice and Ben's sleeping arrangements. With a quick glance around the living room, I spotted a pillow on top of a neatly folded blanket and sheets. One of them was sleeping down here.

I guessed it was Alice, for the warmth of the stove, the proximity to the bathroom, and to avoid the stairs.

The walls in the great room held half a dozen poster-sized photographs in simple black frames. To my surprise the pictures weren't Maine scenes of lupines, lighthouses, lakes, and mountains, but instead they were photos of children. The images were so arresting, so compelling, they drew me to them, each in turn.

I thought at first they might be travel posters, but quickly concluded that was wrong. There was no text, for one thing. And the images weren't advertisements. They were art. There was a boy, caked in white clay, staring into the camera, his eyes great, dark pools. A curly-haired toddler in a ruffled dress danced on a table as her adoring, multi-generational family looked on. A blond boy sat on a rocky hill, dressed in a black tunic, a knife in his belt, embracing his dog. An exhausted young woman, barely out of her teens, dressed in blue coveralls, smoked a cigarette. A boy lay on a doctor's examining table, the stump of his leg bandaged, a look of pain, both physical and existential, on his face. A girl, a bright scarf covering her head, stared at the camera, her knees flexed as if she wasn't sure if she should run. Each photograph was breathtaking and arresting in its own way.

"Please, make yourself comfortable," Alice said.

By wandering around her room, staring at the photographs uninvited, I already had. "These are beautiful."

She smiled, acknowledging the compliment. "Taken by a good friend."

I sat on the sofa opposite her. It looked as old as the house.

"So what brings you all the way out here today?" Her light blue eyes were alive with curiosity.

"You will have heard about Phinney Hardison." Alice might not have many visitors, but there was a smartphone in a flowered case on the table by her chair, along with a box of tissues, a glass of water, and a mystery novel. The Busman's Harbor grapevine would have kept her up on a story as big as Phinney's murder.

"Yes, yes. A terrible shame."

At that moment, Ben returned carrying a tray holding three ceramic mugs and a plate of golden-brown cookies. He stood in front of me and bowed, lowering the tray so I could take a mug, a napkin, and a cookie. "Butterscotch," he said. Then he went to his aunt, plucked a mug off the tray, and put it on her table along with two cookies. Finally he proceeded to the armchair next to his aunt and lowered the last mug and the cookie plate to his side table. He caught me staring when he turned to sit down.

"Julia has come to talk to us about Phinney," Alice told him as we passed around the cream and sugar.

"Terrible." Ben raised a quizzical eyebrow under the flop of brown hair. Why would I have come to them to talk about that?

"He was killed in the basement of his shop." I figured they knew that but I needed a warmup. "And that got me wondering about who owned the property." I looked directly at Alice. "I thought it might be you."

Alice's blue eyes returned my gaze, no averting, no blinking. "Whatever made you think that?"

I should have anticipated the question but I had to think quickly about what to say. I decided on the truth. "There was an incident at the shop yesterday. Someone broke into Lupine Design and smashed all the pottery in the showroom. And then the murder this morning. In neither case was there any sign of a break-in. That got me wondering about the keys. Zoey Butterfield can account for all her copies. She said she wasn't sure who owned the building. She sent me to Oceanside Realty. The woman there sent me to the Town Enforcement Office. Mark Hayman gave me an address for a law firm in Cincinnati. My mother said your family is from Cincinnati . . ." I let the sentence trail off.

"My, you are a clever girl." Alice spoke with apparently genuine admiration. "I do own the building. I own quite a few in town. Whenever I see a place that is in trouble or in danger of being torn down or becoming entirely derelict, I buy it. The agents know I'm often the buyer of last resort."

This was news to me. "How many properties do you own?"

She drew her thin lips together. "I'm not sure. Twenty? Twenty-five."

That was a lot of real estate in our little town.

"You must remember that building from when you were a child," Alice said. "It could never keep its tenants. The previous owner was close to bankruptcy, ready to walk away. The folks at Oceanside Realty got wind of it—they always know everything that's going on—and came to me."

I took advantage of Alice's explanation to devour Ben's cookie. I love butterscotch in any form and the cookie was crunchy and buttery and perfection.

"At first I had trouble keeping the building rented," Alice continued. "Every season brought a new shop, another person full of hopes and dreams that would be dashed. Finally, Stowaway Resortwear moved in and Claire Reagan made a success of it. When she moved her shop farther downtown, I rented to Lupine Design."

"And Phinney?" I asked.

She paused, clasping her blue-veined hands in her lap. "After his mother died, Phinney needed a place to sell her things. She was a bit of a hoarder, as they call them now. In my day, we just called them Mainers."

I smiled appreciatively. The front yards of rural Maine were often littered with things people, "might need later."

"I rented him the other storefront," Alice said. "It was almost fifteen years ago now."

Ben sat, looking comfortable in his overstuffed chair, sipping his tea and moving his eyes from his aunt's face to mine like he was watching a tennis match.

"When Zoey Butterfield came along, she wanted the whole building," Alice said. "But I couldn't do that to Phinney. I had the folks at Oceanside assure her that when Phinney left, she'd have first option in his space. I assumed his mother's stuff would all be gone eventually."

"I'm not sure if selling it was the point." My memories of the times when I'd walked past Phinney's display window and looked inside were mostly of him yakking it up with his cronies, not bargaining with tourists.

"You may be right," Alice allowed. "Now I wish I'd made him leave. Perhaps he wouldn't have been murdered."

"You don't know that," Ben said.

"Well, he wouldn't have been murdered *there*," Alice shot back.

"Did you know Phinney?" I asked. "Is that why you rented to him?"

Alice shook her head. "It was all hands-off, through Oceanside. I'm not even sure he knew I was his landlady."

"Do you have a key to the building?" I asked.

"Ben," Alice said. "Open the second drawer in my desk." She pointed to an old oak teacher's desk on the wall behind me.

Ben walked over and pulled on the wooden handle of the second drawer down. It jingled and clanged when he opened it. "There's like a hundred keys in here."

"They're all labeled." Alice was absolutely confident.

I admired her certainty. Ben pulled out the keys, singles and sets, big Yales, tiny padlock keys, and skinny skeleton keys. He read off each label as Alice shook her head. "No. No. Don't own that property anymore. That was a neighbors' house I used to look after. They're both dead." And so on.

Ben looked at me helplessly. "I'll go through these and see if we have it. Then what?"

"Let the state police detectives know if you do have it. Or if you don't. They might be more interested in that. I'm sure they'll figure out who owns the building eventually. But you might want to call them before they call you."

He nodded. "Will do."

I gave him Flynn's name and cell number.

"Thanks." He put the number in his phone. "Why don't you give me your number, too? I assume you want to know if I find the key."

"Yes, please." I rattled off my cell number.

Ben passed the cookie plate around again. He must have seen the longing in my eyes. I ate the second one as soon as I got it.

"These are delicious." I meant it.

"Thanks." Ben sat back down. "Enough murder. Other

subjects, please. I've been to your clambake, you know. A few times. It used to be favorite stop when I stayed with Aunt Alice."

"I'm glad you've enjoyed it. That's our aim. This will be my fifth summer back running it."

"Five years," he said. "I don't think I've been there during that span. I'm sure I would have noticed you."

I blushed a little, then stood. "I need to get back to town, but thanks so much for seeing me. And for the tea . . . and the cookies."

Ben rose as well.

"I won't get up," Alice said. "It's been lovely to have company no matter how grim the subject. Ben will see you to the door."

"How will you vote on the pedestrian mall?" I asked her before I turned to go.

"I haven't made up my mind, dear."

Ben let me out onto the front porch where I pulled on my wet boots. The rain had slowed but the day was still raw. Great puddles sat on top of the mud in the car park. I slogged back through them to my car, noticing that my tires were in about six inches deep. I stepped into the Subaru, trying to keep my muddy boots on the rubber mat, though it was hopeless, started her up, and put her in reverse.

The wheels spun. "No, no, no." I put the car in drive and tried to move forward. I had a couple of feet available in front of me. But the wheels spun again and I knew from both mud season lore and bitter experience that I was only making things worse.

I was about to get out when Ben appeared on the

porch. "Stay there!" he shouted. He sat on the wet steps, took off the leather slippers and pulled on his boots. He'd put on a navy windbreaker, which might, just might, protect the beautiful sweater. As he came toward the car, he craned his neck to look at my tires.

I opened my window. "This isn't embarrassing at all."

He shrugged. "Mud season. It happens." He trudged toward the big SUV, opened the back and pulled out the enormous floor mat.

"Don't," I said when he returned. "It will get wrecked and you'll get filthy."

"No worries."

"At least use my car mats."

"It's fine. Car mats are made for mud. I'll hose it off tomorrow." He bent and pushed the mat under the car behind my back wheels. I could tell from looking at the top of his head through my rear window that he was kneeling in the mud. My face was burning.

He came around to my side of the car. "Put it in reverse and back up slowly. If you can get up on the mat, we'll use the traction to help you get a running start in reverse. When you get to the middle of this blasted parking area, turn around and head down the road. If we do get you going, whatever you do, don't stop."

He went to the front of the car and pushed, his face twisted with the effort. His instructions worked. I got the car onto the mat and then was able to turn.

Once I was in the firmer center of the parking area, I slowed down. "Thank you!" His jeans were caked in mud and his car mat was, too. "I'm so sorry."

"Don't stop!" He waved me on, laughing.

I pulled down the long dirt road, careful to stay in the center, until I got to the paved street at the bottom.

When I got home I took the longest, hottest shower our ancient water heater could sustain and then put on my sweats. Mom wasn't there. I figured she'd gone to Livvie's, like she'd said. I made a peanut butter sandwich and a cup of cocoa and built a fire in the fireplace.

Later, I got off the couch and looked out the living room window. The rain had stopped completely, though Main Street glistened in the streetlights. There was a light on the second floor of the Snuggles across the street. Zoey must be there. "Go to sleep," I said aloud. "Get some rest. You're going to need it."

CHAPTER TWELVE

In the morning, Mom still wasn't home, but I had a text to say she'd slept at Livvie's.

I called Livvie's cell. "You have Mom."

"I do. She helped me get the kids off this morning. She's not scheduled to work today."

"How are you doing?"

There was a pause. "Okay. Better, I guess. I spent a long time at the police station last night."

"How was that?"

"Tiring."

She wasn't giving me much, which worried me. Livvie wasn't normally so terse. "Do you think they suspect Zoey?"

"They asked lots of questions about her. Though they asked more about Phinney." The information was top of mind. Her antenna had been up for any hint that Binder and Flynn had their sights set on Zoey. "What did you find out?"

I walked Livvie through my activities of the previous day.

"Alice Rumsford owns the building," Livvie said when I was done. "I didn't see that coming." She paused. "Though I don't see how it helps. Alice barely comes up to Phinney's shoulder blades. No way she . . . did that to him."

"She has a nephew staying with her, though I can't think why he'd kill Phinney."

"Umm." Livvie considered that idea. "Your buddies Binder and Flynn won't let us go back to work," she finally said. "I can't decide if I'm relieved or disappointed. I don't want to rush back into that building. I don't know what's going to happen the next time I have to get inventory from the basement. But I think it might be better if I had something to do."

"I have to go to Morrow Island this morning. I'm finally going to make the decisions Todd has been hounding me about. I've put it off far too long. Do you want to come with me?"

Another pause. "No. Thanks. Mom and I are going to tackle some projects around here while I'm not working. Therapy, she's calling it. But why don't you invite Zoey? I'm worried about her. She doesn't have family and her friends are all connected to the business. I don't want her to be alone. Besides, you can get more information for your case."

"Livvie—" Why was she so committed to this notion?

"You promised you'd help Zoey."

"Which is why I was running around in the rain all day yesterday." I gave up arguing. Besides, I liked Zoey and, after seeing her apartment, I thought she might be particularly good company for this trip. "Fine. I'll go over to the Snuggles and suggest an outing."

The sun was out, the clouds high, so unlike the day before. From the kitchen window I watched the tops of the trees sway in the breeze. Out on the water the day would be cold. I dressed quickly and warmly in my quilted vest, gloves, and scarf, and crossed the street to the Snuggles Inn. On the big front porch, I tried the doorknob. The door was locked, not unusual in the off-season, so I rang the bell.

"Julia! How lovely to see you." Fee Snugg stood in the open doorway, her Scottish terrier MacKenzie at her feet. As she stepped back so I could enter, the rubber soles of her sensible shoes squeaked on the polished floorboards. "What brings you for a visit?"

"Hi, Fee." I stepped inside and hugged her. "Actually, I'm looking for your guest."

"In the dining room." Fee pushed at the plastic barrette that held back her short gray bangs. She was bent from arthritis, but that didn't keep her from walking MacKenzie up and down the harbor hill every day.

When I pushed through the swinging door to the dining room, Zoey was seated with her back to me. There was a spread of food on the table, as big as if it had been surrounded by summer guests.

"Julia, welcome." Vee Snugg bustled through the door from the kitchen. With her upswept white hair, heels and pantyhose—always pantyhose—she was as glamorous as her sister was deliberately plain. "Have you had breakfast? You must eat."

I had eaten a piece of dry toast, but based on the smells wafting in my direction and my knowledge of Vee as a cook, I wasn't going to admit it. "Maybe a little something," I said.

"Hi, Julia." Zoey smiled, apparently happy for the company.

"How are you doing?" I moved around the table to sit opposite her. She didn't look the worse for wear.

"Okay, I think. I was hours at the police station yesterday."

"Have some scrambled eggs and bacon." Vee took a plate from the big china cabinet and handed me the spoon for the eggs. "Fresh fruit?" She indicated the bowl. "Do you want juice? I would have put it out, but Zoey here declined."

"I'll be fine." I dished the eggs onto my plate. I knew from experience they would be fluffy and light, cooked to perfection. "Yum." I took some fruit as well.

"There's coffee in the carafe on the sideboard. I'll leave you girls." Vee turned back toward the kitchen. "Call me if you need anything."

"What could we possibly need?" Zoey asked.

"The sisters are being good to you then?" I waited to speak until I was sure Vee was behind the closed kitchen door.

"Amazing. Fee taught me to play cribbage last night. I know she was trying to distract me from what happened, but I appreciated it so much."

"It must have been a tough day."

"The murder was awful, of course. And then the police and the crime scene people all over my studio and apartment. I know they were doing their jobs, but it was a bit unsettling. Then I spent the rest of the day at the police station answering questions."

A bit unsettling? "Do you think they suspect you?" Might as well ask directly.

She shrugged, more even-keeled about it than I could ever hope to be. "I was, as far as they can prove so far, the only person in the building when it happened. It's natural they would look at me first. But they also asked a lot about Phinney, his habits, his friends. Did he keep a lot of cash in his shop? That one made me laugh out loud."

"Binder and Flynn are good detectives," I said. "They'll be fair. And thorough."

"That was my first impression, too."

"Were you able to suggest any suspects to them?"

"Definitely not. I would have said right away if there was someone obvious." Zoey pushed her plate away and got up to refill her coffee cup. The Snuggles Inn's teacups and delicate saucers were lovely, but barely held a thimbleful of liquid. Hardly enough to get you through the day.

I held out my cup. "Hit me, too, please."

Zoey obliged. "The truth is I didn't know Phinney well." She returned to her chair. "We shared a building, but he had his sphere and I had mine."

"I know who your landlord is." I wasn't sure I should tell her. Binder and Flynn probably wouldn't appreciate me giving a possible suspect information she didn't have already, but I couldn't see the harm in it.

"Do tell." Zoey perked up and sat forward, though whether she was eager for the information or the distraction, I couldn't tell.

"Alice Rumsford."

"Get out."

"The very same. She bought your building years ago

when it was in danger of being torn down. Apparently she's bought a number of endangered buildings in town."

"I never suspected." Zoey looked down at the lace placemat. "I wonder how she feels about my advocating for the pedestrian mall."

"I doubt she minds. She says she hasn't decided how she'll vote." It was time to issue my invitation. "I have to go out to Morrow Island this morning. We're renovating a house my mother owns there and I've got to make some decisions. Do you want to come? I could really use your advice."

"To Morrow Island where you run the clambakes? Livvie is always talking about it. Yes, please."

I warned Zoey to dress warmly and cleared the plates and food to the kitchen. Vee was thrilled to hear the plan. "I'll pack a picnic lunch."

"Please don't go to any trouble." We'd just eaten.

"It's no trouble. It's a good idea to get that poor girl out into the sunshine."

"How has she been?"

"You've seen yourself. Surprisingly calm. Surprisingly fine." Vee pulled a loaf of wheat bread out of the old-fashioned metal breadbox. "Honestly, Julia, if someone was murdered in our basement while I was asleep upstairs, I would lose my mind."

CHAPTER THIRTEEN

Zoey stood in the bow of our Boston Whaler, her brown hair blowing around the blue bandana and her coat billowing in the wind. "I love this!" she called back to me as I steered us out of Busman's Harbor.

I nodded and smiled, no use yelling over the noise of the boat.

When we passed out of the harbor and into the cold North Atlantic, Zoey moved back to sit where it was more protected. "Imagine, this is your commute every day in the summer. It must be glorious."

I laughed. "I usually go out to the island on our tour boat with the lunch group. There's a whole narrated tour, but I rarely hear it anymore. It's just like when I lived in New York and I'd suddenly be at my subway stop and have no idea how I got there. You tune it out."

"I guess that's right. My commute now is sixteen steps from my apartment to the shop."

"Mine, too, in the winter, now that I've moved back into my mom's."

Her expression turned sympathetic. "Livvie told me you broke up with your boyfriend."

"And lost my apartment." I smiled to show it was an okay place for the conversation to go, but she didn't follow up. Instead, we talked about where we'd lived in New York (she in Brooklyn, me in Tribeca) when we'd been there (she'd arrived a year before I left), and then played a short game of "Do you know?" (No one in common, even though I went through everyone I knew in the art world and she tried everyone she knew in finance.) The game had been a longshot, anyway.

As we pulled up to the dock on Morrow Island, Zoey returned to the bow. "Oh, wow. Oh wow, oh wow, oh wow."

Exactly the reaction I loved to hear from our guests. The island stood in front of us, the little yellow house to the right of the dock, the flat sandy space where the clambake fire cooked the guests' dinner on the left. Up a set of wooden steps, a grassy plateau held the fields for games—bocce, volleyball, croquet—and the dining pavilion, where about half of our visitors ate. The rest dined at picnic tables scattered across the site. The pavilion also contained the tiny kitchen where Livvie and three helpers cooked the clam chowder and blueberry grunt, the first and last courses of the clambake meal.

"Look at this!" Zoey ran up the stairs from the dock to the great lawn and turned around. "Look at the view!"

"It gets better," I told her.

"It couldn't. I see Spain."

I climbed up to meet her and stowed Vee's picnic basket in the dining pavilion. Then we continued on the path up the hill toward Windsholme, the mansion my mother's ancestors had built and the destination for our journey.

"That's the mansion you're renovating," Zoey said. "It's breathtaking."

"And why we're here today." I bent to clear a broken branch that blocked our path. In a couple of weeks Sonny, Livvie, and I would be out here cleaning away the winter debris.

Windsholme looked good, or at least better than it had for decades. The outside was almost finished. There was new siding, and all new windows. The hole a fire had burned in the roof five summers before had disappeared under new, weather-resistant rubber shingles that replaced the old slate. Only the unpainted pillars on the two porches, the long one across the front and the other off the dining room, indicated the house was still a work in progress.

The inside was a different story. "Holy smokes." Zoey stepped over the threshold.

The work had gone on for two summers, most of it things that were decidedly not fun—plumbing, heating, electricity, insulation, and basic structural work. Finally the drywall was going up on the main floor. It was so much easier to envision the rooms.

I gave Zoey the tour. "The first floor is for the business. Having an indoor function space will allow us to do more and larger events, weddings, corporate retreats and the like. We do a little of that now, but we have to keep events small because we're so weather-dependent."

I led her from the big front hallway into the dining room, where the murals on the walls, wainscoting, and fireplace had been preserved.

"Imagine this place in its day." She traced her hand

along the walls painted with rivers and ships. "These are gorgeous."

Ever since I was a kid, I'd imagined Windsholme in its day. "That one over there"—I pointed to the mural on the back wall—"that's how the people who built this house made their money." In the mural, a team of draft horses walked across a frozen river pulling something that looked like a cross between a plow and a sled. Behind it, the frozen water broke into huge strips that more men pushed toward a causeway that brought the giant pieces into the icehouse. The banks of the river were covered in dark pine trees.

I responded to Zoey's puzzled look. "Selling ice. Exporting millions of tons of it all around the world. We're not sure why, but this mural was hidden under paneling when all the others in the room were left uncovered. The builders found it and saved it, thank goodness."

"Amazing." Zoey stood directly in front of the mural. "That's why it's less faded than the others, and cleaner."

"The fireplace has done a number on them. They'll be professionally restored before the job is done."

I took her through the butler's pantry to the brand-new professional kitchen. The old two-story room with its ring of second-story cabinets for china and crystal, linens and silver, was gone. I'd hated demolishing it, but modern cater-waiters weren't going to love running up and down those old stairs. We needed a workable space to serve food to hundreds of people.

We walked around the main floor while I described the rooms, their old functions, and the new ones we planned. Zoey ran a hand along the drywall. "How do you get the materials out here?"

"Every piece comes out on a barge, and the debris left

after demolition and construction goes off the same way. It's been a thing." A really expensive thing.

I'd originally been against my mother's plan to spend an unexpected inheritance on the renovation. Then I'd been very much for it, the project's main cheerleader. Now that the end was, if not in sight, at least imaginable, I was having, not second thoughts, but second *feelings*.

After we climbed the rebuilt staircase, I briefly showed Zoey my mother's summer apartment, created out of the old master bedroom, bath, dressing rooms, and study. On the second floor, the studs were still visible. The drywallers hadn't gotten there yet. I led Zoey to the other side of the house, to the space that was meant to be mine.

"I have to order the kitchen cabinets at least. Ideally the tile, plumbing, and lighting fixtures, too. Our general contractor is all over me. I've delayed and delayed and delayed. I can't seem to figure out what I want." My mother had made the decisions for her apartment in fifteen minutes. She was so sure. I was not. "Your apartment and shop are so perfect. I was hoping you would help me choose."

To nudge me along, Todd Cochran, our general contractor, had left samples of cabinet doors, countertops, faucets, and tile on the floor of the apartment. Zoey immediately began moving the samples around into different piles. "I love this stuff." She made a face and swapped a piece of granite from one of her groups to another. "What color is the floor?"

I pulled back a piece of the brown paper that protected the oak flooring. "The original floor in this room has been saved. We didn't have to move any walls. It will be sanded and stained, probably a lighter color."

"Are you sure about that? Maybe go darker." She

stood and put her hands on her hips, taking in the full space for the first time. "This room is huge."

My open living-dining-kitchen space was made entirely from the original nursery, which stretched from one end of the house to the other, giving me views of the water from windows on three sides.

"That's the problem," I said. "Everything affects everything else. Once I make a single decision, every other decision will flow from that. It makes me an anxious mess."

"You don't seem like a mess to me. Give me a tour so I can get a feel for the place."

I stayed where I was, standing by the door. "This is the kitchen, as you've no doubt figured out."

She eyed the rough plumbing on the outside wall. "You'll have a view of the water over the sink. Nice."

I led her to the other end of the room by the original fireplace, red brick with a dark wood mantel. "I figured this would be the living area." Though the renovation included heat and air conditioning, we would rarely use either. The fireplace would come in handy in June and September in Maine. And occasionally on nippy evenings at the end of August as well.

I took her into the space off the living room. It had been the nanny's room when the children of the original owner were small, and then the governess's room when the children were school-age. It had been the scene of a horrendous sexual assault in the 1890s and was sealed up after that awful event. Our architect had divided it into a bathroom, walk-in closet, and a passageway to the old family bedroom beyond. I wasn't sorry to see that space broken up. The room seemed ripe for haunting.

"I need to pick out counters, countertops, and tile for

the bathroom, too," I told Zoey. "And plumbing fixtures and faucets, though I'm told those can come later."

"Don't order a sink." Zoey's tone was firm. "I'll make you one."

"I can't accept that." I wasn't sure if she was offering it as a gift or as a purchase. Her custom sinks had to cost a fortune. Either way, the offer was too generous, too much.

"Don't argue." She took a quick look around the bedroom. "Nice light," she said, and headed back to the kitchen space. There had been a plan for a new staircase to incorporate the bedrooms on this side of the third floor into my apartment. But it had been expensive and I'd called it off. There didn't seem much point to it.

I started to follow Zoey back to my kitchen, then stopped. It hit me all at once why I'd lost my enthusiasm for the project. I had never pictured living in this space alone. In the imaginary world I'd built to fill what had been at the time very much an imaginary space, Chris was with me. I'd imagined that later there would be children to occupy those third-floor bedrooms, to have the same idyllic island childhoods Livvie and I had, and Page and Jack were now having. I wanted my kids to live in a place where you could run free as a child and feel productive as a teenager, working with the family.

I hadn't gone off the space, I'd gone off my dream for it.

In the kitchen, Zoey was excitedly changing up the groupings of items. "Favorite color?" she asked.

"Blue. Almost any shade."

"Like the sea," she said. "Hmm." She moved the piles again. "This one."

The cabinets were a deep blue, the countertops white.

Zoey held up a sheet of white tiles, some almost transparent, others milky. "For the backsplash and the shower."

"That's it," I agreed. "You're a genius." It was so simple. On my own I never would have been brave enough to choose blue cabinets. I went to the window that would be over my sink and looked out at the ocean. Maybe I could make this place my own.

We walked back down the hill, the item numbers for the cabinets, tile, and countertops we'd chosen safely in my phone. Todd Cochran would be thrilled.

The beautiful day and the sense of accomplishment combined to put me in a buoyant mood. I steered us to the dining pavilion and spread Vee's picnic lunch out on a table that was protected from the wind but had a great view.

Vee had outdone herself. There were thick sandwiches filled with some kind of roast meat, as well as oranges, enormous gooey chocolate cookies, and a thermos of coffee.

Zoey bit into her sandwich eagerly. The salt air had done its work for both our appetites. "We had this pot roast for dinner last night," she said. "I tried to turn it down. I said, 'This is a bed and *breakfast*,' but they insisted I join them. And I for sure didn't want to eat alone at Crowley's with everyone in town asking me a million questions about things the detectives have asked me not to talk about. Those ladies are so nice."

"They are."

We were quiet for a while, enjoying the food. "How did you become a potter?" I asked between bites.

"I went to art school for college. I got a good scholarship, which I needed because I was, you know, an orphan." She smiled to let me know it was okay, a little joke.

"How old were you when your mom died?"

"Sixteen."

"That must have been rough. My dad died when I was twenty-five and I can't even imagine—" I had been an adult and still had my mom. "What happened to you? Who did you live with?"

"There wasn't any family or anything. My dad was never in the picture. I was in foster care for a couple of years, which was fine, nice people. By the time I went to college I was on my own." She paused, then went on. "I was a good artist in school. I knew I had the eye, and the hand. I applied to art schools with some vague notion of becoming a painter, or an illustrator, like my mother should have been. But most illustrations are done on computers now, at least that's what they were training us for, and I didn't like my classes at all. I was seriously thinking about dropping out when, second semester, I took a pottery class and that was it, always and forever."

"What was it about pottery?"

"I could get my hands dirty, literally. You feel such a connection with the earth when you're working with clay. You can take out all your frustrations—pounding, pulling, squishing. It's as good as therapy and you get art at the end of it. I'd been a city kid, never cared much for gardening or landscaping. At the potter's wheel I realized everything I'd been missing, in my other classes and in my life."

"What was next, after school?" I asked.

"After school I bounced around from studio to studio, learning, looking for mentors, at first only for my art and later for both the art and business side of it."

"Did you always want your own business?"

"I knew I wanted to create my art. It was fabulous to learn by creating someone else's, but ultimately unsatisfying. I knew the only way I would have control would be to take it."

"And now you're so successful." Zoey was an impressive person. "How did you do it?"

"Long hours, hard work, single-mindedness," she answered. "The same way most people do it. I blew up every relationship I ever had, left friends behind without looking back. It hasn't been without a cost. And with no guarantee of success."

She peeled an orange. "In the beginning it was so crazy. I'd pull up to the big trade shows in New York with my VW filled to the roof with boxes of ceramics. Friends would help me carry them onto the floor and set up my booth. Then I would spend hours talking to retailers, shop owners, and buyers for chains and major home-goods websites. My reputation grew a little every year, and then four years ago something about my collection that year met the moment and I stood in my little booth taking more orders than most people would have believed I could produce. More than I had money to buy the materials for." She looked out at the sea. "I was an overnight success after ten long years."

"What did you do?" I sat forward, eager to hear what happened next.

"I borrowed the money for the materials from a bank on the strength of the orders. I called everyone I could think of, old friends from art school, potters, painters, mold-makers, everyone who was any good in any studio I'd ever worked in. Not many could come, but enough did. We stayed in my studio space for two months, eating together, sleeping on the floor, when we did sleep, and working all the time. When we shipped the goods out and the cash started coming in, I gave everyone a big bonus and banked the rest. I had plenty of offers to partner, both from artists and businesspeople, but I wanted to keep Lupine Design as my own."

"I love this story," I told her. "This is what I used to do back in the world. Invest my firm's money and help young businesses." They had been technology and bio-tech businesses, not pottery, but Zoey's story sounded so familiar, and like so much fun.

"Where were you back then when I needed you?" she teased.

"Was your company always called Lupine Design?" I asked.

"Always. I love them. They're such beautiful flowers, wild and free. I didn't name my company Lupine Design because I was in Maine. I came to Maine because I'd named my company Lupine Design. That's why I bought that travel magazine I told you about."

I was more impressed by her willingness to take risks than I had been before.

After lunch we hiked all the way around the island, taking advantage of the beautiful day. Zoey oohed and aahed over every view. As the day went on, my mind kept returning to what Vee had said. Zoey seemed fine. But how could she be? A man had been killed in her base-ment. Not just any man, someone she'd seen on a daily basis. They may not have been friends, or even liked one another, but she had to be feeling something. She had seemed more upset about the destruction of her shop than she was about a murder. Perhaps she was, as therapists say, "well defended."

We were already back on the boat before it occurred to me that despite Zoey's strange detachment, it had never once crossed my mind that I might be alone on an island with a killer.

CHAPTER FOURTEEN

We hugged good-bye on the pier and then Zoey went back to the Snuggles to get some work done. "I can't go to the studio, but the emails and orders don't stop."

I checked on our shuttered ticket kiosk, something I did from time to time during the off season to make sure a substitute mail carrier hadn't pushed letters through the slot. Then I started for home. As I passed Stowaway Resort-wear, I caught a flash of movement through the window.

I put my hand over my eyes, leaned in, and peered through the big picture window. The glass felt cool on my forehead. Sure enough, there was someone moving around the dark store. I raised my fist and knocked. The figure, slender and smartly dressed, moved toward the door.

"I'm sorry, we're not open for the season." Claire Reagan was a pretty woman with an elegantly cut head of highlighted blond hair and a pair of reading glasses hanging around her neck. "I'm pricing stock. We'll be open Memorial Day weekend."

"I'm not here to shop."

She looked me up and down, taking in the T-shirt, flannel overshirt, quilted vest, jeans, and work boots. "I'm not surprised." Which sounded kind of snotty, though not inaccurate. Then she smiled. "You're younger than my usual clientele."

"Ms. Reagan, I'm Julia Snowden. Can I come in?"

"Are you Jacqueline's daughter then?"

"I am."

She stepped aside and gestured for me to enter. The small-town open sesame that came from knowing someone in common. "Call me Claire."

Inside the store, the racks of sleeveless dresses, sporty blouses, and brightly colored slacks and shorts were less than half full and there were piles of clothes on the checkout counter and several chairs. Many of the fabrics had nautical themes. There were lobsters and lighthouses, sailboats, whales, and seals. There were also a lot of floral prints, lupines included.

I wondered what my mother's connection could be to this woman. I couldn't see Mom in any of the high-end resort wear. It wasn't the sort of thing she'd ever wear to her jobs running the gift shop at the Snowden Family Clambake or at Linens and Pantries. My mother didn't go to parties, or at least not anything beyond a birthday party for a grandchild or other member of the family.

I put a hand out, unthinking, and felt the silky fabric of a sleeveless dress in a red and white print of swimming fish. My mother could have worn dresses like this. If she had married the doctor or lawyer or banker her father expected. But she'd married the boy who delivered groceries to her private island in his little boat, the son of a local lobsterman, and her life had taken a different turn.

"I'd like to ask a few questions about your previous location," I said.

Claire's face softened. "Ah, Phinney. Such a shame. What has that to do with you? Are you a journalist?"

"Not at all," I assured her. "My sister works at Lupine Design and I happened to be there right after the vandalism was discovered. Maybe you heard about that, too? And then I was there again later on, the morning Phinney Hardison's body was found."

"You do seem to have a knack for being in the wrong place at the wrong time." Claire stood, unmoving, in the middle of the shop. "I still don't get it."

I drew a big breath and told her the same story I'd told Alice Rumsford. "There was no sign of a break-in, either time. I got to wondering who had access to the building. That led me down a rather crooked path to Miss Rumsford. And led me to you."

Claire's face relaxed, and then she smiled. "Ah, Alice has sent you to me."

I didn't correct her.

"I loved our old Main Street location. I was there for twenty-five years. It was the second location for the shop. I started down here on the waterfront, but when I wanted to expand there was nowhere to go. Alice's building worked out well for me. It's a nice big space and there's more parking down at that end of the street. A lot of my customers are summer people and snowbirds who drive into town."

"You knew Alice was your landlady?" This was a contrast to Zoey, who apparently had no idea.

"Not for the first several years. Everything was through the rental agency. But then Alice started coming to the shop. She liked my taste. She said I made Maine more beautiful. Alice doesn't buy dresses or separates. I can't imagine her wearing them. But she's a devoted customer of my accessories—scarves, belts, bags, and hats, especially hats."

There were some belts and bags hanging on a back wall, but the only sign of hats were some bald-headed white busts with featureless faces.

Claire followed my gaze. "The hats are in the back and I have more coming. They'll go on display closer to opening." She turned back to me. "Alice prefers straw, wide-brimmed, with a colorful ribbon or scarf. She's been a wonderful supporter of the shop."

"Why did you leave Main Street?"

Claire gestured around the store. "I remember when the stores along this row looked like they were going to fall into the harbor. Now, the buildings have been fixed up so beautifully, inside and out. Everything is new—plumbing, electricity, Wi-Fi. The shops have been rebuilt from the inside out."

I'd watched the renovations as they'd been done, from our ticket kiosk across the pier. The gleaming white storefronts with the matching display windows looked bright and clean and new, which as a neighbor, I appreciated.

"There are always trade-offs," Claire was saying. "The parking is tougher down here for my regulars, but they've continued to support me. A lot of them shop early and late in the season, when it's not so crazy. And at this location,

I get so many more tourists." She paused. "Alice is lovely, but she wasn't going to invest in her building that way. Look at all the money her current tenant has put into it."

I felt a little defensive on Zoey's behalf. "She got a reduced rent and a long lease."

"And that was something I wasn't prepared to do. I'm at an age where I'm thinking of winding down, not taking on huge projects. I've worked every day of my life for decades." She fussed with the sunglasses on a rotating rack, making sure they were perfectly straight. "It's time to relax a little. One of the stores had to go. I asked myself where I'd rather spend the bulk of the year. I didn't have to think hard. Busman's Harbor was the answer. I sold my business and my house in Florida and bought a little condo down there where I can stay during the worst of the winter. That's why I'm back so early this year."

"How did you get along with Phinney back when you had neighboring stores?"

"At first I wasn't happy when Alice rented him the space next to me. I didn't think we were after the same customer. But it turned out a surprising number of the people who came to my shop would go next door to root through his late mother's costume jewelry and knick-knacks. And on slow days, weekdays in the spring before business picked up, Phinney would invite me over and throw a couple of tea bags in a set of chipped mugs. We'd take our breaks together and chat. He was a terrible gossip."

Claire's relationship with Phinney had been so different from Zoey's. Why had this woman selling expensive dresses been acceptable to him while Zoey and her $92.00 plates were not? "Did he ever sell anything?"

She laughed. "Goodness, yes. He'd sell anything that wasn't bolted down." Her smile faded and she turned wistful. "Except his old guitar. He kept it on display, front and center, right as you walked into his shop. It seemed like every customer who went in there asked about it and tried to bargain with him. 'I'll never sell,' he would say."

What a strange story. "Did he play?"

"I asked him that. He said, 'Not anymore.' Which made me wonder again why he didn't sell it. Finally, I realized it was the only thing in the shop that was his. Everything else had been his mother's. I suppose he wanted to hang on to some little piece of who he'd been." Claire stared at the floor, her long, mascaraed lashes resting on her high cheekbones. "Poor Phinney. I feel awful about what happened to him."

It was the best opening to ask my question. "Do you still have keys to the building?"

She didn't hesitate. "I turned them in to the real estate office right after I moved out."

"Do you know of anyone else who has a key? A former employee perhaps, or a cleaner or caretaker?"

"Absolutely not. I kept careful track of the copies and threw them all away before I turned in my key as required." She paused, thinking. "Why are you even asking? In a huge renovation, like Lupine Design did, I'm sure the new tenant must have changed the locks and installed a security system. Like at this place. I have the works. Alarm system, cameras inside and out."

But Zoey hadn't done that. "Who owns this building?" I asked.

"Karl Kimbel. He is wonderful. Such an eye for design." Kimbel, the developer who'd been Zoey's ally at the public hearing.

As she finished speaking there was an authoritative rap on the door.

"A busy day for a closed shop," Claire muttered. But when she looked at the figure through the glass she positively beamed with pleasure. She rushed to open the door.

"Karl." She was blushing. "Speak of the devil. Your ears must be ringing. I was just this moment singing your praises as a landlord to this young woman."

He took her hand. "Claire, I heard you were back in town and had to stop in. How is everything?"

"As I was telling Julia here, everything is wonderful. The building has weathered the winter beautifully."

When he heard my name, Kimbel turned to me.

Claire put a hand on his shoulder as she introduced us. "Karl, this is Julia Snowden. Her family owns the Snowden Family Clambake." She pointed toward our ticket kiosk on the pier.

He smiled at me and offered his hand. "Pleased to meet you. I'm an admirer of your business."

I took it and shook. "Have you been to the clambake?"

"I've never had that pleasure. But your reputation precedes you. Everyone in town says you offer a quality dining experience. Anything that attracts tourists and keeps them happy, I'm all for."

He wasn't wearing a suit as he had at the public hearing. Instead he wore a sweater over a plaid shirt with a crisp collar, well-cut trousers, and a puffy hunter-green vest. His glasses had clear-rimmed plastic frames. He was present, powerful, charismatic, the type of person your eyes were drawn toward, even in a crowded room.

"Julia came to talk about Phinney Hardison's murder," Claire told him.

"Terrible business," he said. "Not good for tourism."

I stuck up for my detective friends. "I'm sure the state police will have it cleared up before the season starts."

"You have more faith than I do." His eyes widened and then pulled into a squint. "Didn't I see you at the public hearing the other night?"

Had I worn a sign on my head? First Ben and now this guy. "I'm surprised you noticed. I didn't say a word."

"When you've been to as many of these things as I have over the last few years, you notice the new faces. Mostly it's the same old people having the same old arguments." He looked through the glasses directly into my eyes. "What are your feelings about the pedestrian mall? Were you there because you have a business interest?"

"I haven't made up my mind," I answered.

"I'm a man who loves a challenge. Come have a drink with me and I'll persuade you."

"Sure. Right now?"

"No time like the present." He turned to Claire. "You'll excuse us?"

"Of course." Claire walked us to the door and locked it behind us. As I left I looked back through the shop window. Disappointment was etched across her face. I didn't think it was because *I* was leaving.

CHAPTER FIFTEEN

Outside, Karl and I turned toward Crowley's, the ware-house-turned-bar-and-restaurant at the end of the road. It was the only place to get a drink in the harbor at this time of year. It had been closed down for the season until the end of March and had since reopened with a slowly expanding set of hours of operation.

As we walked, I turned to look back at the buildings Kimbel owned. They were sturdy, white, identical, a neat row of adjoining storefronts. In addition to Stowaway Resortwear, there was an elegant art gallery, a high-end gift shop, and a store devoted entirely to Christmas. None of them were open yet for the season. I had never been in any of them; there was no reason why I would. The fifth store stood empty. I wondered what kind of tenant it would attract.

When the paint had been flaking off the clapboards

and the buildings had leaned precariously, the tenants had been a marine supply store, a shop that sold cheap T-shirts and sweatshirts to tourists, and a fish shop. The new stores were definitely prettier, but which was more authentically Busman's Harbor?

We reached Crowley's a few seconds later. Kimbel held the door for me and I entered for the first time this year. The big place was quiet in the late afternoon. The owner, Sam Rockmaker, was behind the bar. He waved us toward the tables in the main dining room. "Sit anywhere."

Kimbel marched to a booth on the wide aisle next to the bar. He graciously gestured for me to sit down and then sat himself, facing the door. It was the most visible seat in the place. He obviously liked to see and be seen.

I sat for a moment, thinking about the dizzying speed with which this meeting had come together. It seemed absurd to think that the dapper man sitting across from me could be a murderer. But if Binder and Flynn could suspect Zoey of Phinney's murder because she'd argued with him about the pedestrian mall, then Karl Kimbel had to be equally suspect. As a developer, Kimbel had a lot more to gain than Zoey did. On the other hand, Phinney *had* been murdered in Zoey's basement, while she apparently slept alone and alibi-less upstairs.

Sam came out from behind the bar and took our order himself.

"Beer," Kimbel said. "Best you have on draft."

I hesitated, but then said, "White wine." It was late in the afternoon, but the sun definitely wasn't over the yardarm. My second session of day-drinking in a row.

Sam hurried back to the booth with our order.

"Tell me your concerns about the pedestrian mall."

Kimbel moved his beer glass to the side and leaned forward on his elbows, getting right to the point.

"I don't have specific concerns." I answered him honestly. "I'm not sure it will affect my business either way and I think it will be good for the town."

"I knew you were a young person with vision." He sat back in the booth and smiled. His teeth were white and straight except for one that was crowded forward on the bottom. "That's the problem with this town. No vision."

I would have said the problem was a decimated fishing industry and few year-round, lucrative jobs for young people, or anyone else. But I had to admit, vision was part of it. Busman's Harbor had to figure out what it wanted to be in a changing world.

"I have a vision," Kimbel said. "I see a high-end resort, similar to Kennebunkport or Ogunquit. Why can't we have that on the mid-coast?"

Because those places are closer to New York and Boston? Because they have a housing stock of seaside mansions and a history of famous residents? I didn't say what I was thinking. I let Kimbel continue.

"I've been working hard, both publicly and behind the scenes, to make that happen. I own three of the hotels on the east side of the harbor."

"So I've heard."

He smiled in acknowledgment of his local fame. Of course, I had heard. "I've been working quietly, buying them up," he continued. "I'm waiting for some zoning changes and then I plan to replace all three. Sure, the seaside rooms are 'charming' and 'quaint.'" He used his fingers to draw quotes in the air. "But that's not what today's visitors are looking for. They want luxury: a spa, a fancy restaurant, heated pools indoors and out. They want snack bars where they can send the kids for meals. They want room service."

The Bellevue Inn was the Grande Dame, the biggest and best-known hotel in that group, the one that had a No VACANCY sign out when the others were less than half full. But for all its vaunted history, the original Victorian building had been added on to with a collection of hotel- and motel-like rooms that gave it a ramshackle, almost comical appearance. The hotel had a nice dining room that served three meals a day on white tablecloths with a focus on New England offerings like Yankee pot roast and Indian pudding. The Bellevue was often full, despite the large number of rooms, but it was not luxurious in the way modern tourists might expect.

The next hotel in the row was the Seasider, a utilitarian place that focused on tour groups. The staff had the skills to turn over beds and feed big busloads of people, who arrived throughout the summer and in leaf-peeping season in the fall. The concierge often arranged to have the groups visit the Snowden Family Clambake, for which I was grateful. The rooms were clean and affordable for their clientele, who were often senior citizens on bucket-list trips. The Seasider was not luxurious.

The third hotel Kimbel owned, the Lobsterman's Inn, was a three-story motel-like structure with outside walk-ways, not inside halls. It was favored by families and heavily advertised its "housekeeping units" where you could bring and make your own food. It had a restaurant on its dock open for breakfasts and lunches during the sea-son and a little general store that gave it a campground-like feel. It was the opposite of luxurious and had struggled for years. I wasn't surprised its owners had been willing to listen when Kimbel and his moneybags came calling.

"The big thing the Lobsterman advertises is kitchenettes in the rooms, like that's some kind of selling point," Kimbel said. "Women should go on vacation, too. They shouldn't be buying groceries and cooking."

I ignored his rather quaint notion of how women and men divided chores in modern families.

On the one hand, Kimbel's prospective rich guests could more easily afford the price the Snowden Family Clambake had to charge. On the other, people at every income level loved to complain about the price of things, so I wasn't sure these fancy guests would mean any more business for us. "Focusing on the luxury market prices out a lot of people," I pointed out. "What about families and senior citizens?"

"That's a nice thought. Don't get me wrong, but working families don't take vacations anymore. It's not like the mill closes down for a week in the summer and the whole family goes off to a rental cottage by the sea. Nowadays, they can't afford it. Or if they can it's because every family member is working two or three jobs and their time off never gets synchronized."

"That doesn't seem good or fair," I said.

Kimbel shrugged. "I didn't create the economy, but I'm clear-eyed about it and run my business accordingly. We can't have a tourist industry that caters to a clientele that doesn't exist anymore. If it weren't for the Canadians we'd have been done for, years ago. The people who can afford to go on vacation want to stay in some place nicer than their homes. They don't see the charm in staying in a shack that smells of mildew."

Was that true? Maybe he was right. I wasn't prepared to debate the fallout from income inequality with Karl Kimbel.

"I'm not proposing we put a barrier at the top of the highway at Route 1 and become the world's largest gated community," Kimbel said. "I'm saying we must face the realities of the current economy and flex to them. Clinging to the past is the best way to go broke."

I sipped my wine, thinking about what he said. Plenty of people in Busman's Harbor longed for old days that were never coming back. We didn't control the economy. We reacted to it. Perhaps there was something in what he said.

"The kind of guest I plan to attract will expect more of the town, too," Kimbel continued. "They'll want shops with luxury goods. They don't want peeling paint and novelty T-shirts. That's why I've been buying properties in the harbor as they've come on the market." He looked into my eyes to see if I was following, to judge if I agreed. "We already attract the yachters. They'll appreciate the more upscale retail environment, too. I'm also working on the select people to extend the pier here so bigger cruise ships can unload their passengers right downtown. That will bring more people in as well. Energy. What this town needs is energy."

He was a powerful man, his confidence in his vision absolute. I'd met his type before, when I'd worked in venture capital. I was skeptical, but I wasn't immune to the strength of his conviction. It signaled a safe harbor in the sea of an uncertain future.

"And then," he said, "we'll tackle the back harbor. All those shanties will have to go. We want to put our best foot forward as boats come into town."

The back harbor was our working waterfront. It housed the lobster co-op where the lobstermen sold their catch, Bud Barbour's boat repair yard, and Gus's restaurant. Gus's building was a part of me, and the idea that it would be gone made my eyes sting. I swallowed to steady my voice. "I don't think Busman's Harbor would feel like Busman's Harbor without those places. And where would the lobstermen take their catch? We don't want to chase them out of town. Where would you get the lobsters for your pricey restaurants?"

Kimbel sent a short burst of air from his cheeks. I wasn't the visionary young person he had hoped I was. "The co-op can stay. We'll offer tours. But the rest of that mess . . ." He didn't finish the thought. "When you're a little older you'll realize the world is always changing. I've never been in a resort town in any decade where the old-timers didn't tell me, 'You should have been here ten years ago. Things were so much better then.' This town needs to keep moving forward or it will die." He shifted in his seat and looked me in the eye again. "You're rebuilding that old mansion out on your island. That's a good start. You might want to think about investing in the rest of the place, too. A new clientele is coming and they want a more refined experience."

"You said you'd never been to the clambake," I protested.

"I keep a pretty good finger on the pulse of this town." He stated it as a fact, which it undoubtedly was. "I have a big stake in the future, so I like to know what's going on."

There was a tiny commotion behind me and out of the corner of my eye I spotted Sam at the bar waving hello to someone. The hair on the back of my neck stood up. I knew without looking what had happened. My ex, Chris, had arrived and taken up his post for his second job as the bouncer at the door. It was early in the season, too early to truly need a bouncer, especially as no musical act had been advertised for that evening. Sam was probably looking out for his longtime buddy.

I took a last swallow of my wine and pushed the glass forward on the table to indicate it was time to go. Kimbel understood my meaning and signaled for the bill. I fished around in my Snowden Family Clambake tote bag and pulled out my wallet.

"My treat." Kimbel was firm.

I didn't argue. He'd been the one lobbying me for my vote on the pedestrian mall. He paid with a credit card and we waited while it was processed. I read the slip upside down as he added the tip and signed it, a skill you pick up if you've been in the food service business long enough. We stood and he walked ahead of me, parting the crowd around the door in a way that I never could. I waited a moment and left a five-dollar bill on the table to augment Kimbel's ten percent tip. I'd been serving food most of my life and I knew how important that extra money could be.

At the door, Kimbel stepped aside so I could go ahead.

Chris stared with open curiosity as Kimbel trailed me out the door, smiling graciously as we left. "Bye, Julia."

Kimbel and I exited into the late afternoon daylight. Somehow, whatever time of day it was when I left Crowley's, I was surprised the sun was out.

"Bye, Chris." My throat was dry and the words came out in an ugly croak. Then to top that off, I blushed. Chris was already closing the door. I hoped he hadn't noticed.

"I'm parked on Main," Kimbel said as we walked along together.

"I'm staying at my mom's, also on Main Street," I told him without further explanation. "Where do you live?"

"I own a house on Thistle Island," he said. "But it's

tied up in my impending divorce at the moment. I'm staying at the Bellevue."

I didn't know what to say to that. We passed his row of neat retail establishments. Stowaway Resortwear was dark. Claire Reagan must have gone home for the day. "Who's going to rent the fifth store?" I asked him.

He beamed at me, happy for the question. "I'm hoping to get us a Starbucks."

Kimbel and I said good-bye at the corner of Main and Main and I trudged up the hill toward Mom's. I blushed again thinking about my high red color when I'd passed Chris. Eleven months. I should have been done with this. I wished I'd at least brushed my hair and put on a little makeup. Which was ridiculous because in our three years together he had seen me in pretty much every state in which you can see a person. He'd be the last person on earth to be fooled by a little concealer under my eyes.

I had been the one to break us up, so I should have been the one to walk away with her ego intact, right? But I still had deep regrets. Not for the breakup, which was the right thing to do, the only thing to do, but for the reasons behind it. Chris and I loved each other. There was no doubt of that. But a corner of his soul held dark secrets, secrets that in ways big and small kept me on the outside of his life. He couldn't get past them and I couldn't live with them. It was all a terrible waste.

I turned my mind, forcefully and deliberately, to something else. What, truly, did I make of Karl Kimbel's plans for Busman's Harbor? He was right that the town had to change with the times. Throughout our history, farms, shipyards, canneries, and fishing fleets had come and then gone. We'd remade ourselves again and again. He was correct that the vacationers had become more upscale over the course of my lifetime. I could see it in the clothes, the conversations, and the sense of entitlement from some guests at the clambake.

I hated to think about Busman's Harbor without Gus's restaurant or Bud Barbour's boatyard. Neither was pretty, but each helped to define the place. I had nothing against Starbucks. I had drunk, eaten, worked, and even occasionally napped in many as I'd traveled the country in my former job. But I dreaded the idea of our waterfront looking exactly the same as every other place in the country. Would people make the effort to come to Busman's Harbor if it was like everywhere else? There were more convenient places to go.

I let myself into Mom's back door and pried off my boots in the mudroom. The house was quiet. Mom must still be at Livvie's. I crossed the kitchen, opened the fridge, and leaned on the door to peer inside. Nothing looked appetizing. My stomach growled. I ignored it and made my way through the darkening house to the living room. I knelt in front of the fireplace. There were plenty of dry logs and kindling. A fire would be just the thing.

I was about to strike the match when my cell phone buzzed, jangling on the enamel top of the kitchen table where I'd dropped my tote bag. Running to it, I hit my knee on one of the chairs in the dining room. "Oww!"

My phone said the number was unknown. "Hello?" said the man on the other end.

"Hello," I echoed back.

"Is this Julia? Ben Barlow." I recognized the voice as he spoke the words. "I wanted to let you know, I found the key. I called your Sergeant Flynn and told him Aunt Alice is the owner of the building. We had a nice talk and then he spoke with her. He seemed grateful for the call."

"Thank you for telling me."

"I was wondering," Ben continued on the other end, "I know it's last minute, but would you like to have dinner tonight? I thought we hit it off yesterday and much as I love my aunt, I don't think I can eat another dinner on a tray while listening to Vivaldi on the stereo."

"You're saying I'm a better alternative than an eighty-year-old?"

"No, no." He didn't get that I was joking and I felt bad for teasing him. "Not at all. I'm saying I would like to have dinner with you."

"Sure." I'd enjoyed his company, too, and it seemed rude to say no after he'd gotten filthy helping me out of his driveway the day before.

"Great!" he said. "See you at Crowley's at eight?"

I hesitated just a moment. "Great. See you there."

CHAPTER SIXTEEN

Back to Crowley's. If I'd had my wits about me I would have suggested going off the peninsula to a town with more open restaurants—Damariscotta to the north, or Wiscasset to the south. But that idea carried its own freight, like the possibility of a long, awkward car ride together. What if we had a miserable time and were trapped in the car on the way home? Crowley's was open; it was close. I could see why Ben had assumed we'd go there.

At least I had time to pull myself together a little. I changed into nice slacks, flats, and a blouse I would have worn to work in the days before my daily uniform had become flannel overshirts. I brushed my hair and my teeth and put on a little lipstick. I didn't want to overdo it. This was a casual, last-minute invitation to dinner by someone I'd met only the day before. I wanted to look pulled together. As much for Chris as for Ben, I had to admit.

I left the house at eight. I didn't want to be the first one to get to Crowley's. Nothing would look more pathetic than hanging around waiting for someone. I didn't know if Ben was the type to be early, late, or right on time. As luck would have it, he arrived the same moment I did. He wore a long-sleeved, button-down shirt under a maroon sweater. I was glad he had another sweater with him, since I'd probably been a party to destroying the one he'd worn the day before.

Prepared this time, I greeted Chris as I came through the door. "Hi." It would have been weird to walk right by him.

"Hey, Julia." He gave me a grin, an open look of curiosity on his face.

"Um . . . Chris, this is Ben." I could feel the blush returning. Darn. "Ben, Chris."

"Hey." Ben smiled.

"Hey." Chris gave a curt nod.

I hustled Ben over to the host station. "Can we sit in the other room?" Crowley's occupied a cavernous former dockside warehouse. It would be packed in the summer, but we should be able to sit where we pleased tonight, and I didn't want to feel or see Chris watching me during this whole . . . whatever it was.

"The other room is closed. No wait staff assigned there tonight." The hostess was a high school girl I recognized from my niece Page's swim team.

"Then can we sit as far back in this room as possible?"

She took two dinner menus and two drink menus off the stand and cradled them in one arm. "Sure."

At the table in the farthest corner, I took the seat facing the wall and let Ben climb into the banquette. I wasn't going to spend my night listening to Ben while staring at Chris.

The conversation didn't flow quite as easily as it had the day before. Ben squinted at the drinks menu. Though Crowley's looked like a place where a wise person would order beer, in the last few years Sam Rockmaker had gotten quite creative with his cocktail offerings.

Our server came, a skinny kid with thin brown hair, who didn't look old enough to serve alcohol, though I knew Sam was meticulous about that sort of thing.

I removed the menu gently from Ben's hands. "Allow me." I turned to the skinny kid. "Two Pine Tree States, please."

When the waiter moved off, I folded my arms on the table. "So," I said.

Ben smiled back. "So."

"So Alice Rumsford is your aunt." Inane, but it turned out to be a good conversation starter.

"My great-aunt, actually. My grandfather's sister."

"It's nice that you're so close."

"Believe me, I get more out of the relationship than she does."

That seemed unlikely. "Is your whole family close?"

He relaxed visibly, leaning back against the banquette. "The opposite, actually. My mom and her siblings and cousins grew up barely knowing Aunt Alice. She was always off, traveling the world. She came home for weddings and funerals, the occasional christening. To me she was this glamorous figure who swooped in, entertained us with her stories, and left just as quickly."

"She traveled the world?" I had never heard this about her.

"Taking pictures. She was a ground-breaking photographer for *National Geographic Magazine*."

This was new information, thought it did explain something. "The photos on the walls at her house. She told me they were taken by a friend."

He smiled. He had a nice smile that emphasized his cheekbones and crinkled the corners of his eyes. "She does that. It's not any kind of false modesty. It's that she's endlessly curious. She wanted the conversation to be about you, not her. She says she's heard all her stories before."

"Those photos are amazing."

"There are thousands more like that, each one as beautiful and as moving as the ones in the cottage. Alice's brothers, my grandfather and great-uncle, thought she was rebellious and eccentric. My mom's generation wasn't close with her at all, because she was always gone."

"She never married?"

"I don't even remember a boyfriend, ever. Her job wouldn't have allowed it. I heard rumors of a young love, a summer romance when she was in college. My grandfather and his brother forbade the relationship, apparently. Which is hard to believe because as far as I can tell she never listened to a word either of them said about her life ever afterward."

I tried to imagine what Alice's life had been like, traveling the world to take pictures.

The cocktails arrived. Ben eyed the drink, which was garnished with an orange peel and a spring of rosemary, with suspicion. Cautiously, he picked it up, sniffed and took a sip. "Mmm. What is that?"

"Muddled orange and rosemary, pine syrup, pine bitters, rye whiskey, and soda."

"Pine syrup? What is pine syrup?" he asked.

"Delicious," I answered.

I drank, too, enjoying the cocktail as I'd known I would. It tasted like the air around a campfire deep in a Maine forest—earthy, piney, fruity, effervescent.

The young waiter returned. The special was lobster stew, which pretty much decided things for me. "A bowl of lobster stew, house salad," I said.

Ben handed his menu back to the kid. "Exactly the same." He looked at me. "You haven't steered me wrong so far."

"I'm glad you like the cocktail." I raised my glass to his and we clinked. "Cheers. You were telling me about Alice."

Ben took another swallow and then continued the story. "Twenty-five years ago, Aunt Alice announced she was going to retire and she wanted to buy the family cottage and make it her home. My granddad and his brother were both in Ohio and they and their kids could only get to Maine for a couple of weeks a year. It seemed like a good idea to everyone except me. I loved Busman's Harbor and I loved the cottage. I made a huge fuss in the way only a selfish adolescent can. So Alice said I could spend the summers with her. It was a promise she didn't need to keep, but she did."

"You've been here every summer?"

"From age thirteen until I got my undergrad degree. The first two years I worked for Alice, fixing up the cottage, which had been neglected, and creating all those garden beds in the yard. After that I worked summers at Gleason's Hardware." He sat back in the booth. "I'm surprised we never met."

"In the summer my family lived on the island where we run the clambakes."

"Ah, that explains it. I'm sure I would remember you." He smiled and I smiled back. Automatically. I couldn't help it.

"Your aunt doesn't live at the cottage full-time." I would have known if she did.

Ben shook his head. "No. She has a little place in Arizona where she goes for the worst of the winter, but she gets back here as soon as she possibly can, always in time for town meeting season." His smiled disappeared. He downed a big slug from his cocktail glass. "I'm here this month in part because the family is worried about how much longer she can stay here on her own."

I hoped Alice could stay in the cottage as long as she wished. "Does she still take photos?"

"Not one since she retired. When she first took over the cottage, I tried to convince her to go out and take pictures. She wouldn't have had to go much farther than the yard to get some great shots."

"Your view."

"Our view," he agreed. "But she wasn't interested. She said, 'I'm retired. I'm finished worrying about the light and the settings and whether some wild animal is going to stand still. I've captured the world's beauty all my life. Now I want to make the world more beautiful.' Busman's Harbor became her project."

"And we're grateful." We were. We accepted changes that Alice suggested, which we would have rejected completely if they'd been put forward by Karl Kimbel.

The skinny kid came back with the stew and the salads and a basket of Crowley's warm, crusty rolls.

Ben stared at his bowl. "I thought this would be, you know, a stew, with vegetables and potatoes and stuff."

"Nope, just big chunks of lobster, butter, and cream. Taste it."

As Ben brought the stew to his lips, he closed his eyes. "Mmm. You're right. Creamy, buttery, lobster-y." He opened his eyes. "There are some other flavors in there."

Like Ben, I closed my eyes when I tasted the stew. "Pepper. And sherry, I think. But subtle. What really comes through is the lobster."

"If there's no vegetables in lobster stew, what's the difference between lobster stew and lobster bisque?" Ben was enjoying himself, challenging my Maine knowledge.

"Bisque often does have vegetables, but they're ground up. The bits of lobster are usually smaller and the soup is much thicker. It used to be thickened by ground lobster shells. Some people still do that today." Bisque. The same word as the one for the white, unglazed pottery in Zoey's studio.

Ben was impressed with my food knowledge. "How do you know all this?"

"My ex is a chef." Chris would have corrected me and said he was a cook, but after he'd cooked for our restaurant for three winters, I'd conferred the title and told him he couldn't argue.

Ben's eyes flicked over my head. "You mean the ex staring at the back of your head right now?"

"How did you—?"

"I like to think I'm fairly perceptive, but this one doesn't take a high emotional IQ. If looks could kill I'd have been dead twenty minutes ago."

"I'm sorry."

"No worries." He reached across the table and gave

my hand a squeeze. "Though I'd love to know what you did to that poor guy."

That wasn't a topic for a first date, if that's even what this was. I steered the conversation in another direction. "Your aunt's cottage—?" I started to say.

"You're wondering why it's never been modernized."

"I don't mean to pry, but yes. Most people sitting on a piece of property like that, who like your aunt are committed to being here so much of the year, would have put in heat, insulated, put dry wall up to the ceiling—"

Ben took up the list. "Divided the room upstairs into proper bedrooms, added another bathroom, a washing machine, and a dishwasher." He paused. "I expected that would happen when she bought the place. I've urged her to make some modifications, at least for her own comfort, but she resists. She thinks if the house feels like a regular home, with TV and cable and internet, eventually she'll forget to look out the window or sit on the porch and it will be just like living anywhere else."

She had a point. You never look out the window enough when you're staring at one screen or another. "When you stayed for the summers, where did you sleep?" I asked.

He did the crinkly-eyed thing again. "You're asking if Alice and I both slept in the big room upstairs? Not hardly. I know that's how families did it in the olden days. I slept in the daybed in the glassed-in porch in the spring and moved to the one on the screen porch in the summer. I loved it." He smiled at the memory. "Now I sleep upstairs and Alice sleeps in her recliner. It looks uncomfortable to me, but she swears it helps her heartburn."

We were quiet for a moment while we ate the delicious stew. "I know who your aunt is," I said to Ben. "But I don't know a thing about you."

"Not a lot to tell. I live in Cincinnati and work in finance."

"No kidding. I did, too. What do you do?"

"Consulting for a Big Four accounting firm. You?"

We talked for a time about our careers, my former, his current. Ben said, "Then you chucked it all and moved back here? I admire that."

"It's a longer story. My dad died and my family needed me to run the business. I don't regret leaving my old job. The travel and separation from my family were killing me."

"I hear you. The only reason I can be here now is because I'm between onsite assignments. I start a new one the first of the month. As it is, I drive down to the Busman's Harbor library to work every day because there's no internet at the cottage. Also, to warm up my feet, which have been cold since I arrived in Maine. I'd just got back from the library when you arrived yesterday. I'm glad I didn't miss you."

"Even though you had to push me out of the mud?"

"Even though."

We passed a pleasant evening after that. We talked about our families and played "Do you remember?" about Busman's Harbor when we were teenagers. Some of the time, though not often, I even managed to forget about Chris standing guard by the door.

I pulled out my wallet the moment I saw the server heading toward our table with the bill and offered to pay. "I'll get it this time," Ben said and I let him. But what did that mean? That there would be a next time, presumably.

On the way out, we passed behind Jamie, who was seated alone at the bar, nursing a beer. I clapped him on the shoulder. "Tough day?" I asked. "You look tired."

He smiled when he saw me. "Long. You know how it is at the beginning of an investigation. The state cops have us running around, doing the grunt work. Do you want to sit?" The stool next to him was empty.

"Can't. I'm on my way out. I'm here with—" I turned to introduce him to Ben, but Ben had gone ahead and was almost at the door. "Someone," I finished lamely. Jamie followed my eyes to the door where Ben and Chris stood talking. "Gotta go." I speed-walked out of there.

Ben walked me all the way home, even though we passed right by his big SUV, which was parked down the block. But there was no brush of the lips to my cheek, not even a hug.

"Goodnight," he called when I was safely on Mom's front porch. Then he stuck his hands in his pockets and walked back toward his vehicle.

I watched him go, wondering what had just happened and how I felt about it.

CHAPTER SEVENTEEN

I woke up thinking about Phinney's murder and the vandalism at Lupine Design. With no sign of a break-in, I'd reasoned that access to the building had to provide a clue. But the idea was getting me nowhere.

If Zoey hadn't killed Phinney, then there was only one other possibility. Phinney had let his killer into the building. Therefore, the killer had to be someone Phinney knew.

Who would Phinney trust enough to let them into his store in the middle of the night?

Which also begged the question, what had Phinney been doing in the store at that time? Someone must have lured him there. Perhaps they said there was some kind of emergency, a flood or more vandalism, perhaps. Had that person called Phinney at home or on his cell? Binder and Flynn would be working on that.

I called each of the detectives. Neither picked up. I left

a vague "checking on when my statement will be ready to sign" message and asked for a callback.

I went to the clambake office next to my bedroom, opened my laptop, and searched for information about Phinney online. Le Roi jumped into my lap, happy to find me sitting still. I wasn't the least surprised when nothing turned up but a mention of Phinney in his mother's obituary. No other family members were named.

I looked out my office windows. It was another beautiful day. Two in a row, though I was too smart and too experienced with Maine weather to be tricked by Mother Nature into false hope. I gave Le Roi a last, attentive pat and helped the big guy off my lap. In the back hall, I grabbed my quilted vest and my Snowden Family Clambake tote bag and headed over the harbor hill to Gus's restaurant.

With luck, I'd hit the quiet time between breakfast and lunch. I climbed down the stairs from the street level into the restaurant. Only one couple lingered over coffee in a booth in the dining room. The front room was empty of customers, the stools unoccupied, except for one. Bud Barbour sat hunched over the counter, deep in conversation with Gus. Bud's ever-present, mostly-black-Lab, Morgan, lay quietly in the corner created by the counter and the wall. I sat one stool away from Bud.

"What's up?" I addressed them both.

Gus brought his great white eyebrows together in his death stare, but three-plus years of living in the apartment upstairs and running a restaurant in his space had bought me some immunity from their effect.

"Hello to you, too," he said.

"Are you of all people calling me out for an impolite greeting?" I laughed.

Gus had the grace to laugh, too.

"We're talking about Phinney," Bud said. "Stands to reason the police will release his body soon. We're trying to figure out if there's anyone besides us to bury him."

"Are there no relatives around?" I asked.

"Not that I ever heard," Bud said. "Phinney and I graduated from Busman's Harbor High together. I don't remember it was ever more than him and his mom."

"No dad?" Not that his father would still be alive, but knowing who he was might lead to cousins.

"No. Phinney said his dad died when he was young, before he and his mom moved to Busman's Harbor."

"They came here from somewhere else? Might there be relatives there?" I asked.

"Rockland, I think," Bud allowed. "But he never mentioned relations."

"Tell me about Phinney." I scooted forward, settling in on the stool.

Bud started the tale. "Phinney went to school here, like I said. He was a smart guy, but not motivated. Today they'd say he had ADD, or XYZ, or some such. In those days they just said we had 'ants in our pants.'"

"Phinney was a good guitar player," Gus added. "And he had a passable voice."

I remembered what Claire Reagan had said about the guitar in Phinney's shop.

"Which caused nothing but trouble," Bud grumbled.

"Why trouble?" I wondered.

"It got him in with the wrong crowd." Gus wiped down the countertop with his usual ferocity. I moved my elbows so he didn't run right over them.

"Summer people's kids," Bud clarified, in case I didn't know who the "wrong crowd" was.

Gus nodded, acknowledging the truth of Bud's statement. "Phinney learned all that folk music—the Kingston Trio; Pete Seeger; Peter, Paul and Mary; Bob Dylan, even. The summer kids ate it up. They thought he was soulful."

That brought a guffaw from Bud.

"They invited him to their campfires on the beach," Gus continued. "Made him feel like he was part of the gang."

"Dirty hippies," Bud interjected.

"That was before the hippies," Gus corrected. "What did we used to call them? Beatniks," Gus remembered.

"Dirty beatniks," Bud added. "What do we call them now?" he asked Gus. They were enjoying themselves.

"Hipsters," Gus answered.

"Dirty hipsters," Bud said.

That time even I laughed. Not that I had anything against hipsters, but I appreciated Gus and Bud's pure, bloody-minded consistency.

"The dirty beatniks were the problem," Bud said. "Phinney had a job lined up at Herndon Yachts for after graduation, a good one, just like me. But he kept pushing back his start date. I was sure he'd join me there after Labor Day when the summer kids took off. Next thing I knew he joined the merchant marines. He sailed the seven seas in giant cargo ships for over thirty years."

So that's where Phinney had been in the years before he came home to care for his mother.

"He'd come home from time to time to see his mom," Gus said. "Not often. For a month or so every few years. He'd tell us about the ports, the sea, the sunsets. He could be very poetical if you got him going. Which was rare, but it did happen from time to time."

"He went all over the world," Bud added. "Far East,

Middle East, Europe, Africa, South America. He went through the Panama Canal more times than he could count."

"Sometimes the ship he was on was too big for the canal," Gus said. "And he had to go all the way around Cape Horn."

Really. This new information put a different spin on Phinney for me. "Did he go to school for it?"

"Nope. He walked onto a ship, unlicensed. It was a lot more common in those days. He had enough sea time. He could have applied to take his exams and move up the ranks, but he never had an interest. He worked with people from all over the world. Picked up a lot of their lingo. He could speak French, Portuguese, Tagalog. A smattering anyhow, enough to get by."

Phinney was becoming more and more interesting. Hidden depths. "Tell me about his mother," I said.

"Maureen? She was a good person," Bud responded.

"Lovely," Gus agreed. "She worked in the canneries when Phinney was young. That's what brought them here. When those jobs went away she worked in housekeeping at the Bellevue."

"Head housekeeper," Bud said. "She was on the shyer side. Can't say I knew her well."

"No, not well." Gus shook his head in agreement.

"Was there ever a woman in Phinney's life?" I asked. Gus had been married to Mrs. Gus for so long they had a son who was retiring and taking my apartment. I had never heard of any woman, or any person, past or present, linked to Bud.

"Not that I ever heard," Gus said.

"I think there was at one time." Bud looked up at the ceiling and wrinkled his forehead, concentrating. "It's not something I ever knew for sure, just something I felt. It was around that time after high school, when he was hanging out with the beatniks and dithering about the job at Herndon Yachts. I had the notion it might be a girl causing the trouble. I thought maybe she lived in another town and that was why he wouldn't commit to the job. Anyways, the relationship must have ended because he went to sea not long after." Bud smiled at me. "I never saw a whisper of anyone after that. The life Phinney lived wouldn't have had room for it. If you're thinking some long-lost child is going to turn up to claim the Hardison fortune, you're mistaken."

"Or pay for the funeral, for that matter," Gus groused. He and Bud had a good laugh at the idea.

"Who does inherit?" I asked.

"Inherit what?" Gus answered my question with a question. "Phinney sold his mother's house after she passed. He rented the place where he lived after that. There's nothing left but the dusty stuff in that old store. The best of it will end up donated to the Star of the Sea Church auction. Most of it will get hauled off to the dump."

"Which is exactly what Phinney didn't want." Bud's voice was thick with emotion. "He loved his mother."

"That he did," Gus agreed. "Came home when she declined. Nursed her for ten years. Didn't leave that house except for groceries the last two. Kitty Fenwick finally convinced him to get some help. He let people come in to bathe Mrs. Hardison and move her limbs and such, but he'd never leave them alone with her. He was gone all those years, but when he came back, he was as devoted a son as there ever was."

"Kitty Fenwick?" I latched on to the name.

"Yeah. They were next-door neighbors," Gus said.

"John Fenwick's late wife was great friends with Mrs. Hardison. She called on her daily, right to the end when you'd think it wouldn't have mattered. It was she who got word to Phinney it was time to come home, when his ma couldn't live on her own anymore. If I wanted to know more about Phinney, I might pick at John Fenwick's memory." Gus looked at me meaningfully. He knew exactly what I would do with that kind of information.

"If no one turns up, you and me will have to see he gets a proper burial," Bud said to Gus.

"Yes." Gus was an old skinflint, but fiercely loyal. Bud wouldn't be able to contribute much. Gus would see that Phinney was done right by.

"Who would want to kill Phinney Hardison?" I asked. "And why?"

"You mean aside from the Butternut woman?" Bud answered my question with a question. "Not a one. Sure, Phinney could bluster, but he wouldn't hurt a soul."

"I can't imagine anyone wanting to kill Phinney." Gus turned around and pushed a giant pickle jar aside on a high shelf. Behind it was a bottle of Allen's Coffee Brandy, the best-selling liquor in Maine. Gus poured an inch in Bud's coffee and in his own. He fetched a half mug of coffee for me and poured in the Allen's. It was just past eleven in the morning. My third day of day-drinking in a row. Great.

We raised our mugs.

"To Phinney," Gus said.

"To Phinney," Bud and I echoed.

Then we all drank the liquid down. Allen's was super sweet with a burnt aftertaste, but in coffee, or mixed with milk, it was pretty tasty.

On the way out, I gave Gus a hug. "I love you," I said.

Because you never know when you might not get the chance to say it.

"Whoa! Am I dying?" Gus stepped back. His upper face scowled, but his mouth smiled. "Away with you. I have to get ready for the lunch trade."

"Bye, Gus. Bye, Bud. Bye, Morgan."

The dog lifted his head in acknowledgment. Neither of the other two turned my way.

John Fenwick's house was not far from where Main Street met Eastclaw Point Road at the head of the inner harbor. It was maybe a quarter of a mile from the Lupine Design building. By the time Fenwick and Jock passed the shop on their multiple daily walks, they'd be nearly home.

I found the mailbox with Fenwick's last name on it and walked up the private road that led to his house and one other. The houses were set back on a steep hill and would have marvelous views of the activity in the harbor. I stopped where the road dead-ended and split into two driveways. A wooden sign shaped like an arrow with the name FENWICK on it pointed to the house on my right. The other house didn't have a name out front and I stood for a moment to admire it.

It had to have been Phinney's mother's house. Someone, probably a second or third owner after Mrs. Hardison, was in the middle of a major renovation. The siding had been stripped and insulation added. There were all new windows with the stickers from the manufacturer still on them. Through those new windows I glimpsed fresh wooden studs, just like the ones at Windsholme.

I wondered how Phinney had felt about the gut renovation of his childhood home. I hoped he'd been happy someone was spending the money it needed and would be putting the house to good use. It could have been so much worse. The lot was huge and with that view all it would have taken was a Karl Kimbel–type with the ability to get a townhouse cluster through the planning board and the house would have been but a memory. But given what I knew and had learned about Phinney, I thought he had probably mourned the loss of every piece of molding, every layer of wallpaper, and every chipped linoleum floor tile.

As soon as I set foot on John Fenwick's driveway, Jock set up a loud fuss up at the house. As I got closer I could hear the scrabbling at the front door along with the furious barking.

"It's okay, Jock," Fenwick shouted behind the door. "Stand down. We know her." I was not quite to the porch when the front door opened and Fenwick and the dog poked their heads out. "See, Jock, I told you. Everything's okay. Come on in," Fenwick said to me.

From the outside I would have described the house as "nothing much." Aside from the location and the huge front porch, it was a two-story bungalow, painted a shade of brown designed to fade into the background. A gray Volvo stood in the driveway in front of the house.

The front door led directly into the living room. A book sat open by a battered olive-green chair with a crocheted blanket hung over its back. The chair was positioned to look out of the big picture window, down the harbor. A pair of gold-rimmed glasses sat on top of the book. The television, over by the big fieldstone fireplace, was exactly like the one my family had in the late nineties.

It had a layer of dust across its top, and I doubted it could be hooked up to receive programs of any kind anymore.

Low shelves ran along the wall on either side of the fireplace, filled with games, toys, and jigsaw puzzles that looked like they hadn't been moved in decades. There were two wooden pull toys with carved letters riding on their flatbeds that said RICKY and TABBY. I wondered who those children might be. Alice Rumsford's unrenovated cottage evoked images of good times and summers filled with family. Fenwick's living room felt like one of those period rooms at the Museum of Fine Arts in Boston. All that was missing was the silk rope across the threshold. A poorly kept museum for sure, but a monument to a moment in the past that wouldn't be returning.

"If you've come to see if I've remembered anything from walking by Lupine Design the morning it was vandalized, the answer is nothing." Fenwick stood casually on the rust-colored carpet, one leg bent.

"No," I assured him. "I'm here because I want to learn more about Phinney. Gus and Bud said your late wife was a friend of his mother's."

"Let me get you a warm mug of tea." Fenwick turned and walked through the archway into the kitchen. "We'll sit out on the porch."

I followed him into the kitchen, which was the same era as the living room. Fenwick put a metal kettle on an electric burner and set it to high. "What do you take in your tea?" he asked. "I'd offer you a bite to eat, but don't have anything on hand. We don't get many visitors."

I told him I'd take the tea with milk and reassured him I didn't need to eat. "I dropped in uninvited. You're lovely to give me tea."

When the hot water had been poured into the mugs and the tea bags added, we carried them back through the living room. I held both mugs while Fenwick shrugged into a lightweight jacket that hung from a peg by the front door. Jock followed us outside. On the porch Fenwick indicated a wooden table that was flanked on either side by straight-backed wooden chairs. The sun and lack of wind made it seem like it should be a great day for sitting out, but it was a tiny bit too cold to be comfortable. I shivered in my quilted vest.

"I don't know as much as you might think about Phinney," Fenwick said when we sat down, "seeing as how we were neighbors. But my late wife, Kitty, was devoted to his mother."

"Tell me about his mother."

"There's not much to tell. She was a widow when she arrived in Busman's Harbor, or so she told my wife. Kitty was never sure there ever was a Mr. Hardison. There were no photos of him in that house, no talk of relatives on his side and so on. Maureen was a good mother, a hard worker. A good provider for her son."

"A blameless life," I said.

"A useful life. She was a kind and caring person. By the time my parents died and I inherited this house, Phinney was already gone to sea and it was only his mother up on the hill. When I married, Kitty reached out to Mrs. Hardison. At first it was visits back and forth, sitting on each other's porches as you and I are doing now. I was still working in Boston, coming up on the weekends, but Kitty was here with two kids all week during the summer. Now I look back on it, I think she was lonely for adult company, too, like Mrs. Hardison.

"As time went on, the kids went on their own way and

Mrs. Hardison got frailer. Kitty started driving her to the library, and the hairdresser, the grocery store, and the bank. What had begun as an equal friendship became more like a caretaker situation. Finally, one year when we were preparing to go back to Boston at the end of the summer, Mrs. Hardison fell. Kitty discovered her the next morning. That's when she told Phinney either he had to come home or his mother had to go into assisted living, maybe even a nursing home. Give him credit, Phinney was on the next boat back. In later years, even when Phinney was living here, Kitty continued her visits. I was retired and we were up here year-round by then."

"And Kitty?" I asked.

"Died a year after Mrs. Hardison. Cancer. All that time taking care of the old woman, and my wife only lived one year more than she did."

"I'm sorry."

Fenwick paused and gathered himself. If his wife had died a year after Phinney's mother, she'd been gone more than fifteen years, but Fenwick's grief was still raw. "Anyway, after Mrs. Hardison died, Phinney sold the place. It's had three owners since then. You can see the monstrosity the third one is making of it now."

It hadn't seemed like a monstrosity to me. But then, maybe I was biased. My family was in the middle of a major renovation, too, at Windsholme.

"I've left our house exactly as it was when Kitty died," Fenwick was saying. "Some friends and relations have chided me for that. They don't understand. They expect me to 'get over it' and other losses. They've lost patience with me. There aren't any visitors anymore."

I looked out at the beautiful view. The harbor was quiet, not at all the bustling place it would be in two months. A lone figure walked across the footbridge. Then I turned around and looked back through the picture window into the living room. "Are Ricky and Tabby your children?" I asked.

Fenwick smiled. "Ricky-Ticky-Tabby I used to call them," he said. "Kitty came to our marriage with both of the kids. But I raised them from the time they were five and seven years old and I loved them as if they were my own. They were my own, just not in the biological sense."

"Do they visit?" The dusty living room with games and toys on the shelves looked like it was waiting for grandchildren who never came.

Fenwick shook his head. "Ricky we lost, too, a year before Kitty. I wished so hard the order had been reversed and she had gone before him. It would have spared her so much pain. Tabby calls herself Tabitha now, her real name. She lives outside Boston, has three kids, a husband, and a big job at an insurance company. It's hard for them to get away. We talk on the phone from time to time to get caught up . . ." His voice trailed off. "It's me and Jock." At the mention of his name, Jock raised his muzzle and thumped his tail. "We do all right, don't we, boy?" Fenwick said. "We've got our walks and I have a little sailboat at the yacht club. Jock loves to take a sail."

"Yacht club" was the hilarious misnomer for the ramshackle building and mismatched collection of boats— from enormous cabin cruisers to kayaks—that rented moorings in the back harbor.

"Did your wife ever say, or did you ever hear Mrs. Hardison talk about how she felt about Phinney being away all those years?" I asked.

"All the time. Phinney was her favorite subject. Early on when we knew her, she was so proud of him. He was good with postcards and such. She was always eager to show off the latest and tell us where he was in the world. But later, as she got frailer, she wished Phinney had taken a more traditional path. Married and settled down nearby, given her a bunch of grandchildren." Fenwick stopped talking for a moment, remembering. "There had been a girlfriend at some point, before Phinney went away. I don't know if Mrs. Hardison actively disapproved, but she certainly withheld her approval. She regretted that a great deal. It's hard, when you come to the sunset of your life, to realize your line is gone. Soon, no one will remember." Fenwick cleared his throat. "When Phinney moved back, she talked about him like he was a saint. She knew how lucky she was to have a son that devoted."

"You said Mrs. Hardison never mentioned any of Phinney's father's relations. Did she have any of her own? Gus and Bud are wondering about the funeral."

"Tell those old reprobates I'll kick in some money to help out." Fenwick smiled. "Better yet, I'll tell them."

"I'm sure they'll appreciate it."

I drained my tea and got up from the table. "Can you think of anyone who would want Phinney dead?"

He looked up at me but didn't rise. "You mean enough to murder him? Aside from Ms. Lupine Design?"

"Do you really think Zoey had a motive for murder? You feel passionately about the pedestrian mall. Would you kill over it?"

His head snapped back. "Of course not. Commit murder over something so trivial? Never."

"Exactly. Then why do you think Zoey did?"

"The pedestrian mall wasn't the only issue between Zoey and Phinney. There were constant skirmishes over that building. Her delivery trucks blocking access to Phinney's parking spot. Her on a tear to upgrade the building, paint, new roof, the works. Him not wanting to pay for the improvements or suffer the increase in rent. It was quite heated between the two of them."

"How did you hear this?" It seemed odd that Fenwick was reporting this news, and not Gus and Bud, who surely had known Phinney better.

"I get around," he said.

CHAPTER EIGHTEEN

On the walk back from Fenwick's house, I stopped at the police station. "Are the detectives in?" I asked the civilian receptionist.

"I'll see if Lieutenant Binder or Sergeant Flynn is available."

"Thank you."

She punched three numbers into the phone on her desk, announced me, and then listened. "I'll send her right in." She pursed her lips in a tight look of disapproval. I'd never understood why she objected to my relationship with the detectives, but she certainly did.

"Julia. Come in." Lieutenant Jerry Binder stood as I came through the door. Sergeant Flynn acknowledged me but didn't turn from whatever he was doing on his computer. "We've got your statement here," Binder said. "Can you review it and sign it?"

"Why didn't you call me?"

Binder smiled. "We knew you'd turn up eventually."

I read the statement. It was pretty straightforward. I'd arrived at the scene after the crime had been committed. I didn't have a lot I could add. Binder handed me a pen and I signed with a flourish. "Any progress?" I asked.

Finally, Flynn looked up from his laptop. He'd always been less open to my help with their cases than Binder, but when I got him on his own, outside the context of an investigation, we'd made halting steps toward real friendship. He grunted and looked at Binder, knowing his partner would be the soft touch in this situation.

"In a minute," Binder responded. "What information do you bring?"

That was the arrangement. They didn't just give information. They expected to get some.

"You will have heard that Phinney and Zoey had a loud disagreement at a town meeting," I said.

They both nodded. "From multiple sources," Binder confirmed.

"There was someone else who fought with Phinney that night. Karl Kimbel. He's a developer and landlord in town and a vocal backer of the pedestrian mall. He has big plans for the town. He and Phinney might have gone on battling each other for years."

Flynn closed the laptop and turned toward me, giving me his full attention. "You're suggesting this as a motive for murder."

"If the fight over the pedestrian mall is a motive for Zoey to kill Phinney, it would logically be a motive for someone else."

"You mean leaving aside the fact that Mr. Hardison was killed in Ms. Butterfield's basement," Flynn said.

"Their shared basement," I corrected. "I don't see what that proves."

"And leaving aside the fact that Mr. Hardison was killed with the lethally sharp wire that potters use to cut pots off the wheel." Flynn was relentless, but this was new information.

"The medical examiner's report has come in," I guessed.

Binder nodded. "Yes. There is no doubt about the weapon. Our people have linked it to the wire found in the Lupine Design studio."

"But you haven't found the actual length that was used in the murder?"

"Not yet," Binder answered. "It could have been dumped in the woods somewhere or in the ocean."

"Do you have any indication Zoey left the building between the time of the murder and the time the body was discovered?" I asked.

"Not so far." Flynn clearly wasn't happy about that answer.

"The killer took that wire from the pottery studio on the first floor down to the basement," Binder added.

"Proving premeditation," Flynn explained, in case I wasn't getting it. "This wasn't an act of self-defense or something that happened in the moment. It was planned."

Great. Intentional murder. But the situation still didn't add up. "Have you figured out what Phinney was doing in the basement?" I said. "He must have let the murderer in. Which means whoever it was probably called and asked to meet him."

Flynn picked a pen up off his desk. He stared at it as he took the top off and put it back on. Multiple times. He seemed very invested.

Binder ignored him. "We have Hardison's phone. It was in the basement with him. There were no calls in or out. In weeks. Verizon verifies there were no calls to the home or business numbers, either."

"Then how the heck did he end up at his store in the middle of the night?" It was hard to imagine.

"An interesting question." Binder stood, pulling his sports coat off the back of his chair. "You'll have to excuse us. We have a meeting with a witness out of the office."

"What witness?" It couldn't hurt to ask.

Binder laughed. "Nice try, Julia. I'm sure we'll see you soon."

On the way back to Mom's, I spotted Zoey sitting on the porch at the Snuggles. I crossed the street to say hello. "How are you doing?"

Zoey looked up from her phone. "Fine, I guess. The truth is, I'm not used to having spare time. I haven't had a vacation . . ." She stopped, her brow wrinkled. "I can't remember ever having a vacation. I worked every minute when I was in school, and then I dove into learning the pottery business."

"I get it." This winter had been the first time I'd had any spare time in years. I hadn't gotten particularly skilled at filling it, either. "Do you want to go to Gus's for lunch?"

A broad smile lit up her pretty face. "Gus's? I've never had the nerve to go in there. I would love to."

Gus was busy cleaning the grill when we came through the back door. I figured as a former tenant I still had the right. He gave me a curt nod, then brought his eyebrows together in a frown when he spotted Zoey behind me. I ignored him and led her to the best booth with the best view in the nearly empty dining room. There was only one table occupied by a couple of snowbirds, back already from points south, who I recognized but didn't know. We had missed the lunch rush.

Despite the empty restaurant, Gus took his time getting to us, which was good because it gave me time to explain the deal to Zoey. Gus's unchanging ten lunch items were listed on a corrugated sign with moveable letters that had never been moved. There were menus somewhere but no one who had been to the restaurant more than once ever asked for one. Hesitating when Gus came to take your order would bring a frown or worse, a bark. "Don't have all day."

Though Zoey had been in town for three years, I wasn't surprised she hadn't been to Gus's. Strangely, perhaps even uniquely for a restaurateur, Gus only served people he knew, or people who arrived with people he knew. Though Zoey didn't seem the type to be intimidated, she was probably right to steer clear of Gus's, especially given her fraught relationship with his buddy Phinney.

"First time here, go with the burger, the BLT, or the grilled cheese," I counseled. "And definitely, definitely get the fries."

"I'm game," Zoey said.

Gus finally arrived with his stubby pencil and an order pad. "Twice in one day," he said to me. "To what do we owe this great honor?"

"I was here this morning," I explained to Zoey. To Gus I said pointedly, "Zoey's never been to your delightful establishment. After three years in town, full-time, fixing up her building and providing jobs"—I emphasized each of Zoey's bona fides—"I thought she should enjoy your hospitality."

Gus grunted and waggled his eyebrows. I shot him a look. *You better behave.*

Gus took our order. I went with the BLT, Zoey the grilled cheese. She was momentarily perplexed when he asked if we wanted tonic. I ordered a root beer so she could guess it was old-fashioned New England word for soda. Zoey got it and went with the root beer, too. All told, the ordering had gone off well, with only one death-ray stare from Gus at the tonic stumble.

"What kinds of pie do you have left?" At Gus's you ordered your slice of the delicious pies Mrs. Gus made when you ordered your meal, otherwise you might miss out. I wasn't optimistic about the selection this late in the day.

"I've got two slices of pecan with your names on them." In the winter and spring when Mrs. Gus lacked fresh fruits, her pies ran to chocolate peanut butter, coconut cream, and the like. Pecan was a particular favorite of mine.

"We'll take them." I looked at Zoey. "You'll see."

She smiled sweetly, not at me but at Gus, working her way in. "I'll take your word for it."

"I had dinner at Crowley's with Alice Rumford's nephew last night," I told her after Gus left us. I didn't know why, in that moment, I was moved to confide in her.

Her eyebrows shot up. "The dishy one who was at the public hearing? Like a date?"

"'Like a date' is a good description. I still don't know what it was, and I was there. Mostly, I think it was two adults, potential friends, having a companionable meal. I would like to count it as a date, because then it would be my first since the breakup and I could check that box and get it behind me."

"Uh-huh." Zoey was thoughtful. "Then count it."

We joked about the pros and cons until Gus brought my meal. At Gus's you get your food when it's ready, regardless of what might be going on with the dishes for the rest of your party.

"Eat." Zoey gestured for me to go ahead.

"Yours will be here soon," I assured her.

"All the more reason."

I bit into my sandwich, which did not disappoint.

"Tell me about your ex," Zoey said.

I don't know what it was about her, but for some reason the whole story came tumbling out. How I'd had the worst crush in the world on Chris when I was in middle school and he was the quarterback on the high school football team. How we had met again in this very restaurant, fallen in love, moved in together, and run a business. And then how it all unraveled. The secrets and . . . "They weren't really lies, more the withholding, the hidden parts of his life. I couldn't trust him so I broke it off. He moved out. Gus needed the apartment back so dot-dot-dot, I'm living with my mother."

In the middle of the tale, Gus had finally showed up with Zoey's food. She'd taken my word for it and put a couple of the best French fries in the world into her mouth. "I see what you mean," she said when she'd swallowed the fries.

I laughed, "Salt, fat, carbs, crunch. What could be better?"

"Mmm-umm. Nothing in the world," she agreed. "Do you regret it? Not the fries. The breakup."

"Every other day." I looked for the right words. "That's not right. I regret that it didn't turn out the way I hoped. I'm mourning something that was never going to be." Just saying it made me feel ridiculous.

Zoey was sympathetic. "It seems to me like thirteen-year-old you fell for eighteen-year-old him. Then he turned out to be a whole lot more complicated than you thought. You're probably a whole lot more complicated, too. So the question is, does the thirty-something you love the thirty-something him? Or is it just the idea of him?"

It was a good question. I had certainly believed that I loved him.

Gus picked up the plates and delivered the pie.

"Can I have a coffee?" I called to his back as he hurried away.

"Me, too," Zoey said.

He made a sound that might have been a yes.

Zoey put a bite of Mrs. Gus's pecan pie in her mouth. "Oh my goodness, this pie." Her face softened as if she were consumed by bliss.

"Told you."

"I was skeptical," she admitted. "Usually pecan pie is cloyingly sweet. This is amazing. So nutty. And spicy. I'm glad I took your advice."

"Real Maine maple syrup instead of corn syrup, lots of nuts and spices—cardamom for sure and some others. Mrs. Gus's recipes are top secret," I told her. "You're welcome."

Zoey took another forkful and our coffee arrived. "I've been seeing someone," she confided.

"Really? Someone in town? Someone I know?" I was sure I possessed a complete inventory of the available men in our age group.

"Yes to here in town. I don't know who you know."

"Tell."

"I can't." She flashed her big smile. "I'm sworn to secrecy."

"By whom? The Secret Romance Society? I just spilled my guts to you."

"I'm sorry. It's too new to talk about. I will tell you this." She leaned across the table. "I'm finding the secrecy adds a little somethin'-somethin'."

"*Really.*" I spent more time trying to persuade her to tell me, with absolutely no results, while I finished the last of my pie. Then a movement in the front room of the restaurant caught my eye. "Geez, not again."

"What?" Zoey turned her head and followed my gaze to where Chris stood at the lunch counter, shooting the breeze with Gus while he waited for his order. Gus didn't believe in food to go. If you came to eat in his restaurant, you ate in his restaurant. But he and Chris had a special relationship. They looked out for each other while each one simultaneously thought it was his job to keep the other in line.

"Don't look!" I said, too late.

"Your ex?" she asked.

"My ex. I ran into him yesterday. Twice." I shrugged. "Small town."

"I've never lived in a town with an ex."

I stared at her. "Never?"

"Nope. Since I got out of school I've taken every breakup as a signal to move on."

"Wow."

"It sounds extreme, I know." She looked down at her empty plate. "But it's only helped me. Whenever a boyfriend and I would part ways, I'd do a general stocktaking.

I'd always find I'd learned everything I could from the current job, or I was feeling creatively thwarted, or both. Time to move on. New town. New situation."

A thought occurred to me. "What about this new guy? If it doesn't work, will you leave Busman's Harbor?"

"Good question," Zoey said. "I hadn't thought about it."

Gus handed Chris a brown paper bag with a Hannaford logo on it. Chris handed Gus some bills, turned, and walked back across the front room in his long strides. Thank goodness, he hadn't spotted us. Zoey was curled around in her seat, staring.

She turned back to me. "You know he's really, really handsome, right?"

On the way back to the house I thought about what Zoey had said. Did keeping a romance a secret add to the intensity? Phinney had a secret girlfriend when he was eighteen. Even his close friend Bud didn't know her identity. Had the secret been part of the attraction?

Back at the house, Mom was stirring the contents of a pot on the stove. The kitchen smelled wonderful.

"Something new," Mom said without looking over her shoulder. "Mushroom soup."

"I love mushrooms."

"I know."

I didn't move from the back hall. I didn't plan to take off my boots. "I had a big, late lunch at Gus's with Zoey."

"You'll eat when you're ready," Mom said. "How is Zoey doing?"

"Weirdly fine," I answered. "Did you ever hear of Phinney Hardison having a girlfriend?"

Mom turned to face me. "A girlfriend? You mean recently?"

"No. Back before he went to sea."

Mom grimaced. "Julia, how old do you think I am? Phinney had been at sea for years before I married your father and moved to the harbor full-time."

"I know, I know. I thought you might have heard rumors."

"Honestly, no. Never."

"Do you know Alice Rumsford well?" I asked. "She told me she thought you were very brave."

Mom blinked. "Brave? Me? I can't think why she would say that."

"She also said she admired you."

"That's nice." Mom turned back to the pot. "She's the one who's admirable. She has done so much for the town."

"You're admirable," I insisted. "You built a business, had a long and successful marriage."

"And two charming and intelligent children," she finished.

"There is that," I agreed. "It must be very satisfying to be my mother."

Mom laughed and turned back to face me. "Why are you asking about this?"

"No reason," I said. "Something I'm noodling."

CHAPTER NINETEEN

The trip to Alice Rumsford's house was shorter than I remembered, so often the way once you know where you're going. I drove up the private road slowly, staying in the center to avoid the muddy ruts on either side. The big SUV wasn't in the parking area. Ben must have been at the library, working. I suspected his absence might be best for the purpose of my visit.

I pulled my car to the center of the parking area, the place where the ground had been the firmest on my previous visit. I trudged up the path to the house and knocked on the door frame.

Alice opened the door. "Julia, how lovely to see you again. Come in."

I kicked off my boots and followed Alice down the hallway. She was much steadier on her feet than I'd expected, given the way Ben had hovered over her at the public hearing, and how she hadn't moved from her recliner the last time I'd seen her.

"So nice of you to drop by," Alice said. "To what do I owe the honor?"

I suddenly wished I'd thought to stop at Hannaford to pick up cookies, or flowers, something, so I hadn't entered this woman's home empty-handed. This conversation was going to be uncomfortable as it was.

The big living room was flooded with light. The view, obscured on my earlier visit, was indeed magnificent. The bright green lawn was in need of a mow, a result, no doubt, of all the rain. The tops of gray boulders peeked out from the grass and led to a steep cliff. The water beyond it was navy blue, its surface rippling in the wind. Three uninhabited islands, thick with stands of pines, were visible. Beyond that, over the land mass of the peninsula to our west, a thick, black cloud was moving quickly in our direction.

"Your view is unbelievable," I said.

Alice smiled. "I would say thank you, but I had nothing to do with it. Mother Nature created the scenery and my great-grandparents chose the location for the cottage."

Once again, I was drawn to Alice's photographs. Now that I knew she'd taken them, they were even more compelling. She had stood in those places, seen those people. I stopped in front of the photo of the blond boy with his dog. "Ben told me you took these," I said to her.

She came up beside me. "He's a big blabbermouth." She said it with affection.

"Were you on the staff of *National Geographic*?"

"Good heavens, no." Alice was still smiling. "There

have only been four female staff photographers in the history of the magazine. I was a freelancer, which suited me better. I could pick and choose my assignments. The editors were generous and offered me many."

"Not generous," I said. "Impressed, rightfully so. These are beautiful."

She followed my gaze to the portrait of the boy. "The Sami are indigenous reindeer herders in the northernmost regions of Scandinavia and Russia."

"I had no idea."

"Few do. That's the reason for the photographs."

We moved to the one of the girl with the veil. "A child bride in Yemen," Alice said quietly. "She was to be married that day to a middle-aged widower."

"No wonder she looks like she wants to flee."

"But has nowhere to go." Alice packed all of the sadness in the photo into a single sentence.

"How did you get these pictures?" The children in the images were so open and vulnerable.

"Do you mind if we sit?" Alice asked.

"Of course not."

She went to her green velvet recliner and sat, pulling the plaid blanket across her lap. "There's a persistent myth that different cultures object to having their pictures taken because they believe the camera steals their souls." She adjusted the blanket. "It does. If you take a photo because it's your assignment, to sell it for money, you're exploiting the subject. You're stealing a peek at their soul for your own selfish purposes.

"The way to get photographs like these is to spend time with people. I was a female in a field where that was a considerable disadvantage, so I turned it to my advantage. I could go where others couldn't. I could sit with the women. For months, if I needed to. I traveled with the Sami for two years as they herded their reindeer. Even when I didn't understand the language, I came to intuit the conversations. And the women came to trust me. In the case of these photographs, to entrust me with the most precious thing they had. Their children.

"The point was to never exploit. To document." She pointed, her finger moving around the room from photograph to photograph. "Imagine. All these people were on the earth at the same time. The same time as you. The girl working in the Russian munitions factory. The Afghan boy who stepped on a landmine. The Greek toddler, so joyful, dancing on the table at a family celebration. The Asaro boy at a tribal festival in Papua New Guinea."

I was so taken by the images and her stories I didn't trust myself to speak. What a life this woman had led.

Alice let me sit quietly, moved beyond words for a few moments. Then she said, "Do you know what I would love? A cup of tea and a couple of Ben's cookies. Would you mind?"

"Not at all."

The kitchen was as simple as I'd pictured it. A big soapstone sink and a freestanding stove ran along the outside wall. On the other side of the tight galley were cupboards, top and bottom, that provided a little counter space. I was relieved to spot an electric kettle. I wouldn't have to try to figure out how to light the old stove. The cookies were in a homemade tin. I put them on a plate I found on an open shelf above the sink and put tea bags in two mugs. The kettle whistled.

When I returned to the living room Alice was in her chair, staring out the window. The big black cloud bank, with lightning visible inside, was moving quickly in our direction. A rare spring thunderstorm. The living room grew dark.

"What brings you back?" Alice asked when I'd sat on the couch.

I took a deep breath. No time like the present. "I've heard two interesting stories in the last couple of days," I said. "One is the story of a boy who grew up in Busman's Harbor. He played the guitar and had a good singing voice. He had a hardscrabble life. His mother worked in the canneries and then as a housekeeper. When he graduated from high school, he was offered a good job at Herndon Yachts. But he kept putting off starting it. All summer he pushed his start date further into the future. And then, one day, he announced he was leaving town to work on a cargo ship. He didn't return to live here for more than thirty years, when his mother got sick. When she died, a kind stranger made sure he had a shop to sell his mother's stuff. Her things weren't worth much, but the stranger knew he couldn't throw them away. She guessed he needed a place to go every day and a purpose for his life."

"Very interesting," Alice said, eyes twinkling.

"Here's the other story. This is about a young woman, a privileged summer resident from an old family. She's a couple of years older than the young man, but not enough so it mattered. She was already in college. She met the young man on the beach where he played guitar for her friends. They fell in love. He begged her to commit to him. He said he would live anywhere she wanted. She didn't answer all summer, but in the fall, when it was time to go back to school, she broke it off. She told him it could never be." I paused, gathering the courage to continue. "Sadly, it turned out he was her one great love. After college she, too, traveled the world. Then she retired, took over the family cottage, and started buying up properties in the town. Including the store she made sure was available for the man, who was no longer young, so he could sell his mother's things."

The room was silent when I finished talking, and so dark we could barely see one another. There was a clap of thunder and the rain poured down. I thought of my car in the parking area and hoped the ground would hold, though it was so saturated I wasn't optimistic. Alice said nothing.

"What do you think of my stories?" I finally asked.

Alice sat forward and took a sip from her mug, taking her time. "Do you remember I told you your mother is a brave woman?"

"Yes. I mentioned it to her. She didn't know what you were referring to."

Alice smiled. "Now you do. Your mother had the courage I lacked. She married your father."

My parents were a generation younger, but I understood what Alice meant. The differences between my parents hadn't been a matter of money, intelligence, or ambition. They had been a matter of expectations—societal, parental, and their own about what kind of a life each would lead.

"My parents were dead," Alice continued. "But my older brothers found out about Phinney. They were horrified, which was rich, since both of them had their share of summer flings. They demanded I stop seeing him. They painted a terrible picture of my future with him—poor, pregnant, barefoot. You understand.

"I gave him up. Almost without a fight, I'm ashamed to say." She closed her eyes and rubbed the blanket on her lap through her fingers. "Who knows what might have happened. We were kids really, Phinney and I. Maybe we would have broken up by the end of the summer on our own. It wasn't uncommon for women to marry before finishing college in my day, but the idea of Phinney living a in college town, working at some job he'd had to take to be with me. My brothers were undoubtedly right. It never would have worked."

Alice rubbed her large, blue eyes with her swollen knuckles. "I do have to correct your story. You said, 'Sadly it was the love of her life.' I have nothing to be sad about. When I got back to college that fall I had a lot of time to think. I decided my brothers, my family, my friends, my social circle, were never again going to tell me what I could and couldn't do." She sighed with satisfaction. "I've had a wonderful life. I've followed my dreams wherever they took me. I wouldn't trade one minute of it for anything. It's a life that wouldn't have been likely or even possible with Phinney. I have no regrets."

"Yet you made sure he got the store."

"It was something I could do for him," Alice said. "I owned the space. He needed space. It didn't require any sacrifice on my part, except maybe a little rent money. I bought the building as an investment in the town, not to enrich myself, so that wasn't a sacrifice, either."

"You knew he was in town and that his mother had died. You kept track of him to that degree."

The look in her eyes was far away and dreamy. "That is, perhaps, the problem with never finding another to love after your first. No one ever supplanted him. He continued on in my dreams, in my fantasies, as the young man I loved. The man with the deep baritone and the guitar, who sang around the campfire at the beach. Speaking of him now, I feel my heart beating faster. Even though I never spoke to him after I turned twenty. Even though I know he's dead. The heart is a curious organ. I'm sure if I'd done what my brothers expected, had a long marriage and a house full of children, Phinney would be a distant thought, a first name and fuzzy face I could barely recall. But as it is, he's a warm, vivid memory."

"There was no barrier to your relationship when you both returned," I pointed out. "You might have been friends."

She shook her head. "No, thank you. I was in love with my memories. I'd seen enough from a distance at town meetings to understand that getting to know Phinney again might spoil them. I didn't want that. Isn't that terrible?" she mused. "When the memory of the person becomes more important than the person himself? But you can understand that, can't you?"

Could I? Chris had been my first crush, the weak-in-the-knees, can-barely-speak kind. When I was in seventh grade, he'd been so cool, practically a grown man. Years afterward, he'd been my first real, serious love and long-term relationship. I'd come to it later than most people, but I'd made up for my tardiness by falling hard and deep. As Zoey had said, Chris had turned out to be a real flesh-and-blood man, not a teen idol. A complicated man, with a hard-lived experience. As the stars fell from my eyes, I had fallen more in love with this flawed person, because, in truth, so aren't we all? His flaws were like his weathered skin and the laugh lines around his green eyes. They were as deep as the dimple in his chin. I fell and fell. Until I hit bottom and was afraid I wouldn't be able to climb out. I had broken it off, but that didn't staunch the hurt.

I dragged my thoughts back to the present. "When you

spoke to the detective, did you tell him you had a prior relationship with Phinney?" I asked.

Alice gave a dismissive shake of her head. "Why would I? I didn't see how it could have mattered." She sat forward in her chair. "To share a story is to lose a bit of it. I've been sharing with you here in the dark. I hope you'll treasure the bit of me I've given you and tell no one."

I nodded my agreement. I didn't see what a romance more than sixty years in the past could have to do with anything.

"So you have no idea who would want to kill Phinney?" I asked directly.

"Not a one," she said.

I looked around the room again at the photos. Each one evoked a powerful emotion and sense of place.

Alice noticed me looking. "Artifacts," she answered. "They're my art, but they're also artifacts of a life well lived." She drained the last of her tea. "It was a selfish life. One in which I had only myself to consider. It was also a life for which I was eventually well compensated. When I retired I found I only had two desires. To spend my summers in Maine in the cottage I loved, and to give something back. Busman's Harbor became the focus of those efforts."

The sound of a well-powered car came from the drive, and then a heavy car door slammed.

"That will be Ben." Alice brightened as she said his name. "He'll be happy to see you."

We sat and waited for Ben. I thought the least I could do was say hello. The minutes ticked by and he didn't come inside. Finally I stood. "Thank you, Alice, for telling me about you and Phinney." I gave her hand a squeeze. "That was so generous to share your story with me."

"The truth is, it felt good to talk about him. There's been no way to mourn him publicly. I needed someone to talk to and you came along at the right time."

"Gus and Bud are planning a funeral," I said. "For when the police release the body."

"Tell them I'd be pleased to contribute as much as they need," Alice said.

Gus would be relieved.

CHAPTER TWENTY

When I got out onto the front porch, Ben stood in the parking area staring intently at my rear bumper. My tires were sunk deep in the mud. The bucketing rain had stopped as quickly as it had started. Big drops dripped from the buds on the trees.

"I think you've really done it this time," he said when he heard the cottage door close behind me.

"It was fine when I parked. The thunderstorm did this." I could feel the flush rising, heating my face. "I'm a good driver and very used to mud. I swear."

He grinned. "I'm sorry our yard is such a mess." He looked back at the car. "I could pull you out if I had a tow chain, but I don't."

I didn't want to suggest he try pushing me again. Not after the mess it had created the last time. "I'll call my brother-in-law to come pull me out." I took out my phone, worried that Sonny wouldn't be available.

"Tell you what," Ben said. "I'll drive you home. I have to be somewhere tonight, but tomorrow I'll come to town, get some chains and pick you up. Then I can pull your car out. Can you live without it until then?"

"Sure. Thank you." The truth was my car spent most of its time in Mom's garage. There weren't many places in Busman's Harbor proper I couldn't walk to. And Ben's offer sounded way better than listening to what Sonny would have to say about me getting my car stuck in the mud. I pointed to my boots, which stood beside me on the porch. "I don't want to get your car dirty."

He came to the bottom of the steps. "It's a rental. Aunt Alice and I flew into Boston where we picked it up. Besides, look at my boots." He tipped his shoe to show me the muddy edge.

"Okay. Thanks," I said. "If you don't mind."

"Just let me stick my head in the house and let Aunt Alice know what's going on."

I stepped into my boots without tying them while Ben dodged around me and yelled into the house. "I'm driving Julia home then straight back!"

We trudged to the big car and got in. Ben turned the SUV around, backing up and edging forward to avoid my car. On the last swing he aimed for the long dirt road and we were on our way.

"It was nice of you to visit Aunt Alice," he said.

I wasn't sure what to say about that, and finally settled on the truth. "I've been looking into Phinney, trying to understand why someone would kill him."

Ben took that in his stride. "And you thought Alice would know something? She told you last time. She was his landlord, but always at arm's length." He turned to look at me as we reached the bottom of the drive. "Wait, do you think the murder had something to do with the pedestrian mall?"

Alice had asked me to keep her secret and I would. "I don't, but the detectives do."

"How do you know that?" He seemed amused.

"I know those guys from other times they've been in town." Ben may have figured out who Chris was, but he didn't know my whole life story along with every move I'd made the last five years. It was kind of nice.

We rode in silence. Not an uncomfortable one. I thought about what Alice had said about how she captured her magnificent photographs. Sit. Listen. Don't exploit. That was why Alice Rumsford was beloved by the town and Karl Kimbel hated. Alice sat with us patiently, shopped in our stores, ate in our restaurants, and patronized our institutions like the library and the Y. Her only desire was to make Busman's Harbor a better and more beautiful place. Kimbel's only interest was to exploit us for his own gain. He wanted to steal the town's soul.

My mind turned to the caretakers. Phinney had returned to Busman's Harbor to care for his mother. Alice's family was worried about how long she could live in the cottage alone. For the first time I wondered if Gus's son was really coming east for the summer because he had retired. Maybe Gus's kids were worried about him and Mrs. Gus. I hoped Alice and Gus and Mrs. Gus would be able to go on as they were as long as they wished.

When I pulled myself back into the moment, we were speeding down the highway to the harbor. It felt like we were going too fast, especially for the wet road. I snuck a look at the speedometer on the dash. From my angle it looked like we were going close to seventy in a fifty-mile-an-hour zone. I thought about saying something; maybe Ben didn't know the speed limit, but nobody likes a back-seat driver in any set of circumstances.

Immediately after I went through this thought process, I heard a siren coming up behind us.

"Shoot," Ben said. "It's a cop." He slowed down gradually and pulled onto the shoulder.

"Shoot," I said when I saw who it was.

Jamie's face appeared behind Ben's tinted window. Ben pressed the button and down the window went.

"Do you have any idea why I stopped you?" Jamie's dark eyebrows rose when he spotted me. He tilted his head in my direction. "Julia."

"I might have been going a little fast." Ben said it in a quiet voice, though he looked Jamie straight in the face.

"Nineteen miles an hour over the speed limit," Jamie said. "License and registration."

"It's a rental." Ben took off his seat belt and pulled his wallet out of his back pocket. "Julia, can you get the registration and rental agreement out of the glove compartment?"

I flipped the door open and retrieved the documents.

"So you two know each other," Ben said into the uncomfortable silence.

"Yeah," I answered.

Ben handed the documents to Jamie, who walked back toward his patrol car.

"Sorry about this," Ben said to me.

"I'm sorry," I said. "This wouldn't have happened if you weren't giving me a ride home."

There was a knock on my window that made me jump in my seat. Jamie's blurry face appeared behind the glass.

After a little fumbling around to find the button, I opened the window. "Ms. Snowden, may I speak with you?"

"Go ahead."

"Outside the vehicle, please."

I opened the door and climbed out. Jamie walked me well off the shoulder, out of harm's way. "Are you okay?"

"What is that supposed to mean?"

He shifted his weight from one foot to the other. "You're in a car with out-of-state plates that looks like it belongs to a drug dealer. I have to ask. Are you okay? Did you get into the car voluntarily?"

"Are you kidding me?" My voice went up to screech level. Jamie cast a worried look in the direction of Ben's car and I brought my volume down. "You don't think if I was being held captive I wouldn't have found a way to let you know? Is that why you stopped the poor guy?"

"I stopped him because he was going almost twenty miles an hour over the speed limit. Stupid tinted windows. I didn't know you were in the car. You're sure this guy's all right?"

"He's Alice Rumsford's grandnephew, for goodness' sake."

My protest did nothing to calm Jamie down. "How could I have known that?"

"You saw him with me the other night at Crowley's. Don't pretend you didn't. And you could have trusted that, as an adult, if I get into a car with someone, it's someone I know and feel safe with. Seriously, Jamie, this is screwed up. Why do you care, anyway? You're not my big brother."

Jamie's hands fell to his sides, Ben's documents still in his hands. "Julia, if you don't get it by now, you never will."

Jamie strode to his patrol car, back hunched. I got into the SUV.

"What was that about?" Ben asked.

"Nothing." My tone didn't invite discussion.

A few minutes later Jamie returned and handed Ben his license and the car's papers through the window. Then he took out his ticket pad and a pen. Ben looked at me and I figured I had to try.

"Officer Dawes"—I cleared my throat—"do you think maybe Mr. Barlow should get a warning? I'm feeling guilty. He's giving me a lift to my house."

"Is your house on fire?" Jamie sounded deadly serious.

I didn't bother to answer. Jamie finished writing the ticket, ripped it off with a flourish, and handed it to Ben.

"Thank you, Officer." Ben didn't look up as he said it. He glanced at the ticket and then put his license back in his wallet. Jamie returned to his patrol car. Ben closed his window and handed the ticket, registration, and rental agreement to me. "Can you put these in the glove compartment?"

"I'm really sorry," I said.

Ben waited until Jamie had pulled out and disappeared down the highway toward town before moving carefully off the shoulder. He drove exactly the speed limit all the way to town, speeding up and slowing down according to the signs. It was common wisdom around town that the speed limit changed so frequently along the highway in order to trick people with out-of-state license plates into speeding, making them easy pickings for the Busman's Harbor P.D.

When we got to Mom's house, I turned in my seat to face Ben. "I should pay the ticket." I was angry at Jamie and imagined marching into the police station and making a big, loud show of paying it.

"It's a hundred and ninety dollars. Besides, you didn't tell me to speed. That was entirely my carelessness." He smiled at me. "My mind was elsewhere."

"At least let me contribute."

"Tell you what. Agree to have dinner with me again before I leave town and we'll be even."

"When are you going back to Cincinnati?" I asked.

"A week from Monday, after the town meeting."

Plenty of time. "Okay. My treat this time. I insist."

"You've got a deal."

Ben waited with the car idling until I opened the front door. I turned and waved to let him know I was in.

Mom was upstairs in her sitting room watching TV when I got home. "I'm back!" I called up the stairs.

"Good."

The mushroom soup was still in the pot on the stove, so I ladled some out and stuck the bowl in the microwave. I broke off a heel of the crusty bread Mom had left on the cutting board and settled down to eat. The soup was everything mushroom soup should be. Earthy. Warm. Satisfying. My mother had made this wonderful meal. Six months ago, if you'd told me this could happen, I wouldn't have believed you.

I called Livvie and put the phone on speaker.

"How are you?" I asked as soon as she picked up.

"Better." Her voice sounded stronger. Almost back to normal. "Zoey called. Binder and Flynn are letting her move back to her apartment the day after tomorrow. She told us not to come into work. She wants some time to herself to figure out what's what. We'll go back to the studio next week." I could hear Livvie moving around doing the dishes in the background. "Have you found anything that will help Zoey?"

"I have found zero things that will help Zoey or anyone else," I answered. "Today I learned more about Phinney Hardison than I thought I would ever know. But nothing that will help solve his murder. Not why he was in that basement in the middle of the night. Not who was there with him. I can't even figure out who he would have trusted enough to put himself in that situation. Unless Bud and Gus killed him, and I think that's unlikely." I stopped for a moment, wondering how to broach the next subject. "Honestly, it's not clear to me Zoey needs or wants my help. She's pretty chill about the whole situation."

"Of course she needs your help."

An unpleasant thought occurred to me. "Did you ask me to help Zoey because you believe she needs help or because you thought I needed a project?"

There was a long silence on the other end. "Yes," Livvie offered tentatively.

"I'm not some kind of reclamation project," I objected.

Livvie ignored my protest. "How are you doing? Really."

"Really, I'm fine. I just got a ride home from Alice Rumsford's cottage with her grandnephew Ben. My car's stuck in the mud up there."

"That's too—wait—is he the good-looking one you had dinner with at Crowley's the other night?"

"How did you—" But I was too smart to finish that

question. A lot of people would have been eager to tell Livvie they'd seen me at Crowley's with a handsome guy From Away. "He wants to have dinner again."

"Interesting."

"Why? Nothing can come of it. He lives in Cincinnati. He's here supporting his aunt for a few weeks. Then he'll be gone."

"Julia." Livvie used the voice she uses when she pretends that she's the big sister. "I got married when I was eighteen to the only man I ever dated, but even I know that the next man after a big breakup is the transitional man. It's not *supposed* to go anywhere. Stop your moping around and go out and have dinner with the man. Goodness."

"I plan to. I kind of owe him. Jamie gave Ben a ticket when he was driving me home. A big one. He was a jerk about it if you want to know the truth."

"Jamie saw you in the car with Ben and acted like a jerk?" Livvie clarified.

"He was rude and he could have given a warning. You'd think with me in the car Ben would have gotten a break."

There was a long silence from the other end. "You never are going to get it, are you?" An exact echo of what Jamie had said. Clearly my lack of enlightenment had been discussed when I wasn't around.

"He's like my brother," I protested.

"He is most definitely *not* your brother," Livvie said. "I am your only sibling and I resent that."

I sighed into the phone on purpose, loud enough for her to hear. "This whole conversation reeks of 'He's the only eligible guy in town.' Be advised, the more you and Mom want it, the more I resist."

"Well, sue us for wanting you to stay in town and be happy." My sister hung up the phone.

When Livvie was gone, I thought about Jamie, his anger—and hurt?—when he'd seen me in the car with Ben. I'd believed our outings over the winter had been pity playdates. Could Jamie have wanted something more?

Could I ever feel differently about him? I didn't know. It wasn't something I'd ever considered.

CHAPTER TWENTY-ONE

In the morning I headed straight to the police station hoping to catch Binder and Flynn at the beginning of their day. When I got there some sort of meeting was breaking up. State police in uniform and plainclothes poured into the corridor, along with four members of the Busman's Harbor P.D. Jamie blushed when he saw me. I was glad he had the good sense to be embarrassed about his behavior the day before.

I took advantage of the confusion to slip into the multipurpose room. Binder and Flynn stood behind the plastic folding table they used as a desk, heads bent, speaking in low voices.

Binder smiled when he looked up and saw me. "Hullo, Julia. What have you got for us?" He reminded me of our bargain.

I racked my brain. Despite being busy the whole day

before, I didn't have much to offer. "Did you speak to John Fenwick, the dog walker I told you about?"

Flynn answered. "Early on. As you suggested, we hoped he could shorten the time frame for the vandalism at Lupine Design. Unfortunately, he was vague about what he'd seen or didn't see. Why?"

"I found out his late wife was a good friend of Phinney's mother. They're neighbors."

"And?" Flynn was unimpressed. I couldn't blame him.

"It's another connection between them," I offered lamely.

"Julia." He was losing his patience. "It's a small town. Everyone and everything is connected."

"If you're following up on the vandalism, you must believe the same person committed the murder," I said.

Flynn shook his head. "Not necessarily."

"It can't be a coincidence," I protested.

"Not coincidence," Binder said. "Causation."

I stared at him blankly.

"It's obvious, isn't it?" Binder continued. "Hardison trashes Butterfield's store. It's the last straw for her. She kills him."

My mouth fell open. "Then why was he there to be murdered in the middle of the night?"

"We're working on that," Flynn said.

I couldn't believe it. "You guys really think all of this is fallout from a town dispute?"

"It wouldn't be the first time." Flynn ran a hand over his close-cropped hair. "A witness has come forward."

"A witness? To the murder?"

"We interviewed a neighbor who had some information about Ms. Butterfield and Mr. Hardison's relationship," Flynn clarified. "She lives above the shop next door."

I pictured Main Street. A storefront swam into focus. Fleet's Children's Clothing. The kind of fancy garments grandparents buy, not the practical things a parent might purchase. Who lived upstairs? I didn't know.

"The neighbor says the dispute between the two went way beyond the fight over the pedestrian mall," Flynn said. "She heard Butterfield and Hardison shouting at each other at the top of their lungs on a daily basis."

"I know about the issues with the loading dock and the parking spaces," I admitted.

"Uh-huh. And other things," Flynn said. "Butterfield played loud music when she worked in the studio alone. Hardison smoked cigars outside the shop, right under her studio windows. It escalated and escalated."

"A dispute between neighbors that got out of control?" I didn't believe it. "You think that's enough to drive a person to murder?"

"If you'd seen what we've seen, you'd believe it." Flynn's tone was grim. I thought about all the terrible things the detectives encountered in their work. Things the rest of us got to avoid. "Our witness believes Butterfield was doing everything she could to drive Hardison out of his space," Flynn continued. "She reports Butterfield said as much, frequently and loudly."

Binder came around the table and put a hand on my shoulder. "Julia, we know you've become close to this woman. I hear you had lunch with her at Gus's yesterday."

How the heck did he hear that? There was *one* other party there, besides Gus. Besides Chris and Gus, I reminded myself. And neither of them would have been talking to the police.

"And there's something else," Binder said. "Ms. Butterfield's mother was murdered."

"What?" I was stunned. Zoey had lost her mother early and had been on her own as a teenager. Both were painful truths. But to add this to it. It was a moment before I could find my voice. "You're not suggesting Zoey *killed her mother.*"

"The mother's boyfriend was tried and convicted. He received a life sentence," Binder said.

"Then what's your point?" I challenged him. "Surely if someone has a loved one who was a murder victim, that person would be less likely, not more likely, to be a murderer."

"Not clear," Binder said. "And not what the department's forensic psychologist thinks."

We were all quiet for a moment. "Did you have anything else?" Binder asked, not unkindly.

"Er . . . no." My head was spinning. I needed to get out of there.

Binder could tell how flummoxed I was by the news about Zoey's mother. Still he thanked me for coming in.

"Bye," Flynn called. He was already seated and typing on his laptop.

I walked back to Mom's thinking about Zoey. The day was sunny and miraculously warm. For the first time, I'd left both the rain jacket and the quilted vest at home.

My phone buzzed with a text from Ben. **Conference call this morning. Will pick you up and we'll rescue your car later. Okay?**

I texted back a thumbs-up and kept walking.

Why hadn't Zoey told me her mother was murdered? Especially given that we were in the middle of another murder investigation.

But then, she didn't owe me anything. Four days earlier we'd been passing acquaintances, people whose conversations were limited to "hello" and "good-bye." Her mother's murder would hardly be the part of her history that Zoey led with. She undoubtedly knew from experience how people reacted. She wouldn't want that single event to define her.

Back at Mom's, I went straight up to my office and opened my laptop. I hadn't had the presence of mind to ask Zoey's mother's name. Was it Butterfield? Zoey had said her father was never in the picture. Perhaps her parents hadn't been married.

Zoey had grown up in California. She said her mother died when she was sixteen, which I judged to be about twenty years earlier. I started with those basics—murder, California, and the year—but the results were way too many. California was a huge state.

Had Zoey been a witness? Had she, God forbid, had to testify at the killer's trial? I entered "Zoey Butterfield" in the search engine and, the same as before, got back hundreds of results about Lupine Design. Image upon image of one stunning piece of pottery after another. Articles in major home magazines, often accompanied by photos of Zoey, standing proudly in the shop with the sun filtering through the windows, smiling broadly.

How was she smiling like that? How had she come back from such a trauma to build a life and a business? I'd admired her before I knew about her mother. Now I admired her more.

Finally, I entered everything I could think of into the same search. "Murder," "California," the three years most likely, and "Butterfield."

Instantly there it was, in words and links on my com-

puter screen. Frances "Frannie" Butterfield was found
dead by her daughter, when she returned home from high
school.

My heart skipped a beat. This was worse than I'd
imagined. Zoey had found her mother's body. I followed
the story in the San Jose paper from the first small article,
barely more than a police report, through the sensational
trial and sentencing.

The suspect, Frannie's live-in boyfriend, was arrested
in Oregon five days after the murder. During those five
days there were several stories about Frannie. A talented
painter, she'd never settled into a career and supported
her daughter and herself by waitressing in a string of din-
ers. She wasn't ever married, the stories emphasized,
usually in a paragraph immediately preceding or following information about her daughter. Zoey's name never
appeared in print, but there was no question who the
daughter was. I wondered about Zoey's friends and classmates and whether she'd had any support. The mother
and daughter seemed profoundly alone.

When the boyfriend, Calvin Erickson III, was arrested,
the focus of the articles shifted to him, the ne'er-do-well
son of an East Coast family. But even the stories about
him dropping out of school, trying career after career,
starting business after business, moving ever westward
across the country, still managed to let readers know that
Frannie Butterfield was a loose woman, often leaving the
impression she was responsible for her own death. "There's
been carryings on in that apartment since she moved there,"
a neighbor was quoted as saying.

I understood why journalists emphasized Zoey's
mother's lifestyle and why their readers lapped it up.

People wanted to believe if they lived more carefully than the victim, if they had more advantages in which to cloak themselves, then they could avoid her fate. People needed to see the victim as "not like them." Still, it was galling. How much had this angle added to Zoey's pain?

After the arrest, the articles disappeared until Calvin Erickson's trial approached. Then they started up again with a vengeance. His family Back East had hired a high-priced defense attorney, whose first tactic was to pile delay upon delay. When that no longer worked and the trial was inevitable, the lawyer managed to get stories in the newspaper, which I could only assume were planted, that made Calvin sound like Mother Teresa. There were articles about the men he'd helped during his stays in homeless shelters. And the ones he'd tutored during his previous stints in prison.

But the reporters hadn't been content to be spoon-fed stories of Calvin Erickson's sainthood. There were also articles about Calvin's ever-escalating violence toward women as evidenced by his previous arrest and conviction records, and interviews, always anonymous, with some of those women.

The trial was sensational and there were stories every day. Zoey was eighteen by then and there were photos of her as she was rushed into the courthouse. She looked young, heartbreakingly so. Her hair was longer, her face leaner and pinched with pain, but the images were unmistakable. My heart broke for her.

According to the reporters in the courtroom, Zoey was an excellent witness. She described her mother's relationship with Erickson, how it had started as deeply romantic but that over time he had become more demanding, controlling, and ultimately violent. Minute by minute she described how she had come home from school that day, hoping against hope that Erickson had moved out. She'd put her key in the lock of their garden apartment and the door had swung open. Her mother was on the floor, her throat cut so deeply her head was nearly off.

I had to stop reading. I hadn't known until a couple of hours earlier that Zoey's mother had been murdered. I hadn't known until that minute that her mother had been killed in the same way as Phinney. And Zoey had discovered both bodies. I could barely think about it, the idea was so painful.

The trial dragged on for two more weeks. The defense attorney tried to paint the picture of an unplanned attack, not intended to kill. But the prosecutor had too much evidence. The lethal knife had been purchased two weeks earlier. Erickson had told witnesses he'd be leaving town. The jury came back in less than a day. Guilty of murder in the first degree. A few weeks later the sentence came down. Life in prison. I wondered if Zoey had gotten any satisfaction from that.

There followed appeal after appeal, all to no avail.

When I couldn't bear to read any more, I took several deep breaths, went down to the kitchen, brewed a cup of tea, and sat at the table. What would I do with the knowledge I now had? Binder and Flynn wouldn't appreciate me talking to Zoey about her mother's murder, particularly if they truly believed it was somehow tied to the current murder. But I didn't see how I could face her, knowing what I now knew, with her not knowing that I knew it. It seemed desperately unfair to her.

CHAPTER TWENTY-TWO

Vee opened the door to the Snuggles, wearing a crisply ironed apron over her put-together outfit of an aubergine twinset over an aubergine and brown plaid skirt.

"Julia. This is getting to be a regular thing. I'm guessing you're looking for our guest."

"Is Zoey available?" I suddenly felt less sure about what I was doing. How was I going to approach this delicate topic?

"In the dining room. She's got her paperwork spread out across the table."

I went through the swinging door and called softly to Zoey. "Good morning." I didn't want to startle her.

She turned and smiled, obviously happy to see me, which made me feel both better and worse. She was, as Vee had said, in the middle of working. "I need to talk to you," I said.

Zoey caught my tone. Her forehead pinched with concern. "About Phinney's murder?"

"Yes," I answered. "And no."

Her face unscrunched and then her eyebrows drew up, her concern turned to curiosity. I sat across from her and looked into her eyes. "I know about your mother's murder."

"Oh." There was a long silence. Zoey finally spoke. "How much do you know?"

"I took a pretty deep dive on the Web this morning."

She looked down, studying the tabletop. "You'll have seen how they made her look."

"Yes," I admitted, "and I'm sorry. There's always a tendency to try to blame the victim, especially if she's a woman."

"She was exactly like they said." Zoey's voice was so low I could barely hear. But then she looked up at me. "There were men, lots of men. New 'uncles' every couple of years. When I was young, I didn't understand it. I gave my heart to the first two that I can remember. Mike, then Joe. Both of them were good to me, pushed me on the swings in our apartment complex, turned me upside down and shook me while I squealed. I loved them the way the kids I knew loved their dads. But they weren't my dad. I didn't understand then that my mother had a type, and hers was the type of man who didn't hang around."

"I'm sorry," I said.

"Don't be. You didn't cause it and no one can fix it now." She spoke matter-of-factly, without a trace of self-pity. "After Joe there were a few whose names I don't remember. I gave up on loving them, even though my mother didn't. But for years, until I was nine or ten, at the beginning of each new relationship, I had hope. Hope that he would stay, that we could stay in this apartment, I could stay in the same school, and we would look, to my classmates, like a normal family. It never happened."

I got up and retrieved the coffee carafe from the sideboard. I refilled her cup and poured one for me. I returned the carafe, grabbed the small tray on which the delicate cream and sugar set sat, and pushed it to her across the table. She poured cream in her cup and pushed the tray back toward me.

"By the time I was in middle school, I had given up my fantasy of a normal family life and I only hoped that whoever he was, if he was paying part of our rent, or if we had moved into his place, he'd last through the school year so we wouldn't have to move. They weren't bad, these men. They were just undomesticated, like tomcats. Or if they were domesticated, it was because they had a family across town. Whether they were divorced or separated, or in some other gray state, these men had no interest in creating another family, though my mother always hoped, always believed.

"Then, when I was a freshman in high school, Cal came along. My mother thought he was the answer to her prayers. He came from money out East. He owned his own business. He showered attention on her. Bought her things, took her out to dinner. He was willing to meet her friends at whatever dive she was working at, something the others were rarely willing to do. He moved in after five days but the romantic gestures continued for months.

"I was wary of him from the beginning. He had an edge, no question. He wasn't violent, not at first. But you sensed he could explode at any minute. At least I did. In that first year, I don't know if my mother didn't see it or decided it was in her interest to ignore it. We could never manage to have a civil conversation about her boyfriends, before, during, or after they left, so we'd entered a silent truce.

"Things went downhill fast that second year. Something had happened to Cal's business. He said he had sold it and was waiting for another opportunity, but I didn't believe him and I couldn't see how my mother could, either. He sat around the house all day. He was always there. He controlled the couch and the remote, the food that was brought into the house. He inspected every trash can, checking for what was thrown away. He would tell you this or that was 'perfectly good' and make you keep it. He'd comment on how many tissues you'd used, always too many. I started carrying the trash from the wastebasket in my room to school in my backpack so I could dispose of it there. I couldn't stand him or the situation, but my mother still believed. He would buy that new business, his family out East would stake him if he found the right opportunity. He was going to propose. It was right around the corner.

"He was worse than the others, not better, and not one of them had proposed. The control and silences escalated into terrible fights, each of them screaming at the other about their disappointments. I joined the art club, which met after school, painted sets for the drama club, knitted socks and hats for kids in shelters, with a group of girls. Anything to avoid going back to our apartment."

"You don't have to tell me." It was obviously painful for her to talk about. I was sorry I had brought it up.

"No." She tossed her abundant brown hair as if shaking off doubt. "I want to. Let me get through it.

"At home things got worse. Mom and Cal had moved from screaming to slapping and punching. Both of them, but he was much stronger. Most of the time when I got home he was on the couch watching sports and she was in her room, crying. I tried to talk to her, but our long silence on the subject made it difficult. That she was still defending him made it impossible.

"I started sleeping out, whenever I could. Weekends at girlfriends'. Even weeknights. I never told anyone what was wrong at home but the mothers could see and were sympathetic. A young waitress who worked with Mom let me stay at her apartment for almost a month."

Zoey didn't talk again for a long time. I wondered if I should say something, but couldn't for the life of me think what. "I'm sorry," seemed so impossibly lame.

Finally, she spoke. "Then one day, I don't know why, but I had a terrible feeling and I decided I had to go home. It was my home more than his. I walked straight from school. His truck wasn't in the driveway, and I was hopeful that either he'd left on his own, or she'd finally told him to go." Zoey paused and took a long gulp of her coffee. "In spite of it all, I never expected what I saw when I walked through the door that day. Never."

Tears welled up in her eyes and spilled over onto her cheeks. "Darn," she said, wiping them away with her wrist. "Sorry."

I was on the edge of tears myself. What had I done to this woman? It was as if someone had asked me to describe those last few weeks of my father's cancer. Only worse. Way, way worse. I went to the powder room off the entrance hall of the Snuggles, brought back a box of tissues, and placed it in front of her.

"Thanks." She blew her nose. She was regaining her

composure. "What made you check the internet for my mother in the first place?"

There was no way around it. I certainly wasn't going to lie. "The detectives, Lieutenant Binder and Sergeant Flynn, know," I said. "They told me your mother was murdered."

"Which made them suspect me even more." It wasn't a question, though it certainly should have been.

"I don't see why," I protested. I still didn't.

"Julia, I know how this works. I found the body. Phinney Hardison was murdered in the basement of my home. I was briefly a suspect in my mother's murder. Not for long, thank goodness. One set of interviews with the neighbors and the police learned all about Cal. But long enough to understand what it feels like."

"Your current neighbor hasn't been nearly as helpful," I said.

She looked surprised, but then said, "Mrs. Bright, next door."

"I don't know her name, but someone told the detectives you and Phinney fought all the time. He believed you wanted him out of the building."

"I *did* want him out of the building." Zoey was defiant. "I never made a secret of it. I asked for the whole space before I even signed the lease. But I wouldn't murder anyone for the sake of a few hundred square feet. I wouldn't murder anyone for any reason. You believe me, don't you?"

I got up and gave her a hug. "Of course I do. I'm so sorry I brought this up."

"You weren't the one who took me back there. It's been sitting close ever since I saw poor Phinney with his head nearly cut off. Just like my mother." The tears started again. She pressed the palms of her hands into her eye sockets in an attempt to staunch the tears. "I've tried and tried to shut it out, push it away. I'm usually good at that." She stepped away from me, gesturing with her hands about the futility of it all. "I'm sorry I didn't tell you. I know from what you said about your ex yesterday that you hate secrets."

"You don't owe me anything, Zoey. This is an entirely different situation."

Zoey sniffled and blew her nose again. We sat down, not saying anything. Finally, she spoke. "To make up for not telling you about my mother, I'm going to tell you a different secret. I want us to be friends." She inhaled deeply and then said it in a rush. "The man I'm seeing is Karl Kimbel."

"What?"

"You can't tell a soul. He's in the middle of a horrible divorce."

I concentrated on my poker face, which had never been a good one.

"You're shocked," Zoey said.

"No," I lied. "I get it. He's good-looking. Confident." *Powerful, charismatic, rich, old enough to be your father.* "You're working on these town causes together. That gives you a common goal. Is it serious?"

"It's pretty new, so I can't say. He's technically not even available."

"I'm happy for you." *Another lie?*

"Thanks." Zoey didn't say anything after that and I wondered if I should go. I was trying to figure out what to say when she spoke again.

"What those articles you read didn't tell you is that Frannie Butterfield was a really good mother. She was impulsive and had terrible taste in men. But she kept a roof over my head my whole life, even when it was hard. I was never hungry. I was always clean. Every time we moved, she registered me in school and took me the first day to make sure I was settled. Even when I was older." Zoey paused, inhaling deeply. "She made the best brownies. I've been trying brownie recipes for years hoping to figure it out. And she loved art. Everywhere we lived she found a place for her easel and her paints. She's the person who made me who I am as an artist. As a person. I hated her when she clung to Cal and I felt exiled from my own home, even though, on some teenage level, I understood why she did. But I also loved her. *Love her.* Always."

Zoey's speech brought the tears back, hers and mine, so I stayed a few more minutes with her. She had wanted to set the record straight. I wanted her to know I had heard.

CHAPTER TWENTY-THREE

When I left the Snuggles, Fee was across the street taking advantage of the beautiful spring day to spread mulch in the garden beds that lined my mother's front walk. The daffodils had finally sprouted and the hyacinths were poking through.

Fee had taken care of my parents' gardens as long as we'd lived in the house. When I was a kid, we'd stayed on Morrow Island all summer. Without Fee our house would have looked weedy and neglected. In return, my dad had plowed the sisters' driveway, shoveled their walks, and raked their leaves in the autumn.

Now that she was bent with arthritis, I hated to see Fee working so hard. I always felt terribly guilty as she toiled away. But she absolutely insisted. Since my dad had died, Sonny had taken over the plowing, the shoveling, and the raking. The Snugg sisters did not take charity. Fee insisted on a quid pro quo.

"At least let me help." I grabbed a shovel that was leaning against the front steps and distributed the mulch to the ends of the walk. Fee could spread it. She wouldn't trust me with the detail work, but I could do the heavy lifting.

"Thanks," she said.

We worked together for a few minutes. "Fee, do you know anything about lupines?" I asked.

"*Lupinus polyphyllus*," she said. "Beautiful flowers, white, pink, purple, almost red, massed in the fields by the side of the road. They bloom in June as the solstice approaches, the symbol of a Maine summer begun." Fee stopped raking the mulch and straightened up as much as she was able. "They're not native, of course."

I stopped shoveling. "You're kidding. You just said they are the symbol of a Maine summer."

Fee chuckled. "They're invasive. They come from the West Coast. They've only been in Maine since the 1960s. They've pushed out our native lupines, *lupinus perennis*, which are extinct in Maine. And with *lupinus perennis* so went the Karner blue butterfly, now extirpated here, though I hear there are some in New Hampshire."

"How did the West Coast lupines get to Maine?" I asked.

"You know how they got here." Fee looked at me like she couldn't believe her ears. "*Miss Rumphius*."

"That's a children's book," I protested.

"Based on a true story," Fee responded. "Hilda Edwards of Christmas Cove. She dropped lupine seeds wherever she went."

"I can't believe lupines come From Away," I said.

"And now they're one of the most beloved sights in

Maine. Something lost, something gained. Change is constant," Fee said.

We had finished up the beds and were tidying up when the big black SUV pulled in front of the house. The window rolled down. "Did you get my second text?" Ben called. "When I said I was on my way to pick you up?"

I hadn't looked. "You're here now," I shouted back. "Let's do it."

I started to introduce Fee but she waved me off. "You young people go along."

Ben had already bought the tow chain and refused payment for it. As we drove up the highway toward Alice's cottage, I spotted Oceanside Realty. "Ben, do you mind stopping here while I run in?"

He gave me a questioning look but pulled into the parking lot. "Are you looking for real estate?"

"Not exactly. I'll only be a minute, I promise."

Judi with the Pebbles Flintstone ponytail was behind the counter.

"Hi. I'm Julia Snowden. I came in the other day, do you remember?"

"Yes. You had questions about 587 Main Street." She said it in a way that didn't encourage further conversation. "Before you say anything, you should know the state police detectives have been here and I cooperated fully. I told them everything I know."

But what did she know? "I'm not here about the murder, specifically," I said, which was sort of true. "I'm wondering if you ever received any complaints from Phinney Hardison about Lupine Design."

She sighed, impatient with the conversation. "As I told the detectives, after Zoey Butterfield rented her space, Phinney called numerous times. He didn't like the renovation. She had approached him about paying for a security system, which ticked him off. She was too noisy, the store attracted too much foot traffic, and on and on.

"Like I told you before, we don't have a management contract for the building. Nonetheless, we investigated every one of his complaints. We asked her to turn down the music in the studio, but that made Mr. Hardison madder, because then he could hear the machinery. We told him it was a permitted use. There was absolutely nothing that rose to the level where we would even recommend to the owner that Ms. Butterfield be evicted. Especially as she was renting three-quarters of the space, had paid for a massive renovation, and had a ten-year lease, while Mr. Hardison's tenancy was month to month."

"How did he take that?"

"About as well as you'd expect. He wouldn't stop calling with complaints that got more and more deranged. Finally, to shut him up, we told him to put his demands in letter form and we'd forward them on to the owner's law firm."

"And did he?"

"He did. The letters have been arriving on the first of the month, along with his rent check, for a year."

"Did you, or anyone in your office, ever read the letters?" I asked.

"Nope, nope, and nope. Thankfully, they came in sealed envelopes. We forwarded them to the owner's lawyers, just like we said we would."

"Do you know what the lawyers did with them?"

"Don't know. Don't want to know." A phone began to ring. "I've got to go. Like I said, we told all this to the police. If you have any other questions, call them."

I got back in the car and we went on our way. When I thanked him for making the stop, Ben gave me another curious look but didn't ask questions.

I thought about what I'd learned. Phinney hated Zoey and wanted her evicted. Binder and Flynn knew that, too, from multiple sources. They'd tracked Phinney's complaints as far as the real estate office. They had probably talked to the law firm and talked to Alice.

Ben pulled the heavy car up the private road to where my Subaru was still stuck in the car park. I got out and inspected the tires. The mud had closed around them like cement.

I stood on the front steps, a useless spectator, while Ben took the rear mat out of his car and lay on it to fix the chain to the Subaru's rear axle. "Let me do that," I said, but he wouldn't hear of it.

The big SUV had no trouble extricating the much smaller Subaru. Ben turned off his car and stood opposite me. "There you go." He was pleased with himself. "We said we'd have dinner, but we didn't set a date."

"True," I replied. "You're the one who's leaving. And has a great-aunt to look after. What works for you?"

"Tomorrow night?"

"Why not?" The thought of Crowley's again, and the risk that Chris would be working the door, was more than I wanted to deal with. "Let's go to Damariscotta. There's a great place there. Several, in fact. No sense in taking two cars. I'll pick you up. It's my treat. I should drive."

He smiled in amusement. "Okay, but maybe call me from the bottom of the road? Let's not do this again."

I laughed.

He glanced at the high-tech watch on his wrist. "Seven thirty?"

"Seven thirty it is." I paused, thinking about how to word my request. "There's one more thing. I'd like to speak to Alice."

"I'm sure she'd be pleased to see you." The skin pinched together over his nose; he didn't understand what I was getting at.

"I'd like to talk to her alone," I clarified.

Ben hesitated, then relaxed. "Let me go in and clean up and I'll get out of your hair." He tilted his head in the direction of the Subaru. "You've got your own ride home."

After Ben's SUV disappeared down the long drive, I took off my boots and padded into the cottage. The hallway was dark, but when I entered the living room the west-facing view was ablaze with the late afternoon sun, low in the western sky.

"Hello, dear." Alice was in the green velvet recliner. "I didn't expect to see you again so soon."

I sat across from her. "Have you talked to Lieutenant Binder and Sergeant Flynn since we spoke?"

"How funny you should ask. They did come around earlier this afternoon with new questions."

"Questions about Phinney," I said.

She rubbed one thin hand over the other and gave a slight dip of her head. "Yes."

"They asked about the letters Phinney sent to your law firm."

She hesitated for a moment, then nodded, her bright blue eyes trained on me. "Yes."

"Did you tell them about your history with Phinney?"

"No." Her voice was low and quivery, not at all the self-assured woman I'd talked to before. She took a deep breath. "It's ancient history. Not anything that could matter now."

She had lied, or at least omitted.

"Except, if the detectives knew you were once in love with Phinney, they would know you had a reason to lie about the letters," I said. "They asked you about them, didn't they? They asked if you had them."

She was silent for so long I wasn't sure she would ever answer. Or answer truthfully. "They did." She hesitated. "I think of myself as a truthful person. *Liar* is a new label for me, one I don't wear easily."

"Lying to the police in an active murder investigation is never a good idea," I responded. "It's a crime."

"I'm sure you're right, dear." She pulled her blanket around her. "Would you like to see the letters?"

I was surprised at the offer and jumped at the chance before she had time to change her mind. I could tell her lie weighed on her heavily. She needed someone else to know about the letters.

She directed me to the same desk where she'd told Ben to find the keys on the day of my first visit. The letters were there, not at all hidden, in the top side drawer in a plastic baggie. There were about a dozen letters in their envelopes, the name of Alice's law firm scrawled across the front in heavily slanted but readable penmanship.

"Read them if you like," she said.

I sat in the desk chair. "I don't think I should touch them."

"I've read them each dozens of times," she said. "I don't think you can hurt them."

I pulled an envelope from the middle of the pile and slid a letter out, holding it by its edges. The letter was dated the previous August and written in the same slanted handwriting, in blue ballpoint pen, that appeared on the envelopes. *To Whom It May Concern*. Then came the same litany of complaints I'd heard about before. Loud music, too many people coming and going, delivery trucks blocking parking spaces, requests to invest money that the author protested he did not have and it wasn't his duty as a tenant to spend anyway. It was signed, *Your tenant, Phinney Hardison*.

I read the next letter, and then the next, moving forward in time. The tone and complaints were the same, until I came to the three most recent.

Those letters contained threats. *I can see you'll do nothing. I will have to take matters into my own hands. If I don't get satisfaction, I'll have to perform a citizen's eviction*. I gathered Phinney thought that was like a citizen's arrest. Throughout the last three letters, the names Phinney called Zoey were increasingly vile. Clearly, he had hated her. She had somehow become responsible for every bit of hurt and anger he felt in his life.

I put the last letter back in its envelope. "I don't understand. Why didn't you evict him?"

She turned her palms upward. "Because it was Phinney. I would have if I'd understood he was in danger."

"You have to give these to the detectives," I insisted. "You can truthfully say they came to you in your role as his landlord. You don't need to disclose anything about your past." I got up from the chair and handed her the plastic bag. "Call the detectives. Now. Or I will."

Flynn's card was on her side table. She picked up the phone in the flowered case and pressed the numbers, moving her eyes from the card to the phone, squinting all the while.

"Detective? Alice Rumsford. You were here today asking about some letters."

Flynn said something and Alice listened.

"Yes. As it happens, I have them. I apologize for not telling you earlier. My young friend here has urged me to call." Alice listened again. "Julia Snowden."

Flynn's voice grew louder.

Alice ended the call. "He'll be right along. He says for you to wait."

CHAPTER TWENTY-FOUR

The meeting with Flynn wasn't nearly as bad as I'd feared. He wasn't even that mad I'd read some of the letters. When he asked Alice why she hadn't turned them over when he and Binder had been there earlier, she didn't lie.

"I didn't want to. Julia convinced me I must."

After he was done, Flynn and I sat on the porch together to put on our boots. "Do you want to grab dinner?" he asked.

I was surprised by the invitation. Then I realized in the day's running around I hadn't eaten lunch. "Where's Binder?"

"Gone to attend to some business in Augusta," Flynn said. "He'll kiss his wife and kids, sleep in his own bed, and be back in the morning."

"Dinner sounds great," I said. "Anywhere but Crowley's."

He gave me a grin. He knew exactly why I wanted to avoid the place. "I have to check these letters into evidence at the police station. I'm staying at the Bellevue. Why don't you grab a pizza and a six-pack and meet me there? We can eat on the deck. It would be terrible to waste the first warm evening of the year."

"Pizza? You?" I couldn't imagine anything that delicious passing Flynn's lips. His body was his temple and nothing as unhealthy as pizza entered its gates.

He stood on the muddy path and faced me. "Anything but anchovy."

"If you say so."

We drove off, me in my recently liberated Subaru and Flynn in a nondescript Camry. Binder must have their state car.

I ordered a veggie pizza just to be safe and picked up six cold bottles of beer made by a local small-batch brewery, wondering all the while what Flynn was up to. His car was already in the lot by the time I got to the Bellevue. I found him on the enormous wooden deck by the harbor. The furniture wasn't out yet, but he'd set up a single table and two chairs he'd taken from a pile in a protected corner beside the old hotel.

I wiped the table with a couple of the napkins and we sat down to eat.

"How did you know about the letters?" Flynn asked.

I wasn't going to give Alice up. "I found out they existed from the woman at Oceanside Realty."

"Pebbles Flintstone?" He smiled.

"You saw it, too!"

He laughed out loud. "And now I can't unsee it."

"The very one. She told me their office forwarded the letters, unopened, to the owner's law firm. I knew Alice was the owner. Presto!"

Flynn was actually eating the pizza. He even seemed to be enjoying it.

"What's with the pizza?" I asked.

"What? I can be flexible."

"Pfft. Not that I've ever witnessed." I smiled to let him know I was teasing. "Why did you invite me to share dinner, anyway?"

His attempt to look insulted was only semi-successful. "For the pleasure of your estimable company. What other reason could I have?" He picked up a second piece of pizza. "Don't change the subject," he chided. "You found out she had the letters, but how did you get Ms. Rumsford to admit she had the letters and turn them over to us?"

"I'd rather not say."

"You may have to eventually." Flynn took a long swig of his beer. "This is good." I had never seen him drink alcohol before, either. "I'm surprised you of all people talked Ms. Rumsford into giving the letters to us. They only reinforce Zoey's motive. Hardison wanted her out. Even if she figured the landlord would let him go before breaking her lease, it can't have been pleasant to live in the same building with someone who hated her so completely."

It was true. The letters did give Zoey all the more reason for homicide, but that wasn't what I thought had happened. "I hope you know I would never keep anything important from you or Binder," I said.

"I do." He opened a second beer, took a swig, and then gave me a meaningful look. "We both know what the letters mean."

I nodded. "Phinney Hardison vandalized Zoey's store."

"Yup." He took another drink.

"Which means the vandalism is a separate crime from the murder." I was trying to work it out.

"Or the vandalism caused the murder, as I've said to you before. The motive was revenge."

I didn't see it. Zoey was not a murderer.

The sun had set behind the hill on the other side of the harbor. The dusk made everything fuzzy, including Flynn. The lights along the dock in front of us blinked on. "I gather, since we couldn't go to Crowley's, that you and Chris are still apart," Flynn said.

"Yes," I answered. "Why would you think we wouldn't be?"

He hesitated. "Those big relationships, the ones where you're in love, where you live together—"

"Run a business together," I added.

"Exactly. They take a while to wear off. Sometimes you have to break up two or three times before you're done hurting each other."

We were silent again for a moment. "Are you speaking from experience?" I asked him.

Flynn had been in love with my friend Genevieve. She'd broken his heart when she decided to continue to pursue her career as a chef on superyachts rather than taking a land-based job and moving in with him. To my knowledge, he hadn't been in a serious relationship since. Beyond that, Flynn's dating life, or any aspect of his personal life, was terra incognita to me. He was attractive. More than attractive. His body was like a piece of art he worked on daily.

"My ex-fiancée," he said.

So not Genevieve.

"We called it quits three times," he said. "The last time, she sealed the deal by sleeping with my brother. When she married him and had his kid, I thought that was carrying the whole charade too far."

His voice was light, like it was all a joke, but I wasn't fooled. "Is that why you moved to Maine from Providence?" I had heard the one-sentence version of this story before, the one that had made it sound like his brother had married Flynn's casual girlfriend when he'd been in Afghanistan with his reserve unit. Girlfriend, not fiancée, had been the way he'd told it then.

Flynn, his brothers, and uncles had all been on the Providence police force. His father had been a chief. I'd assumed, and when pressed he'd always said, that he'd come to Maine because there was too much family in Rhode Island. I'd always sensed there was more to the story.

"I moved to get away from the pity," he said. "The looks on people's faces. My mother, throwing me a big, embarrassing thirtieth birthday party because, unlike my brothers, I didn't have a wife to celebrate with. It was awful."

"My family doesn't feel pity," I responded. "At least I don't think so. Instead it's like they have restless, nervous energy to find me a job and a man that will keep me in town."

"I can imagine who that man is." Flynn grinned at me in the growing darkness. "Am I right?"

"I'm guessing you're right," I admitted.

"Do you love him?"

What a question. "Of course I love him." I searched for words that wouldn't be a terrible cliché and failed. "But not in that way."

"Could you?"

I blushed furiously, grateful Flynn couldn't see in the

dark. "I'm glad you don't turn your interrogation techniques on me often."

"You're deflecting," he teased. Then his tone turned serious. "If you think there's anything there, if you could love him the way he wants, you should give it a chance. The poor guy has it bad."

I didn't know how to respond to that. I wasn't used to Flynn giving me any kind of advice except to stay out of his hair.

Flynn changed the subject, but he wasn't done giving advice. "I know you've become friendly with Zoey. Be careful there, please. She's not being straight with you."

"If you mean about her mother's murder, we've talked about that. You can understand why it wouldn't be something she'd tell a near stranger."

"Is Livvie a stranger to her?" His voice was so low and he'd leaned in so close I could feel his breath. "Besides, that's not what I'm talking about. Did your friend tell you, for example, she's having an affair with Karl Kimbel?"

"Yes," I answered, feeling superior. "He's staying here at the Bellevue, you know."

"I've seen him around. Why do you think we're whispering? Did Ms. Butterfield tell you that Kimbel was there at her apartment the night of the murder?"

My superior feeling melted away. "How do you know that?" I demanded.

"Shh," Flynn reminded me. "The neighbor told us."

"Mrs. Bright."

Flynn nodded, a movement I felt more than saw in the dark. "When Kimbel stays at Zoey's he parks his fancy sports car behind Mrs. Bright's building all night, which annoys her. She saw him coming out the studio door onto the loading dock early in the morning the day Hardison was killed."

The breath was knocked out of me. Not by Zoey's omission, but by what Kimbel's presence might mean. I inhaled deeply, exhaled, and kept my voice steady. "Have you interviewed Zoey and Kimbel about this?"

"This afternoon. They each admitted the affair and each denied he was in the building that night. Zoey insisted Mrs. Bright had her days wrong."

"Kimbel could give Zoey an alibi," I said.

"Or he could be an accomplice." Flynn settled back in his chair. "Julia, it doesn't look good."

No, it doesn't. We sat in silence and finished off the beer as the small harbor waves lapped against the deck footings beneath us. I was strangely depleted by the conversation. I felt like I could go home and straight to sleep.

I stood. "I'm going."

"Leave your car here. I'll walk you to your house."

"I'm fine to walk by myself. I only drank two beers. You'll have to walk back."

Flynn stood too. "I'm state police. I'll walk you home."

We cleared away the leavings from dinner, then meandered across the footbridge into town. The trip to Mom's house took minutes. We stood under the streetlight at the end of the sidewalk. "You and the lieutenant are good detectives," I said. "You wouldn't focus on Zoey without investigating other possibilities. Have you found anyone else, anyone at all, who wanted Phinney Hardison dead?"

"Nope." He shook his head. "Phinney was a blusterer, even a bully. But there's no one. No family, no lover, no business partner. Not a soul on earth had anything to gain from his death. Except your friend Zoey."

CHAPTER TWENTY-FIVE

At ten the next morning, Fee was taking advantage of another beautiful day—two in a row—to work in the gardens across the street at the Snuggles.

"You've missed your friend," she shouted at me. "She's already moved back home. First thing this morning. As quick as she could."

"Thanks!" I called back and started down Main Street.

The door to Lupine Design was locked when I arrived, which didn't surprise me. The shop wasn't open to the public yet. I knocked and got no answer, though I could feel and hear the thump of a heavy bass coming from the studio in the back. I walked around the old building and climbed up the concrete steps onto the loading dock. The thumping was louder and I could make out a melody line, though I still couldn't guess the song or the artist.

I banged on the barn-style door. No response. I'd already turned to leave when the music suddenly stopped. The door rolled open and Zoey peered out. She smiled, happy to see me. I wasn't sure she would be once we had talked. "Julia? Come in. You're just in time."

"In time for what?"

She led me into the big space. "In time for the opening of the kiln. We'd just finished loading it when Livvie persuaded me to call Phinney's cell to check if he was okay. You know what happened after that." She made a face.

"Will the pottery be all right?" I asked.

Zoey was already at one of the kilns, turning the handle. "It should be fine. The kiln was on a timer. Everything has been sitting here, waiting." She swung the door open. "Every time I do this, no matter how many thousands of times, the anticipation is like Christmas morning." She clapped her hands and started pulling pieces from the shelves of the kiln.

They were the white pieces, the ones Livvie had called the bisque, which came from the first firing. "What are they?" I asked.

"New designs, I hope. I've been wanting to expand my Quahog line. It's popular with wedding couples, but they're always looking for soup bowls in addition to cereals, and the wedding guests want serving pieces in a range of prices, for gifts." She continued to pull pottery from the kiln. "These pieces were experiments. I'm trying out new shapes for the bowls—no lip, thin lip, wide lip. I threw the bowls on the wheel and hand built the platters."

As Zoey took the pieces out of the kiln, she put them in three groups on a long wooden table, muttering to herself as she did. "No. No. Maybe. Ugly. Possible. Nice! Cracked.

Broken. Yuck. Oh my goodness, *that* didn't work." Finally she held up a big piece, triumphant. "Gorgeous."

The serving bowl was shaped like a giant clamshell. I could see the hinge would be a little bowl for dip and the big shell would hold chips. Even in its unglazed shape, it was beautiful.

Her reject pile was three times the size of the other two.

"It doesn't sound like Christmas morning to me," I said. "Unless you were a lot pickier about your gifts than I was."

Zoey smiled. "Pottery breaks your heart. Every. Single. Time."

"Even with all your experience?"

"Making pottery isn't like manufacturing. You can guess and hope, but you can never be sure what you're going to get. The pottery gods have to be with you." She paused and held up a soup bowl from the "maybe" pile. "This would be a reject." She handed me the bowl.

"What's wrong with it?" For all the world, it looked fine to me.

She took it back and traced a slight irregularity on the lip. She had to do it twice before I saw it. One curve in the design wasn't quite symmetrical with the others. "That little thing? You can barely see it."

"I agree," Zoey said. "I always say that's how you can tell they're individually made. But I've learned that retailers, who are going to mark these items up forty percent, want perfection. Fortunately, I have a mailing list of customers looking for seconds for our established lines." She put the bowl back in the "maybe" pile. "The design of this piece has possibilities even if the execution is flawed."

As she continued examining the pieces, I worked up my courage. It was time for the question I'd come to ask. "Zoey, was Karl here the night Phinney was murdered? The detectives believe he was."

"Mrs. Bright." Zoey spat out the name. "What an old witch that woman is. And of course Phinney poisoned her against me. They were constantly gossiping across the property line."

"The cops know you're lying," I said.

"Because they believe Mrs. Bright over me." She looked at me, jaw jutting, defiant.

"No," I said patiently, "because you are, actually, lying. I know these guys. They can tell." I tried again. "If Karl was here, he can give you an alibi."

"Can he?" she demanded. "I've thought about this. We were upstairs in my apartment. You can't hear anything that goes in on the basement from there. Karl was asleep. For all he knows, I got up, went down to the basement, and murdered Phinney."

"For all you know, Karl got up while you were sleeping, went down to the cellar, and murdered Phinney." I was talking very fast. My cheeks were flushed. "By lying to the police, you're hiding the fact that Karl was at the scene of the crime. You could go to jail as an accomplice."

Zoey stayed calm in the face of my anger. "Karl? Kill Phinney? That's ridiculous. And the question no one has answered in any of these scenarios is what Phinney was doing in the basement in the middle of the night."

A couple of answers came to me immediately. Karl

lured Phinney there so he could kill him and pin it on Zoey. Or Zoey lured Phinney there in order to have Karl kill him. I was hard-pressed to come up with another explanation. "Zoey," I said, "you need to go back to Lieutenant Binder and Sergeant Flynn and tell them the truth."

"No. Thank you." She spread her hands out wide. "Karl's in the middle of a truly awful divorce. If I place him at the scene of a murder, it's bound to get out. You know it will. And once it becomes public, it will ruin everything. It will probably triple his wife's settlement. Also people will say I'm working with him on these town issues because we're together. I don't want to be known around town as Karl Kimbel's girlfriend."

"Then don't be his girlfriend," I said.

We were silent after that. I knew I couldn't persuade her. Binder and Flynn would get Kimbel to admit he'd been there. I had faith in them.

Zoey went back to examining the pieces she'd taken from the kiln. "This is why I love pottery. I love all of it. Digging for the clay. Shaping a piece on the wheel. Working on the slab. Looking at my glazes and thinking, 'I wonder what this combination would look like?'

"But the thing I love the absolute most, is the constant risk of failure. You can't be a potter if you can't handle the risk of never knowing what will come out of the kiln. You have to be prepared to fail again and again."

Zoey looked directly at me. "When I told you about my mother, I wasn't clear about one thing," she said slowly. "Because it's the most painful thing." Her eyes were suddenly wet with tears and her voice shuddered. "I was ashamed of her. I was embarrassed by our life. I did everything to cover it up. At school, after school, with friend group after friend group, I carried on the pretense that we were like other families. I understand now I wasn't fooling anyone, particularly the grownups, but it was desperately important to me.

"Then it blew up in spectacular fashion. The rest of the kids in my foster homes were there because of private tragedies. Everyone knew who I was and what had happened, even before my name was in the paper. I was mortified, not by my mother's murder, which I knew wasn't my fault, or hers, but by everyone knowing what our life together had been like. We weren't the people I had pretended we were.

"Then I got to college and found pottery. I was a natural talent on the wheel, but I failed again and again. That's the real life lesson of pottery. You have to learn to handle the failure. Some people walk away from clay because they can't handle the losses. Pottery makes you a better, stronger, more resilient person." She paused. "Everyone tried to help me when my mother was murdered. The prosecutors assigned a victim's advocate. The foster system made sure I had a shrink. But it was pottery that healed me and allowed me to go on with my life."

Zoey threw the cracked and broken pieces into a big trash bin. "You could do with that yourself," she said. "Learning how to fail. And then to move on."

"You're talking about Chris." I got angry. "But who are you to lecture me? You're a grown woman with daddy issues, mixed up with a man who isn't even free. And you're *lying* for him. How long are you going to keep this up? Until they send you to prison?" The more I talked the madder I got. I was furious at her. "I am trying to help you!"

Zoey met my anger with deadly calm, though there were two bright splotches high on her cheeks. "I know you are," she said. "That's why I'm trying to help you."

She came around the table and gave me a hug. I remained stiff-backed. Then she walked me to the studio door. "Such a gorgeous day," she said when she rolled the door open. "I should be outside." She hugged me again and pushed me out the door. "You think about what I said."

"You think about what I said," I responded. "Please."

CHAPTER TWENTY-SIX

I stomped up the hill toward Mom's. I was beyond angry. Why wouldn't this woman help herself? And who was she to give advice to me?

But then I began to calm down. If Zoey wanted to have a relationship with a man who was clearly separated from his wife, who was I, getting all judgy? And if she had daddy issues, well, no one I knew had earned them more. I wasn't happy about the lying to the police, but maybe she'd come around on her own. Sometimes demanding someone do something had the opposite effect.

Besides, I had to admit there was some truth to what she'd said about me. As I walked, I thought about how different Zoey's work was from mine. Pottery supported failure, the destruction of the unsalvageable. Every single diner at the Snowden Family Clambake believed they'd paid good money and expected a great time—good food, service, atmosphere—and weather, as if we controlled it.

The goal was to give it to them. Not to screw up a single meal. The margins in the food business were paper-thin. Anything we threw away, anytime I mis-ordered, I berated myself. The Snowden Family Clambake wasn't a business that supported failures, even small ones.

When I'd worked in venture capital we'd had failures. Every firm did. Lots of them. But every business that failed was like a death. The consequences were huge. Loss of shareholder money, loss of jobs. Venture capital hadn't taught me how to fail.

And then there was Chris. He had been, against all probability, both my first crush and my first love. And I had clung to the relationship, even as red flags flapped in the wind around me, because I could not let it fail. Zoey was right. I was afraid of failure.

And yet, despite my fear of failure, and doing everything I could think of to avoid it, I had failed spectacularly. I had no relationship, no meaningful winter work, and I was sleeping every night in the twin bed in my childhood bedroom. I was in the abyss and didn't know how to climb out. Zoey had been trying to show me a way. I had to forgive myself.

Mom's house was empty and silent when I came through the back door. I pulled my phone out of my tote bag and called Livvie.

"Hi. What's up?" she said.

"I thought I was going to call you to tell you I wasn't going to help Zoey anymore, but I've changed my mind."

"Good. What happened?"

"I'll tell you some other time. Right now do you have a minute to talk something through with me?"

She only hesitated for a moment. "Sure, give me the topic."

"Phinney Hardison's murder."

"Oh, thank goodness," Livvie said. "After our last conversation I'm relieved it isn't your love life. I'm sorry if I was snippy."

"I'm sorry, too." I sat at the kitchen table. "I'm oversensitive about the issue. Are you ready?"

"Ready."

"Everyone says no one except Zoey had a reason to kill Phinney. We know the killer wasn't Zoey. What if the intended victim wasn't Phinney?"

"Whoa." Livvie took a moment to process what I'd said. "Who was it then? It has to be Zoey, right? She's the only person the killer could have reasonably expected would be there overnight."

I wasn't going to tell Livvie that Kimbel had been in the building. It would lead down a path that wasn't where I wanted to go. "No one could mistake Phinney for Zoey, even in the dark," I replied. "They're so different physically."

"And why was Phinney there anyway?" Livvie said. "There to be mistaken for Zoey—if that's what happened."

We were quiet, each of us thinking. "What if the point wasn't to kill Zoey?" I asked. "What if the objective was to kill Phinney and frame Zoey?" I started to get excited. We were on to something. I could feel it. "It all works. Lure Phinney into Zoey's basement and kill him with a weapon associated with her."

Livvie took her time to respond, thinking it through before she answered. "It does all work," she finally said. "Except, who would want Zoey to be accused of murder?"

My brain hurt. There was one huge incident in Zoey's

past, the murder of her mother. No one would say murder was too trivial to be a motive. But the killer was in prison and Zoey's mother was dead. How were the two crimes connected?

"Livvie, I've got to go. Thanks so much for helping me think about this."

Livvie laughed. "No problem. I have no idea what I did, but I'm glad you found it useful."

Upstairs in my office, Le Roi on my lap, I reread all the articles I'd found about Zoey's mother's murder. I couldn't see any sign of anyone who was involved who would want to frame Zoey. I confirmed Calvin Erickson III was still in prison. There was no mention in any article that either Frannie Butterfield or Calvin had been involved with a third party. Besides, if Frannie had had another lover, why would he want Zoey in prison?

The murder and trial had taken place in California. What connection did any of it have to someone who was in Busman's Harbor today? Whoever it was had the ability to lure Phinney back to his business in the middle of the night. It wasn't a stranger. It was someone Phinney knew.

Someone Phinney knew who was connected to Calvin Erickson.

I tried to find out more about Erickson, sifting through the thicket of articles about the murder and his earlier crimes. The articles repeatedly stated Cal's fancy lawyer was paid for by his family. But no names were ever connected to that generous, if ultimately unsuccessful, gift. The lawyer must have worked to prevent publicity about the family somehow.

I even located a long, grim, true-crime television show about the murder on YouTube and watched it, hopeful with every pan of the courtroom that Cal's parents would be shown or their names mentioned. They never were.

Time ticked by. I'd wasted hours. It was midafternoon.

Who in Busman's Harbor, I wondered, was connected to Phinney's murder, and had enough money to pay for a fancy lawyer for Cal Erickson? Alice Rumsford did, but she hadn't killed Phinney. She loved the memory of him so much she'd tried to hide facts about his present state of mind from the police.

Karl Kimbel had the money to hire fancy lawyers, but would he have had it twenty years ago when Erickson was on trial? I looked up Kimbel on the Web. The articles I found were about his previous triumphs as a developer in Boston, Baltimore, and Miami Beach. The bio on his company website told a rags-to-riches story about a college dropout who crewed on sailboats and then parlayed his first successful project—a restored house in suburban Boston—to mega-success. The bio mentioned a wife and three children. It didn't mention the pending divorce.

Kimbel might have had the money to pay Cal Erickson's lawyers twenty years ago, but what was his connection to the case? The more I thought about Kimbel, the more unlikely he seemed. He'd been with Zoey in the most vulnerable of circumstances. If he wanted revenge, there were less byzantine ways to get it.

Which led me to John Fenwick. I took a quick look and found nothing, though a thought nagged at me.

"Erickson," I said aloud. "Erickson. Erickson." I stopped. My laptop screen blurred. "Ricky."

* * *

I called Zoey.

"Hi," she said when she picked up. "I'm in my car. Off to dig clay and about to lose service. I'm sorry about earlier."

"I'm sorry, too. I was really mean. Let's talk that through later. It isn't what I'm calling about. This is going to seem out of the blue. I don't have time to explain. When Calvin Erickson was with your mother, was he called by any other names?"

"That is a strange question," Zoey said. But then she was quiet, obviously thinking back to that horrible time, taking my question seriously. "Cal," she said. "That's what Mom called him."

"Anything else? By friends."

"Mom kept her wits about her enough not to encourage his cronies to hang around our apartment."

"What about Cal's family?" I asked. "Did any of them come to the trial?"

Again, she hesitated. "A sister, I think. I never saw her. I was only there when I testified."

"Do you remember her name?"

"I doubt I ever knew it. What are you up to?"

"Untying some knots. Please, please be careful."

"No worries. I always am."

It wasn't hard to find a woman named Tabitha who worked at an insurance company in Boston. It was an unusual enough name. Her name now was Tabitha Wilson.

I called the company directory and ended up talking to her assistant. "Can I speak with Ms. Wilson?"

"I'm sorry. She's in a meeting. I'm happy to take a message."

"Please tell her Julia Snowden called from Busman's Harbor, Maine. It's in regard to her stepfather, John Fenwick. It's critical that she call me immediately."

"I'll find her and let her know."

I called Flynn as I walked to my car. "Phinney wasn't the target of the murder," I told him.

"The killer murdered the wrong person in the dark?" He didn't dismiss my idea out-of-hand, but I could hear the doubt in his voice.

"No. I don't mean the killer murdered the wrong person. I mean the motive didn't involve Phinney. He was collateral damage."

"Wait a minute." Flynn's phone went silent. "I'm back. Tell me."

"Phinney trashed Lupine Design. We're agreed."

"Yes," Flynn said. "Zoey kills him in retaliation."

"No," I corrected. "Try this. Phinney trashes Lupine Design. *Someone else* sees him and turns the situation to his advantage."

"And you have an idea who *someone else* is," Flynn guessed.

"John Fenwick walks his dog early every morning. He walked by Lupine Design and saw Phinney inside, destroying property. At that moment, something clicked for him. He hated Zoey. He'd dreamt of bringing her down for a long time. His revenge fantasy was complex and difficult to execute. When Phinney trashed Zoey's store, at last Fenwick's plan came together."

"He dreamed of bringing Ms. Butterfield down because of the fight about the pedestrian mall?"

I didn't blame Flynn for his skepticism. "No," I clarified. "Because he blamed Zoey for the fact that his stepson was serving a life sentence for murder. The murder of Zoey's mother."

Flynn whistled. "Hold on a minute. I'm going to put you on speaker so the lieutenant can hear." The line went silent again.

"Julia?" Binder's voice boomed into my car. "Flynn tells me you've discovered something interesting."

"John Fenwick's stepson murdered Zoey Butterfield's mother." I swallowed. "Zoey testified against him at his trial."

"Are you certain?" Binder asked.

"Ninety percent. I'm trying to confirm it with Fenwick's stepdaughter, Tabitha Wilson. She works at Liberty Mutual in Boston. She's there now."

Binder said, "Flynn, can you use my phone and—"

"On it."

"So what you think happened was . . ." Binder prompted.

"Fenwick had been holding on to hatred for Zoey since she moved to town. He knew who she was and blamed her for his stepson's incarceration. When Fenwick saw Phinney destroying Zoey's shop, he saw his opportunity for revenge. He gave Phinney an 'Attaboy, I hate her, too,' and talked him into meeting in the basement in the middle of the night to trash Zoey's inventory. 'Let's kick her when she's down,' he might have said. 'That will get her out of your building for good.'"

"There's no indication of a call between them," Binder said. "We've checked out Hardison's phone."

"It must have been in person. Remember, Fenwick walked by Phinney's shop three times a day."

"It will be impossible to prove," Binder said. "Why would Fenwick kill Phinney and not Zoey? And why not kill Zoey at any time since she arrived in Busman's Harbor?"

"Because the objective wasn't to kill her. Fenwick wanted her in prison for life, just like his stepson."

Flynn came back on the line. "I left a voicemail for Tabitha Wilson. Catch me up."

"Julia believes Fenwick killed Hardison in Zoey Butterfield's home with her weapon in order to frame her," Flynn said.

"The day after Phinney had a huge fight with her in front of two hundred witnesses," I added.

"Wow," Flynn said.

"If Fenwick's stepson killed Zoey's mother, at the very least he's withheld important information from us," Binder said. "We'll take a drive over to his house to see what he has to say."

"Good," I said. "I'm on my way to find Zoey. She's digging clay in her favorite spot. I think she should know."

I'd just crossed the bridge from Thistle Island onto Westclaw Point Road when my cell phone rang.

"Fenwick's not home," Flynn said. "A guy up on a ladder working on the house next door told us he left in his Volvo half an hour ago. He came running back with his dog. Put the dog in the house, jumped in his car and peeled out. The workman said it seemed like he was in a heck of a hurry."

"Do you think he knows you're coming for him?"

"Maybe." I could tell Flynn was distracted. There was too much going on. "If he's running, he can't have gone far. One of our people will find him."

"He's got a boat." I said it as soon as I remembered. "At the yacht club."

"Thanks. We'll check it out. We're going to try to get a warrant to search his house. He's withheld material information. We'll hope that's enough."

"I'm going to lose cell coverage soon," I told him. "Officer Dawes knows where Zoey digs. If you need us, he can find us."

"I'll call him now and send him along to you." And then Flynn was gone.

The moment I hung up, the phone rang again.

"This is Tabitha Wilson," a woman's voice said when I answered. "You called about my stepfather. Is he ill?"

"Not physically."

There was a sharp intake of breath on the other end. "Who are you? What is this about?"

"I'm going to lose you very soon," I said. "When I do, please call the Busman's Harbor Police Department and insist they put you through to Lieutenant Jerry Binder's cell phone. Tell him who you are and who your stepfather is. He has some questions for you. Before I lose you, I have two questions myself. Is your brother Calvin Erickson? And was he ever called Ricky?"

Tabitha Wilson gasped. "My grandfather, Calvin Erickson, Senior, was Calvin, and my real dad, Calvin Erickson Junior, was Cal. My brother, Calvin Erickson the third, was called Ricky by the family."

"Ricky-Ticky-Tabby," I said.

"How do you know that?" When I didn't answer, she said, "I'll do what you ask and call the police." She swallowed, loud enough for me to hear. "Whatever your part is in whatever this is, Julia Snowden, be careful. My stepfather is a man obsessed."

CHAPTER TWENTY-SEVEN

I slowed down when I sensed I was close to the turnoff for the Old Culver property. I finally spotted the opening in the vegetation, with muddy tire tracks leading the way. I turned off onto the dirt road, driving carefully, mindful of the mud even after two dry days.

As I started around the big bend, I tapped my brakes. Should I wait for Jamie? But what if Fenwick was there? What if he was hurting Zoey, right now? Maybe I could scare him off. A witness might give him second thoughts. I stepped lightly on the accelerator and took the last curve.

The first thing I saw, even before Zoey's red SUV, even before Zoey, was Fenwick's gray Volvo. I scanned the property and immediately spotted the two of them on the bayfront, ankle-deep in the cold water. Fenwick had Zoey by the hair, a knife to her throat.

Bile rose in my throat. My arms shook so hard the

steering wheel vibrated. I slammed on the brakes, ready
to back all the way up the track, but it was too late. Fenwick had spotted me. I heard him yelling. I couldn't make
out the words through the closed car window, but clearly
he was addressing me. I pulled behind his car, opened my
window, and turned off the engine.

"That's better," Fenwick called. "Now get out of the
car and drop that phone or I'll slit her throat right here,
right now."

I got out of the car and dropped the phone, useless due
to lack of service, into the mud. "Let her go!" I shouted
into the wind, but my words flew away behind me. Fenwick shook his head, though whether it was to show he
hadn't heard or wouldn't comply I didn't know. I moved
closer. "Let her go."

"You don't scare me," Fenwick shot back.

"I don't mean to. But you should know, a Busman's
Harbor police officer is on his way." I wondered how far
away Jamie was.

"I don't believe you!"

"You won't get away with hurting Zoey," I yelled.
"The state police detectives know your stepson killed her
mother. You'll be the first person they'll suspect."

"What?" Zoey shouted.

"His stepson is Calvin Erickson," I told her. "Fenwick
killed Phinney so that you would get the blame. He wants
you to spend your life in prison, like Cal."

Zoey staggered backward. Fenwick yanked her hair
and brought the knife closer again.

"They've figured it all out, have they?" Fenwick answered. "Well, the joke's on you. I don't care if I live or
die. My life hasn't been worth living since I lost my wife.
If you're right and the police know I killed Phinney, then

I have nothing to lose by killing this one, too. A man can only serve one life sentence."

As he spoke, I stepped forward, until Zoey and Fenwick were about fifteen feet away. My boots sank into the sand. Fenwick was strong for his age, and wiry. He kept in great shape. But my bet was that together Zoey and I were stronger. I caught Zoey's eye, willing her to understand what was going to happen. She stared back at me, her eyes reflecting her terror, but I thought I saw a glimmer of comprehension.

I ran into the water and dove for Fenwick's calves. Zoey screamed long and loud and ducked out of the way. He and I came down in a heap in the freezing water. I hoped he'd dropped the knife. We struggled to stand, scrabbling against one another. Twice we fell back into the knee-deep water. In the end we were both standing. Fenwick held me tightly by one wrist and still had the knife.

Zoey had made it to shore and was screaming her lungs out.

"Zoey, go get help!" I cried. "Take my car and drive up the road. Jamie Dawes is on his way. Flag him down. Tell him what's happening."

"I'm not leaving you!" She shook her head so hard her ears must have rattled.

"He doesn't want me." Even as I said it, I wondered if it was true. I'd thwarted Fenwick's last desperate plan to get Zoey.

"You'll do," he hissed.

I pulled away from him, leaning with all my weight toward the water, hoping to escape his grasp. He was a head taller than me and his sinewy arms were much longer than mine. I was overpowered. He yanked me to his side and touched the cold steel of the knife against my neck.

Zoey picked up a big rock from the shoreline and winged it toward him. It fell short, splashing us both.

"Why?" I demanded of Fenwick. I asked more for Zoey's benefit than for my own. "Your stepson killed her mom. He's a troubled man who's led a troubled life. How is that Zoey's fault? And how can revenge against her justify killing Phinney, your friend—or killing me?"

"She killed my wife!" Fenwick howled. He moved the blade away a little. Heart pounding, I assessed how quickly I could move in any direction. Could I get away?

"How?" Zoey screamed at him. "How did I kill your wife?"

"Ricky had his problems," Fenwick answered. His voice was strong and calm. "I don't deny it. But my wife, my Kitty, believed he'd turn around. She believed it with all her being. Every arrest. Every jail stint. I paid. I gladly paid it all—the lawyers' fees, the rehabs, the shrinks. I invested in the businesses. Not his useless father. I was the father. And not because I believed Ricky would get better. I paid because I had to give Kitty hope. Hope to her was like oxygen. I knew without it, she would die.

"That girl," he shouted toward Zoey, "took away Kitty's last hope. The prosecutors, police, and medical examiner all did their damage, but she was the one who made him out to be a monster. Our lawyer told us she persuaded the jury, not that he *did* do it, but that he *could*. The lawyer said he knew the case was lost by the time she got off the stand."

Fenwick's voice had turned ragged, but he held the knife steady, inches from my throat. I'd gotten soaked when we'd fallen into the water and every time the wind blew, I shivered, though whether from cold or fear I didn't know.

"Kitty got the cancer diagnosis less than a month after the trial ended." Fenwick's voice was raised enough that Zoey could hear. "Even before the sentencing, though we knew what the sentence would be." He paused. "It says cancer on her death certificate, but on my copy, the one I keep in my files, I wrote over top of it, 'broken heart.'" Fenwick's voice cracked this time. His pain was real even if the fantasy of revenge he'd built around it was not.

"I tried to forget," he said. "I tried to forgive. I buried my wife. I kept in touch with my stepdaughter. I got a dog. I tried to be a good citizen of this town." He let out a sob. "But I couldn't forget or forgive."

"But why me?" Zoey's voice shook with emotion. "Why don't you hate Cal?"

"Because he's been punished. You, on the other hand, flaunt your happiness and success. You push it in all our faces. 'Look at me! I'm making a fortune. I'll gut your buildings and close down your streets. Because I can.' Not while I have a breath left in my body, you won't." Fenwick shouted over the sound of the gulls and the water. "I did everything I could to teach you a lesson, to punish you as my family has been punished. But even with the weapon and the murder in your home, the police haven't arrested you. I've had to take matters into my own hands—yet again."

"They didn't arrest me because I didn't do it," Suddenly, Zoey straightened and stood still. It took me another moment to hear the sound, over the lapping of the water and my own breathing. Sirens, far away but getting closer.

"Jamie!" I didn't realize I'd said it out loud until Fenwick spoke.

"Shut up!"

"Drop the knife," I begged. "Drop it in the water and we'll all walk out of here safe and whole."

"Not likely," he hissed back. "You've told me yourself the cops know I killed Phinney."

"Do you think they're going to let you walk to your car and drive away with me?" My mind spun, trying to imagine a good ending to the situation. I couldn't.

The vehicles, a Busman's Harbor patrol car, a state police cruiser, a county sheriff's car, two ambulances, and Binder and Flynn's unmarked car pulled up behind my Subaru. There was the sound of doors opening. The officers peered out, shielded by their car doors, assessing the situation.

"Julia!" Jamie yelled.

Binder shot him a venomous look, then stepped out and walked toward the shore, evidently satisfied Fenwick didn't have a gun. Jamie and Flynn advanced as well. A uniformed state police officer took Zoey by the shoulders and guided her to one of the ambulances.

Binder got within thirty feet of us when Fenwick growled, "Hold it right there." He slid the blade across my throat. I waited for the warm trickle of blood on my neck, but it didn't come.

Behind Binder, the police drew their guns. All were pointed at Fenwick, which meant it looked for all the world like they were pointed at me. My knees buckled. Fenwick hauled me back up to standing and touched the knife to my throat again.

"Let her go," Binder commanded. "She's not a part of this."

Fenwick's response was to pull me even farther in front of him, so I was shielding almost his entire body. "She wasn't before, but she is now. She put herself in this situation."

"What do you think is going to happen, John?" Binder shouted. "There's one road into this place and it's jammed with cop cars. I don't see you driving away from here, even with a hostage."

"I want a boat!" Fenwick yelled.

"Pardon?" Binder looked like he couldn't believe his ears. I couldn't tell if it was for effect or a genuine reaction.

"You heard me," Fenwick shouted. "Call your buddies on the marine patrol and tell them I want to get picked up and taken to my boat at the Busman's Harbor Yacht Club. I'll let her go when I get there."

What did he imagine would happen then? There was no way he could get away. He was clearly buying time. But for what?

Binder astonished me with his answer. "Okay. I'll call them." He must be buying time, too. He walked to his vehicle and picked up the radio handset. It would work where cell phones did not. Flynn and Jamie walked back and huddled with him for a quick word.

"The marine patrol has sent a boat." Binder came back to the edge of the bay. "It'll take a little time."

"Time, I've got," Fenwick growled. "Don't come any closer."

We settled in to wait it out. Noisy gulls circled overhead. My feet were so cold they'd lost all feeling and I wondered if there came a time when I had to run, whether they would move.

"Go! Go! Go!" Binder screamed and ran toward us, Flynn, Jamie, and the other officers fast on his heels.

I felt the knife press more tightly against my throat. Then, seconds later, there was a crash and Fenwick let go. He and Flynn roiled beneath me in the water while Jamie swept me into his arms.

When Jamie deposited me in the ambulance, the EMTs took my wet clothes and boots off so fast I didn't understand what was happening. They gave me scrubs to put on and I sat on one of the gurneys, booties on my feet, a mylar blanket around my shoulders and another across my lap. Zoey was on the other gurney.

The bayfront swarmed with police. Fenwick was taken to the other ambulance and then away from the scene. In the melee he'd dropped the knife in the water. Flynn found it, holding it up and shouting in triumph when he did. They brought him back to the ambulance and gave him scrubs, booties, and a mylar blanket, too.

He stood and talked to Zoey and me for a few minutes. "Officer Dawes was on Eastclaw Point when we reached him. It took him time to get back to town and for us to follow him here. I'm glad you're both okay." He turned to me. "You should have waited for Officer Dawes." He didn't sound happy.

"I know. I'm sorry. But Fenwick had Zoey. I couldn't wait."

"She saved me." Zoey made her feelings clear. "And so did you. Thank you, Sergeant."

"Yes, thank you, Tom." My voice was thick with gratitude. I was so happy to be alive.

Flynn surprised me by pulling me off the gurney for a hug. "Don't ever do that to me again," he said.

And as quickly as he had come, he was gone. Zoey and I sat on the gurneys, waiting.

"You saved my life," she said. "Let's never fight."

I reached across the space between us and took her hand. "I can't guarantee we'll never fight. But let's always be friends."

The sun was setting by the time the EMTs decided we were neither in shock nor hypothermic and the scratches on my throat were superficial. A police photographer took pictures and then the paramedics put a bandage on my neck. They told us we could go. Binder and Flynn gave us a ride back to the station to give our statements.

The detectives spoke to Zoey while I waited on the wooden bench outside the reception area. Hours later, after I'd given my statement, Jamie drove me home. My car was still at the Old Culver property.

He stopped the patrol car in front of Mom's house. The front porch light was on and Livvie's car was in the driveway.

"Julia," Jamie said, his voice low and thick. "If anything had happened to you."

I reached across and took his hand. His strong arms scooping me out of the water had felt like safety itself. "It didn't. Thank—" My throat spasmed on "you."

"Why did you do it?" His voice had a husky, pleading sound.

"She was alone and afraid, and he would have killed her. Why did you run at a man with a knife?"

His shoulders relaxed a little and he smiled. "Why did

I, and five other trained men, run at a seventy-two-year-old with a kitchen knife? It's not the same."

"To me it was." I gave his hand another squeeze. We were going to have to talk, really talk, sometime, but tonight was not that time and a patrol car was not the place.

The front door burst open and Livvie ran down the walk. "Julia!" I got out of the car and she pulled me into a hug. "I'm so sorry I got you into this. I thought you needed something to do. It was meant to be a distraction."

"Don't apologize," I said. "Your heart was in the right place. I love you."

"I love you, too. Come inside. You, too, Jamie. You both look like you need coffee. Or something stronger."

Jamie followed us up the walk. When we got on the porch, he fished something out of his pocket. "Your phone. You dropped it by your car. The detectives are done with it."

"You guys go ahead," I said. They went inside. There were ten texts and a string of missed calls, including four from Ben. The last text said, **I guess our date is off.**

CHAPTER TWENTY-EIGHT

By Father's Day the lupines were in bloom along the roadsides, glorious brushstrokes of color across the landscape, symbols of a Maine summer to come. The Snowden Family Clambake had been open for two weeks and the kinks were nearly worked out. I hoped for a calm and profitable season.

On Morrow Island, at lunchtime, I greeted the first boatload of passengers disembarking from the *Jacquie II*. I was surprised to see Zoey walk down the gangway carrying a large box.

"Julia!" Her smile was huge.

"I didn't know you were coming today." I wanted to give her a hug, but the big box got in the way.

"I've brought your sink," she said.

I had completely forgotten about it. "Thank you. That's so lovely. The plumbing won't be hooked up for ages," I told her, "but the sink cabinet is here. As soon as I get this crowd settled, we can go take a look."

"Great. Where's Livvie?"

"In the kitchen. Go back through the dining pavilion. She'll be busy, but she wouldn't forgive you if you didn't poke your head in. Leave the sink here. I'll take care of it."

Zoey went on her way. I stowed the box in the little house by the dock without peeking, and got to work. I made sure all the tables were set with nutcrackers and picks for the lobsters, and the mason jars on each table were filled with cutlery, ready for our guests. I found bocce balls for a group beginning a game on the great lawn and directed another group to the beach on the other side of the island. Finally, I grabbed the box and found Zoey chatting with Mom in the gift shop. "C'mon," I said. "We have fifteen minutes before lunch service."

We hurried up the hill to Windsholme, as fast as I could move carrying the awkward box. We climbed through the ugly orange hazard fence and ducked under the white tape printed with NO TRESPASSING in bold black letters that was strung across the front porch. Both had been added in a mostly successful attempt to keep the clambake visitors out of the construction zone. Inside the house we zoomed up the stairs.

The drywall was up on the second floor. You could really envision what my apartment would look like. The cabinets for the kitchen and bathroom had been delivered and stood in clumps under tarps in the center of the main room.

Zoey immediately went over and pulled back the

tarps. "Let's find the cabinet for the sink." She spotted it right away. It took some maneuvering to move it to a place where we could both stand in front of it.

With a flourish, Zoey pulled a bundle, swathed in bubble wrap, from the box. "Let's see if this thing fits."

Once unveiled, the sink was gorgeous, deep and round and painted with lupines. "Zoey, I love it."

"Moment of truth." She placed the sink in the hole in the top of the cabinet. It fit perfectly.

I threw my arms around her. I couldn't think why tears had sprung to my eyes. It was a beautiful sink, but . . . "Thank you, thank you, thank you."

Zoey hugged me hard. Harder than necessary or normal. "How have you been? I've hardly caught sight of you since the clambake opened."

We'd seen each other constantly for weeks after Fenwick had threatened to kill us, but now that the summer was upon us those visits had ended. "Fine," I said.

"Truth?" she demanded.

"Okay, truth. Since the clambake opened, the nightmares have subsided. I'm so tired when I fall into bed at night, nothing wakes me, and I hardly remember my dreams in the morning. It's just me in my solitary little bed."

She laughed at that. "How are things in the Chris department?"

"I finally saw him with another woman." It had happened at Crowley's. The music was back, on the weekends, and I'd gone in with a gang of our young, single employees, straight off the last run of the *Jacquie II*. I didn't know why I'd gone. It wasn't the kind of thing I normally did.

Chris had been working the door, as always, and when I came in we'd nodded in that cordial-awkward way we'd developed. Later, he'd taken a break and sat at a nearby table crowded with off-shift Crowley's employees and guests of the band. I'd sat at that table with him so often, feeling like one of the cool kids. A tanned brunette woman sitting next to him had reached for his hand and held it on the tabletop. They looked happy and relaxed as they shouted bits of conversation at one another over the raucous music. I tried not to look too often. I didn't want him to catch me. But of course, I did, and he did.

"How was it?" Zoey asked.

"Terrible." I was honest. "But I have no right to be jealous. This is all my doing. It had to happen sometime." Chris had dated through a wide swath of the town before me, and I had every expectation he would after me.

"What about Ben?" Zoey wanted to know.

We'd finally had that dinner and he'd gone back to Cincinnati, as predicted. Then he'd dropped off the face of the earth. "Nothing to report. At least I've gotten that first date over with."

"And your cop friend?" she asked.

"I'm using the busy season to avoid that," I said. "Jamie and I will need to talk, really talk, soon."

Her brows drew together in confusion. "Jamie? No, I meant—" But then she thought better of it and shook her head.

"How about you?" I was eager to change the subject. "How are you doing?"

"I'm good." Zoey's smile disappeared. "Like I told you, I locked every door in the building and lay in bed with my eyes wide open for weeks, but I'm sleeping better now. Also in my solitary bed."

"Karl's gone?" He was still a delicate subject between us.

"He was never destined to be around for long." She laughed. "I never admitted this to you, but once you accused me of having daddy issues, I could never look at him the same way."

"But you're not moving away?" I was suddenly worried. "I thought you never lived in a town with an ex."

"Or his ex-wife. Or kids. But no, I'm not moving. In fact, Alice Rumsford's offered to sell me my building. Lupine Design will be taking over the whole space. And since the proposal for the pedestrian mall was passed during the town meeting, I feel responsible to help make it a success. Besides, I've got too much going on in Busman's Harbor—the business, friends." She colored slightly. "I'm dug in. I've put down roots in spite of myself."

"I'm glad you're staying."

The ship's bell rang to let our guests know it was time to find their tables. "Let's go," I said. "I want to get you settled."

I took Zoey to the "family table," two picnic tables pushed together in a quiet spot on the lawn with a fabulous view. Jamie was there with his parents, who were up from Florida for the summer, along with his sister and brother-in-law, who cared for them down there. The Snugg sisters were also in attendance, for a first and last gasp of summer before the B&B got too busy. Sonny's brother, and his father, Bard Ramsey, were with us for Father's Day, as was Jerry Binder with his wife and two boys. Flynn had tagged along, too.

"Can we make room for Zoey?" I asked them.

Everyone scooched and Zoey sat down.

After the meal, when the bowls from the blueberry grunt had been cleared, I thanked everyone as they boarded the *Jacquie II* for the trip back to the harbor. When Zoey left, I gave her another hug. "Don't be a stranger," I said.

She squeezed back. "I won't be."

RECIPES

Refrigerator Soup

Julia and her mother, the two non-cooks in the family, have been marooned together through a cold and rainy spring. One of their solutions is Refrigerator Soup, a concoction made with whatever ingredients might be at hand. The recipe for this version comes from my husband. I loved it so much, I begged him to make it the same way again, something he's almost never willing to do.

Ingredients:

1 Tablespoon olive oil
1 onion, chopped
2 carrots, chopped
2–3 ribs celery, chopped
3–4 rashers bacon, cooked or uncooked, chopped
1 6-ounce can tomato paste
1 15-ounce can diced tomatoes
2 quarts chicken stock
1 15-ounce can of cannellini beans
1½ cups (uncooked) of small, dried pasta like small
    shells, ditalini, etc. cooked to al dente.
1–2 cups of shredded, cooked chicken meat

Instructions:

Heat olive oil in large soup pan. If bacon is uncooked, add at this point and cook until crisp before adding vegetables and sautéing for 5 minutes. If bacon is cooked, sauté vegetables for 2–3 minutes, then add bacon and cook 2 minutes more.

Add tomato paste, fill the can with water and stir the liquid into the vegetables. Add diced tomatoes with their juice and stir. Cook for 3 minutes.

Add chicken stock. Bring to a boil and lower heat to simmer for 15–20 minutes. Add beans, pasta, and chicken. Cook for 10–12 minutes more.

Serves 4–6

Butterscotch Cookies

Ben makes these butterscotch cookies for his Aunt Alice. In real life, they came from a book of handwritten recipes my grandmother made for me. Like Julia, I love butterscotch, so these are a particular favorite.

Ingredients:

3½ cups flour
1 teaspoon baking soda
1 teaspoon cream of tartar
½ teaspoon salt
½ pound butter, soft
2 cups dark brown sugar
2 beaten eggs
1 teaspoon vanilla
1 cup chopped walnuts

Instructions:

In a large bowl, mix dry ingredients—flour, baking soda, cream of tartar, salt.

Cream together the butter, sugar, and vanilla. Stir in beaten eggs. Add dry ingredients. Mix well. Add chopped walnuts. Mix.

Form into logs, approximately 1½ inches high by 2½ inches wide by 6 inches long.

Place in refrigerator 4 hours or overnight.

Slice the logs into 1/4-inch slices. Place each slice on parchment paper on a cookie sheet.

Bake at 400 degrees for 10 to 12 minutes until golden.

Makes approximately 60 cookies.

Lobster Stew

I include a lobster recipe in each Maine Clambake Mystery, no matter the subject matter of the book. Since this book takes place during a cold Maine spring and the recipes focus on soups, we thought lobster stew, which is a particular favorite of my husband's, would be just the thing. My son-in-law tried the stew and said it should "definitely go in the book."

Ingredients:

4 cooked lobsters
8 Tablespoons butter, divided in half
1 onion, chopped
1 fennel bulb, top removed, sliced thin and chopped
Salt & pepper
½ cup dry sherry
4 cups milk
2 cups heavy cream

Instructions:

Remove meat from lobsters and store overnight, reserving shells. In a separate bowl, reserve any tomalley, roe, or juices.

In a large saucepan, melt four tablespoons of butter. Add onion and fennel, salt and pepper to taste, and sauté for 3–4 minutes. Add reserved lobster shells and continue to cook for 5 minutes. Stir in sherry and allow to bubble away for 2 minutes. Stir in tomalley, roe, and any accumulated juices.

Stir in milk and cream. Slowly bring to a simmer (do

not boil) and cook for 15–20 minutes. Remove from burner and allow to cool.

Store the mixture in the refrigerator overnight, allowing flavors to blend.

The next day, drain through a sieve to remove solids and reserve the strained liquid. Melt the remaining four tablespoons of butter in a large saucepan. Add lobster meat and gently sauté until warmed through. Add reserved milk and cream mixture and slowly reheat (do not boil). Adjust seasonings.

Serves 4

Mrs. Gus's Cardamom Pecan Pie

Mrs. Gus gets up at 4:00 every morning to bake the pies for her husband's restaurant. In the winter and spring, when fresh local fruit is unavailable, Mrs. Gus gets creative with non-fruit options. In the real world this is a variation on the pie my sister-in-law, Maria Kent, makes every other Thanksgiving for the big Carito family gatherings. Though it seems like there are a thousand dessert offerings available at that feast, I always go for this one.

Ingredients:

Crust:
Make or buy your favorite single-crust pie crust

Filling:
1 cup real maple syrup
1 cup light brown sugar
½ cup whipping cream
1 Tablespoon molasses
4 Tablespoons butter, cubed and softened
½ teaspoon kosher salt
1 teaspoon ground cardamom
½ teaspoon cinnamon
¼ teaspoon ground nutmeg
6 large egg yolks, lightly beaten
2 cups pecan halves

Instructions:

Roll out dough into a 9-inch pie plate. Refrigerate for 30 minutes to an hour.

Preheat oven to 350 degrees.

Toast the pecan halves by spreading them on a baking tray and baking them for 8–10 minutes. Allow them to cool.

Preheat oven to 425 degrees.

Combine maple syrup, light brown sugar, whipping cream, and molasses in a sauce pot. Cook over medium heat, stirring until sugar dissolves, about 3 minutes. Remove from heat. Let cool 5 minutes. Whisk in butter, salt, cardamom, cinnamon, and nutmeg. Whisk in egg yolks.

Spread pecans evenly over the crust. Pour syrup mixture over pecans.

Place in preheated oven and reduce heat to 325 degrees. Bake for 45 to 50 minutes until filling is set and center jiggles slightly when gently shaken.

Cool completely on a wire rack.

Serves 8 to 10.

Mushroom Soup

My husband, Bill, contributed this recipe. It's perfect on a cold, rainy day, spring or fall.

Ingredients:

1 stick (4 ounces) of butter
2 medium onions, chopped
3 cloves garlic, chopped
2½ pounds mixed, sliced mushrooms, your choice
1 Tablespoon dried porcini mushroom powder (grind dried porcinis in a coffee grinder used for grinding spices)
1 cup dry white wine or dry sherry
2 teaspoons dried Herbs de Provence
2 teaspoons kosher salt
2 teaspoons ground black pepper
8 cups mushroom or vegetable stock
2 cups heavy cream
½ cup cornstarch

Instructions:

Melt butter. Add onion and garlic and sauté for 4 minutes. Add mushrooms and sauté for 6 minutes. Sprinkle with porcini powder and sauté an additional 6 minutes.

Add wine or sherry and cook 2 minutes. Stir in herbs, salt, and pepper. Pour into a slow cooker. Add stock. Cook on high for 2 hours. Whisk cream and cornstarch together and stir into pot. Cook on high for 30 minutes longer.

Adjust seasonings, if necessary. Blend with an immersion blender leaving the mushrooms in small chunks.

Serves 8–10

Pine Tree State of Mind Cocktail

When I announced the coming release of Muddled
Through, *I said that I loved the title (which was suggested by a reader), but that it was a little different because, unlike many other Maine Clambake Mystery
series titles, it did not have a food connotation. Many
fans wrote back to assure that it did. "Muddled" is a
word used in the preparation of many types of cocktails.
To muddle is to lightly mash fruit, herbs, and spices to release their essence and flavor to the drink. I had known
that but hadn't made the connection. Once it was made
for me, I had to add a cocktail recipe to the book.*

Ingredients:

2 thin slices of orange, quartered
1-2 sprigs fresh rosemary
1½ ounce Vena's Fizz House Maine Pine Syrup
A few drops of Vena's Fizz House Maine Pine Bitters
2 ounces Rye whiskey
Club soda or seltzer
Maraschino cherry and/or twist of orange peel for gar-
nish

Instructions:

In a cocktail shaker, muddle the orange and rosemary.
Add syrup, bitters, and whiskey. Shake well and strain
into a large rocks glass filled with ice cubes. Stir. Top
with club soda or seltzer.

Add cherry and orange peel

Note: Syrup and bitters may be purchased at www. venasfizzhouse.com

Makes one cocktail.

Acknowledgments

Thank you so much to the three wonderful potters who gave up their valuable time to answer my many, sometimes crazily naïve, questions. Malley Weber (https://www.malleyweber.com), specifically, educated me about digging local clay in Maine. Alison Evans (https://aeceramics.com) gave me particular insight into what it takes to run a business of the scale and type as Lupine Design. Jan Thomas Conover (https://www.instagram.com/jtcpottery/) walked me through the skills she uses to create her beautiful pottery. Each of these woman creates in unique ways, and each has a different business model and approach to the commerce side. Yet they all spontaneously expressed the same joy about working with clay and mastering the many techniques and stages that creating pottery demands. Each spoke about the important lessons making pottery teaches about learning from failure and facing the future with resilience and optimism. Please visit their websites and buy their beautiful goods. All mistakes in this book, both inadvertent and deliberate, are mine.

Thank you to author Maureen Milliken for coming to my house (our first visitor as the pandemic ebbed the first time) to talk to me for hours about Maine town meetings, a subject she's well-acquainted with as a journalist and as a citizen. Her Bernie O'Dea mysteries are terrific, and you should read them.

Many thanks to reader Lorna Doran, who suggested the title *Muddled Through*, in response to a call for help in my author newsletter. The title perfectly captures not only the season of the book and its subject matter, but also Julia's emotional journey.

Two books were critical to my understanding of the women who have traveled the world taking photographs for *National Geographic* magazine. They are *Women Photographers at National Geographic* by Cathy Newman (National Geographic, September 2000) and *Women of Vision: National Geographic Photographers on Assignment* by Rena Silverman (National Geographic, March 2014). These books are fascinating and made me regret I wasn't writing a historical novel. I borrowed parts of some of these amazing women's lives and approaches to photography, along with descriptions of some of their photos, for Alice Rumsford.

Many readers will recognize in the character of Alice Rumsford strong echoes of the classic children's book *Miss Rumphius*, written and illustrated by the singular talent that was Barbara Cooney. (Originally published by Viking Penguin, 1982.) Like Miss Rumphius, Alice Rumsford travels the world as an adventurous, independent woman and then comes back home determined to create beauty in her world. As I prepared to write this book, my granddaughter Viola and I read *Miss Rumphius* over and over.

Thank you, always, to the Moore family, owners and operators of the Cabbage Island Clambake http://www.cabbageislandclambake.com/ for their support for the series.

My friend and fellow Kensington author Sherry Harris always takes the time to read my manuscripts and give me brilliant comments no matter how late I get them to her. Her new Sea Glass Saloon Mystery series is fantastic. Read one soon, if you haven't yet had the chance.

As always, I want to thank my agent John Talbot, and all the folks at Kensington, especially my editor, John Scognamiglio, and my publicist Larissa Ackerman, for their unwavering support.

And, of course, my family: Rob, Sunny, and Viola Carito and Kate, Luke, Etta, and Sylvie Donius. I could not do this without your love and support. And to my husband, Bill Carito, who develops so many of the recipes for the Maine Clambake Mystery series, and who runs the house and our lives when I am in "book jail," words cannot express my love and gratitude.

Visit us online at
KensingtonBooks.com
to read more from your favorite authors,
see books by series, view reading
group guides, and more!

BOOK CLUB
BETWEEN THE CHAPTERS

Visit us online for sneak peeks, exclusive
giveaways, special discounts, author content,
and engaging discussions with your fellow readers.

Betweenthechapters.net

Sign up for our newsletters and be the first
to get exciting news and announcements about
your favorite authors!
Kensingtonbooks.com/newsletter